MW00415202

God, he was ⌐ him down to her in a long, hard kiss.

She turned from him instead.

"Now that is the most British thing you've ever said to me." She stalked down the street toward the restaurant.

Callan appeared right at her side. "I mean it, Dawn. What were you thinking, wandering alone in a strange city by yourself?"

"I was thinking I'm a tourist in a crowded city, and it's only eight thirty at night." She glanced at her watch. Whoops. Make that nine thirty. "It's not like I'm lurking in a seedy part of town at three a.m. Those guys were assholes. They probably wouldn't have done anything anyway."

He stopped her. "But what if they had?"

"I don't know, Callan. What if they had? How would you have reacted? Like a professional coworker?"

He ran a hand through his hair and scowled again. "No, damn it. Not like a coworker. I know we said this morning we'd keep things professional, but today, in the car, you drove me crazy and then, all evening, I've been searching for you. All my calls to you went straight to voicemail. I finally find you, and you're being accosted by those arses, and I snapped. So, no. Not like a coworker."

Drove him crazy? Searched for me all evening?

"Callan—"

"Dawn—"

And then, in unison. "We need to talk."

Just a Fling

by

Katherine Grace

This is a work of fiction. Names, characters, places, and incidents are either the product of the author's imagination or are used fictitiously, and any resemblance to actual persons living or dead, business establishments, events, or locales, is entirely coincidental.

Just a Fling

COPYRIGHT © 2022 by Katherine Grace

All rights reserved. No part of this book may be used or reproduced in any manner whatsoever without written permission of the author or The Wild Rose Press, Inc. except in the case of brief quotations embodied in critical articles or reviews.
Contact Information: info@thewildrosepress.com

Cover Art by *Diana Carlile*

The Wild Rose Press, Inc.
PO Box 708
Adams Basin, NY 14410-0708
Visit us at www.thewildrosepress.com

Publishing History
First Edition, 2023
Trade Paperback ISBN 978-1-5092-4585-7
Digital ISBN 978-1-5092-4586-4

Published in the United States of America

Dedication

To my family and friends who have been along for the ride, especially Michelle, Dana, and Martha. Thank you for your input and encouragement!

And to Rich, who played the role of cheerleader, babysitter, and chief motivation officer. I love you.

Chapter One

New York, NY—Present Day

Crawling around on her hands and knees in front of her boss, Dawn Mathison questioned her life decisions.

Again.

"I need that contract in thirty minutes," Mr. White demanded.

Dawn scuttled over to another banker's box and quickly shuffled through the stack of legal documents. "Maybe it's on your desk," she suggested.

Her stern, middle-aged boss was not amused. "Unacceptable, Ms. Mathison. Find it."

"Yes sir," she muttered but he'd already left the storage room.

Off to torture someone else.

Dawn tightened her ponytail and glanced at her smartwatch. Twenty minutes left. This was what hustling in law school had done for her. Landed her a prestigious job at the exclusive New York law firm of White & Halston LLP, where she now filed papers, scanned papers, and looked for papers. Not exactly like the legal dramas on TV.

"Lucky to be here, lucky to be here," she chanted.

And she was lucky. White & Halston was the crème of the law firm crop. An old school firm known to Wall Streeters and Ivy Leaguers as the firm-of-choice for prominent corporations and banks. White & Halston took "old school" seriously, operating the firm as if it were preserved in a 1990's time capsule. While other firms wooed law students with trendy Gen Z perks— Advanced technology! Wellness and mental health days! No suits required! Work from anywhere!— White & Halston did the opposite. The firm's prestige and outrageous starting salaries were more than enough to lure the best students from the top law schools.

And Dawn was the best of the best. Second in her class—second only to Mae Lin—and driven to succeed, she was an ideal associate.

Too bad she hated it.

But she just had to stick it out here for a few years. Then, with White & Halston on her résumé and her student loans paid off, she could write her ticket to anywhere, do anything. Her career was right on track; she knew exactly what she wanted and where she was going.

Right?

You're twenty-five years old with over $300,000 in student loan debt. So yeah, you'll crawl around all morning until you find that freaking contract.

Dawn sifted through another box and struck gold. "Yes!" She pulled out the missing contract and raised the papers over her head triumphantly. Completing a task for Mr. White was like advancing to the next level in a video game when you had zero lives left.

On to the next bullshit assignment.

A sunny blond head popped through the storage room doorway. "Hey, you found it."

Dawn grinned at her friend, Kurt, and lowered her arms. "Was I that loud?"

"Nah, I was passing by and thought I'd give you a hand. But it looks like you've got it under control."

"You're so nice, thank you." At least she had some fellow associates to commiserate with, like Kurt. He'd clerked at White & Halston last summer, so he'd known what he was getting into. He'd given Dawn the scoop on the firm and her coworkers when they went through orientation together last month, and they'd become fast friends.

She stood and swatted at the dust balls clinging to her black suit. "I have to rush this to Mr. White and then get started on my memo for Mr. Halston. It's due by five."

"Get Halston's memo in on time so you can come to happy hour with us. Remember, five-dollar pitchers until eight."

Kurt winked and sauntered off. Kurt had told the firm he'd accept an associate position if he could work with Mr. Gandry instead of Mr. White. Mr. Gandry, who billed thousands of dollars an hour, was semi-retired, and spent most of his time at his vacation home in the Caribbean.

Kurt planned all the associate happy hours.

Dawn shoved the document into a manila folder and hurried toward Mr. White's office. Happy hour wouldn't be in her future if she couldn't get through the mountain of work on her plate. She scanned the cubicles grouped along the long hallway to Mr. White's corner office. Kurt may be coasting through life, but the other five associates in her first-year class looked as freaked as she felt.

Their group sat in what the other firm lawyers and staff called the "kindercubes," a block of cubicles spaced in two neat rows surrounded by the windowed offices of more seasoned attorneys. They were zoo animals on display. Fish in a fishbowl. At the mercy of any partner or senior associate who walked by.

They'd started together at the firm a month ago in July after taking the New York Bar Exam. Their entire careers hung in the balance while they waited for the results to be released in October, which was absolutely nerve-racking since the New York Bar was a notorious bitch to pass. As Mr. White liked to remind them, they were not real lawyers until they passed the bar, and they would *never* be lawyers at White & Halston if they had to retake the bar exam.

Waiting for the results was taking its toll on the kindercubers. And it was only August.

Dawn rounded the corner and passed the cubes where anxiety hung like a thick, dark cloud. Matt, hyped up on coffee, gave her a quick nod and zoomed past. Hannah scowled and banged on her keyboard; she still hadn't recovered from Mr. White accusing her of "lazy" research. Olivia mumbled into her headset, her face shuttering in sheer panic. Abbey stared off into space, semi-catatonic. And poor Natalie. She chewed on her hands so much they'd be down to stumps by Halloween.

This might not be Dawn's dream job—not even close—but Mr. White would not crack her.

"He's in the main conference room," Debbie, Mr. White's assistant, said. Dawn thanked her and turned on her black pumps to speed-walk down another hallway. She halted in front of the large conference room reserved for important client meetings.

Dawn grabbed the mahogany door's heavy brass handle. A round of masculine laughter erupted from inside the conference room. *Ugh.* Her clammy hands fluttered to straighten the collar of her white blouse. *Come on, grow a vagina and get in there.*

She pushed the door open. Seven men, all in gray suits, sat around the large conference table. They stopped talking and stared when she entered the room. Mr. White beckoned her forward.

"Here's the contract." She handed Mr. White the folder and turned to leave.

He raised his hand, stopping her. "One moment, I need seven copies of this contract. And make sure you copy every page. Some of these are double-sided. And keep them in the right order."

She pursed her lips and waited. Being treated like an imbecile in front of Mr. White's clients was not the most ignominious thing to ever happen to her, and it probably wouldn't be the last.

She pasted a polite smile on her lips and surveyed the men around the table. One of them was Mr. White's father, Bill White Sr., the firm's founding partner. Well into his eighties and hunched with age, Bill White Sr. still came to work every day for a few key clients. How a man as lovely as Bill White Sr. had produced such a jerk for a son, she'd never understand. She gave him a big smile, which he returned through his oversized dentures.

She scanned the faces of the other men in the room but didn't recognize them.

Until her gaze landed on a pair of beautiful hazel eyes.

Shock zipped down Dawn's spine. A high-pitched sound rang in her ears, muffling Mr. White's blathering. She reached out to grip onto something, anything, but there was nothing to steady her, so she clasped her hands together instead. She swiveled back to Mr. White, who held the papers out to her with an expectant glare. A creeping heat suffused her neck and climbed up her cheeks. She had to get out of there. Now.

Why is he here?

"Here you go." Mr. White's annoyance prompted Dawn into action. She grabbed the papers like a lifeline. Like they were the only thing keeping her grounded in reality. She raced from the room, her stomach flip-flopping. The heavy door closed behind her with a *thud*. She drew a long, shaky breath.

What. The. Fuck?

The trip to the copy machine was an out-of-body experience; she barely registered walking. In front of the copy machine, Dawn punched the numbers by rote.

He's not here. He's not here.

Oh, God. Ice shot down her extremities and the hairs on her arms stood on end. The copy machine sputtered out the final page, but she didn't move. She stood frozen like a rabbit caught in a snare.

She couldn't face him again. No freaking way. Maybe Debbie could deliver the copies. But then Debbie would want to know why, and it would turn into a whole thing. Besides, Mr. White was waiting for *her*. Waiting with *him. Oh, God.*

Was passing out a viable option?

Oh, God. She had to do it quick. Get it over with. In and out. Ignore him.

Dawn threw her shoulders back and returned to the conference room. She opened the door and walked with purpose toward Mr. White, head held high.

Inside she was a freaking wreck.

Do. Not. Look.

But her heart and her brain weren't on the same page. She had no control. Against her will, her gaze slid to the right of Mr. White, and their eyes locked.

His stare was an atomic blast, and her legs wobbled from the impact.

Callan...

Those hazel eyes burned her.

"Your copies," Dawn muttered. She thrust the papers into Mr. White's hand and ran like holy hell from the room.

****

"Jane, oh my God. Callan is here." Dawn cupped her hand over her phone and kept a lookout through the glass door of the empty conference room she'd chosen as her hideout. There was no way she could go back to her kindercube. Not when *he* could saunter by at any moment.

"You mean your hot but emotionally unavailable British fuckwad? Why is he in your apartment?" her best friend asked. Kids screamed and splashed around in the background. Jane must be lounging in her usual poolside spot at the country club. Jane was "taking a break" and living with her parents in between getting her master's degree in early childhood education and getting a job. So far, Jane's break had lasted over a year and would probably continue until Jane's boyfriend, Todd, proposed to her.

"No, I'm at work, Jane. My freaking job. I don't know why, but he's here." Dawn craned her neck, but only a sliver of the lobby was visible down the long hallway. When would it be safe to come out of hiding?

"Is he stalking you?" *A Killer in Our Midst* was

Jane's favorite show, next to *My Out of Control Teen* and *Bride Wars of Dallas*.

"I doubt it. I think he's here on business. What if he's a client? I can't believe he might be a client. What are the odds?" Dawn's voice pitched higher and higher. She had to get a grip.

"Okay, calm down," Jane said soothingly. "I agree it's crazy. You haven't seen him for almost a year. Are you sure he didn't know you work there? Do you think he'll come find you?"

"I hope not. I'm hiding out in a random conference room. I have no idea what I'd say to him." The conference room window faced the front of the building, and she smashed her face against it to scan the sidewalk twenty stories below. Maybe she could make out the top of his head as he left the building.

"You say, 'Hey, shithead, thanks for nothing last year. I thought you meant it when you said you wanted to be with me. Now, get the hell out.' " Jane always did have a way with words.

This was not good. She had so much work to do on her memo, and it was already past lunchtime. She couldn't hide in here forever.

Why, why, why did Callan have to appear back in her life now? She'd spent a year trying to forget him. It had been a struggle to dive back into school last fall and maintain her perfect GPA. But she'd done it. She'd graduated number two in her class—Mae Lin was a freaking savant, okay?—and had done it despite her feelings for Callan. Hell, *because* of her feelings for Callan.

He had no right to be here now. Not when she'd recommitted to her career path. Put her dreams in a box and shoved them away.

She stood on her tiptoes and plastered her cheek even harder against the glass, squinting at the sidewalk below to catch a glimpse of the thick crop of curling golden-brown hair she'd recognize from twenty stories up. He needed to leave. *When* would he leave?

"Dawn?" A deep rumbling voice called from behind her.

Dawn jumped and turned from the window. Callan Marlowe stood in the doorway. His tall, muscular frame filled the space and sucked all the air from the conference room. A faint smile played across his sculpted lips, but his eyes were so intense... Meeting his dark gaze made her pulse leap and shot a fission of heat straight to her core.

Stupid, traitorous body.

"Uh, I'll call you back." She ended the call without waiting for Jane's response and tossed the phone down on the conference table.

Callan stepped into the room and shut the glass door behind him. The conference table separated them, but it wasn't enough. She backed away until her shoulder blades pressed against the window. If she'd had a parachute, she might've broken the glass and jumped.

Her senses exploded. She *smelled* him, for God's sake. Sandalwood and bergamot, a mix of the shampoo and body wash he used. That body wash... *Flashes of a steaming shower, the soapy ripples of his golden torso, her hands slowly following the trail downward...*

She shifted uncomfortably. She knew his body as well as her own, knew the hard planes of his chest, the ridge of muscles along his hips, the firm curve of his ass. And yet, this man who stood before her felt like a

9

complete stranger, like she didn't have the right to know all those intimate things about him.

Was he, right now, remembering their time together last summer? Did she measure up to his memories? She should've popped by the ladies' room to check her teeth and reapply some lipstick. Maybe camped out there instead. A conference room with a glass door probably wasn't the smartest hiding place.

His gaze traveled up and down her body, lingering on her lips. She licked them. His eyes narrowed; a lion ready to pounce. Her breath caught, and her body froze. Electricity, silent but powerful, crackled between them, and she locked her knees to keep herself from melting down the glass.

But then Callan's face changed abruptly, as if he'd slipped on a mask.

He put his hands in the pockets of his gray suit trousers and assumed a casual stance. He relaxed his shoulders, and a slow dazzling smile spread across his impossibly handsome face. "It's great to see you, Dawn."

Her stomach clenched in response to her name on his sexy British tongue. The clipped sound was a freaking Pavlovian bell. His smile—bright white teeth shining against golden skin—amplified the pounding in her chest. He was dressed as Mr. *GQ* today, in his bespoke gray suit, crisp white shirt, no tie, and tanned skin peeking out from the collar. The man was too good-looking for any sensible woman. No wonder she'd been so bamboozled by him.

She blinked several times. How could he appear before her so unruffled, so *casual*? Meanwhile, she was either going to pass out or hurl all over the conference table.

"I couldn't believe it when you walked into the meeting," he said when she didn't respond.

"Yes, well." She shifted on her heels and smoothed her long ponytail. She made a snap decision. She'd act breezy and professional. Callan may have torn her heart out last summer, but the asshole would never know. She forced her nerves to settle down.

She stretched her lips into what she hoped was a polite smile. "So, are you a client here? Is Gemma with you?" she asked, referring to his business partner and chief legal officer. She mentally kicked herself in the butt for her curiosity. *Don't ask him questions. Get him the hell out. Now.*

Callan shook his head. "No, Gemma's back in London." He smiled pleasantly, though his smile didn't quite reach his eyes. Maybe he wasn't so unruffled after all. "We have a large solar project in the works. It's in Granada, Spain."

"Spain…" she whispered.

His gaze pierced hers, but he continued, "Your firm is representing our US investors. I'm here to meet with them and hammer out some details." He paused and stepped forward. His strong thighs hit the conference table, and he ran his long fingers in a smooth line on the table's surface. Her breath hitched. Could a person be jealous of a table?

"So, you seem to be doing well. I take it you're an associate here?"

Dawn jerked her gaze back to his face. "I am. After I graduated, I moved to New York to study for the bar, which I took last month. I started working here, but I can't officially practice until I pass the exam—" She stopped her rambling. He didn't care about her. *She'd* been the idiot who'd fantasized about their future together. Not him. How humiliating.

"I see," he said. "And did you graduate number one?"

"Number two, actually," she replied, embarrassed now by her juvenile desire to be first in her class.

"Mae Lin?" he asked sympathetically. Though his eyes held a glint of teasing in them.

"Yes." She ground her teeth. Was he making fun of her?

"It's hard to compete with someone who has a photographic memory."

He still remembered her prattling from last summer? "It doesn't matter anymore," she said. His teasing smile faded, replaced with a flash of pain, and her throat constricted.

There was so much to say between them. So much hurt and regret and longing. Why wasn't he saying the things she needed him to say? Because he didn't freaking care. He was an illusion, a myth of her own design. He'd used her, filled her head with pretty lies, and discarded her.

Dawn inhaled slowly. *Do not melt down in front of this man.*

Callan shoved his hands back into his pockets. "I'm surprised you are working for a firm like this."

"Why?" she asked him sharply.

He shrugged. "I thought you'd decided to change course." She knew what he meant.

"It's a great job," she said, defensive even to her ears. *This job is sucking my soul.*

"Of course," he murmured.

He stared at her. She stared at him. A memory invaded her thoughts: lying in bed with him, memorizing his chiseled, handsome features, getting lost in his beautiful, changeable hazel eyes. She used to love staring at him. She shook the image away. Now it took all her willpower not to back down from his heated gaze.

Even from across the room, his presence engulfed her, suffocated her. She wanted to claw her way around him and escape, but—*oh, God*—she also wanted him to come to her. To touch her as he once had. Hold her in his strong arms and tell her he'd made a mistake. He'd been an asshole. And he was sorry. So sorry.

Dawn blew out the breath she'd held. "It was nice to see you, but I have a memo due." She didn't care about being rude. She needed Callan gone from this room. Gone from her life. Her thoughts. Forever.

He gave her a hard look and nodded. "Nice to see you as well. I realize you must be very busy. I'm sorry we couldn't catch up more." He backed away but then hesitated. His expression cracked, and his eyes filled with regret.

She braced for an apology, fully prepared to tell him to go to hell.

"Dawn, I—" He shook his head. "Perhaps another time." His face a mask again, Callan nodded once, opened the glass door, and walked down the hallway, his broad back and long legs moving with a preternatural grace no man should have. He disappeared around the corner, and her body sagged. She placed her palms on the conference table and shut her eyes. Her throat tightened, and tears pricked her eyelids.

She inhaled, long and deep. The worst was over. She'd pull herself together and get back to work.

She'd forget him. Put the memories back in a box and lock them up.

Again.

On her way back to her cubicle, Dawn stopped by Kurt's workstation.

"Where did you say happy hour is?" she asked. She needed to forget hard tonight.

Chapter Two

Callan could not get over the coincidence. Dawn Mathison. Here in New York. Waltzing right into his damn business meeting.

The second she'd appeared in the conference room doorway, it had taken everything in him to keep calm, to not leap to his feet and shout her name. He'd managed to rein himself in, but *bloody hell*.

That fucking black suit of hers...so ridiculously sexy, showcasing her long legs and fit body. A body that melted to his touch and still drove him crazy, even with a year and three thousand miles separating them.

He'd itched to sink his hands into the long russet curls of her ponytail. He remembered twining his fingers around her locks, feeling the silky strands against his lips, watching them glimmer red and gold in the sunlight. Her hair was glorious. He'd say it was her crowning feature if she didn't have so many others. Like her eyes. Brown lashes fringing a striking green like he'd never seen. Clear and sparkling when happy, dark and mossy when upset.

Her eyes had been mossy today.

But her smile had undone him. When she'd given old Bill White Sr. the full wattage of her smile, his heart had lurched, and he'd thought to himself, *there's my sunshine*.

He was the biggest arsehole in the world.

He knew he'd fucked up but seeing her today gutted him. He ran a hand over his face. It was all so complicated.

Outside the car window, the midtown skyscrapers crawled by as the driver lurched from stoplight to stoplight. This solar deal was too important. He didn't need the added distraction of Dawn Mathison working for the law firm of his goddamn investors.

The car approached Callan's hotel. "I'll drop you off out front," the driver said, interrupting his twisted thoughts.

"Thank you." Callan exited the car, nodded to the doorman, and strode through the gilded lobby toward the elevator bank.

"Mr. Marlowe." A concierge approached him. "I have a message for you from Ms. Chadwick. She said it's urgent."

Callan checked his phone. Three missed calls from Gemma. What's wrong now?

He thanked the concierge, rode the elevator to his floor, and dialed her number. "Christ, this better not be more bad news."

"Where have you been? We have a problem with the power agreements." Gemma's voice was steady, but he knew her well enough to tell she was stressed.

Callan swiped the key to his room and entered. "Shit," he said after Gemma detailed another complication. "We'll straighten everything out when we get to Granada." He swallowed the rising panic. This project was supposed to put his company on the map, but it was turning into a first-class clusterfuck instead.

"We can't wait a week. I'm going to set up a video call for tomorrow before your flight."

"You're right. Gemma, thank God you are in this with me."

"Thank God when this is finally done," she responded and launched into their action plan.

When they'd finished mapping out their strategy, Callan paused. "Gemma, there's something else."

"What? What else is wrong?"

"Nothing. It's just...I saw Dawn today."

Gemma sucked in a breath. "Oh?"

"She works for White & Halston."

"What are the chances?"

"Yeah, I know."

"Hmmm." Gemma could say so much without saying anything.

"She was...not happy."

"Well, in all honesty, I can't say I'm surprised."

"She was angry, actually," he said. "And rightly so. I know," he added in response to Gemma's silence. "We didn't talk for long."

"I imagine she was surprised to see you at her workplace."

"To say the least."

"Are you going to contact her again?"

Good question. Was he going to contact her? Should he?

He'd become an expert at blocking Dawn from his mind during the day. But at night...he dreamed about her sometimes. Okay, maybe more than sometimes. Foggy, hot, hungry dreams, which ended with him waking to find his hands clutching a pillow or, more often, himself. Then the emptiness would hit. And he'd shake off the dreams and push her to the back of his mind.

But the shock of seeing her today had blasted

through all the idiotic denials and self-delusions he'd built around himself when it came to Dawn.

Underneath her anger, there had been a flash of *something*. A charged heat between them, which had never gone away. He'd had a strong urge to walk around the conference table and pull Dawn into his arms. Taste her lips. Run his hands down her curves. But also tease her. Make her smile at him the way she had last year. Have a real conversation with her instead of the rubbish they'd exchanged today.

"Ahem. You still there?" Gemma prompted.

"Fuck," he swore. "This is ridiculous. Dawn and I are in the same city. What if I called her? Just to clear the air, no expectations."

"I think no expectations is what got you in trouble last time."

"If we can't be together, shouldn't we at least part on good terms?" He was like an addict who'd fallen off the wagon, and Dawn was the drug. He'd rationalize anything to get another hit.

"Sure. Go ahead and tell yourself parting on good terms is all you want from her."

"Gemma—" Callan warned.

"Callan"—Gemma's voice was serious—"if you do contact her, which it sounds like you are going to do, please have an *honest* talk with her. Tell her how you feel, and tell her the truth, for God's sake."

"I'll think about it."

"Don't think too hard," she said and hung up. Probably as sick of his bullshit as he was himself.

Callan shrugged off his suit jacket and threw his phone to the side. He flopped back onto the bed. A memory came to mind: *Dawn dancing in a slinky green dress, her smile bright as the sun, him turning her in his arms, stripping off her clothes, kissing her, then an all-consuming frenzy...*

He groaned and sat up. He had to stop. He was getting hard and wallowing in a fantasy that would never happen. He'd made promises he couldn't deliver, and Dawn hated him for it. Hell, he hated himself for not being able to live up to her expectations. For not being able to *move on.*

"Fuck," Callan swore again and picked up his phone. He stood and strode in front of the window overlooking Central Park and the city beyond. Dawn was somewhere out there, and he was just sitting here, morose, in his hotel room. Pathetic.

He didn't know what he needed to say to her, but it wasn't the "perhaps another time" he'd given her today. He owed her a lot more than that.

It's now or never. He unlocked his phone and typed in the number he knew by heart.

****

"Damn, this is good." Dawn tipped her glass back and finished off her Pimm's Cup. She'd joined Kurt and her fellow associates for happy hour in a dive bar downtown and, surprisingly, was having a great time. She'd only thought about Callan once every five minutes. Way better than she'd anticipated.

Now it was late, and she and Kurt sat alone, side by side in a worn leather booth. Strands of Neil Diamond struggled to push through the loud din of the crowd. Even though cigarettes were banned in the city, a faint smokiness drifted over the patrons, creating a tableau of dirty angel vignettes. Kurt draped his arm casually over the padded seat behind her, a dazed smile on his face.

She had a feeling Kurt liked her. She considered liking him back. *Go back in your box, Callan.*

"I'll get you another," Kurt said and slid out of the booth to order more drinks at the crowded bar.

Her phone buzzed with a text from Jane.

—*What r u doing? What happened?*—

—*We talked.*—

—*And?*— Jane accompanied the text with an eggplant emoji.

—*Nothing happened.*—

—*Details!*—

Kurt made his way back, drinks in hand. Dawn typed —*Can't talk right now. I'll call you tomorrow.*— Jane responded with an emoji smiley face sticking out its tongue.

"Who's texting?" Kurt asked, scooting in beside her. She accepted the drink from him. Was he trying to find out if she had a boyfriend?

"My best friend from high school. She wants to catch up." She took a sip, and her phone buzzed again.

—*Where are you?*—

She threw Kurt an apologetic smile and quickly responded, —*A bar called The Thirsty Thistle. Wish u were here.*—

Jane didn't respond. Dawn put her phone away and turned to Kurt.

He leaned in closer. "So who do you hang out with in the city?" He was definitely probing.

"I have a couple of friends from law school who also got jobs here. One's in the DA's office; another's at a smaller firm. But honestly, I usually just go home and catch up on my shows." Kurt's eyes lit up, and they launched into a lengthy discussion of the finer plot points

20

of their favorite fantasy show.

Watching him talk, Dawn realized Kurt was cute. *This is the guy I should be into.* She tucked closer to him, so close she could see the dark flecks in his sky-blue eyes as he became more animated. She laughed when he got worked up, waving his hand all around.

Kurt paused, a sheepish smile on his face. "Sorry, I get really into the fan theories." Dawn's laughter turned to a shy smile. His gaze dropped from her eyes to her lips. He was going to kiss her, and she was going to let him. Sparks could fly with non-British-kinda-cute-guys too, right?

Kurt leaned down, brushed his lips to hers, and pulled back. She smiled slightly, but inside, disappointment hit her. No fire, not even a spark. More like a nice, cozy blanket. Still, she'd been burned by fire in the past. Maybe security and comfort had their own merits.

"Dawn, I've wanted to do that since I met you."

The bar hummed around them while she debated her response.

"I think—" She broke off when a waiter approached their booth and set down a beer and another Pimm's Cup on their table.

"From the guy at the bar in the black shirt," the waiter said, gesturing toward the bar.

Dawn looked past the waiter, and her jaw dropped.

Callan. In the flesh and sitting on a barstool squarely facing her. Clad in jeans and a simple black button-down with the sleeves rolled up over his impressive forearms, he looked like a Nordic god trying hard to blend in with the humans. He held up his glass in a mock salute, a tight smile on his face.

Make that a pissed-off Nordic god.

"Who's the guy?" Kurt asked, frowning.

"Uh, he's doing a deal with one of our clients," she hedged.

Kurt cast her a doubtful look as Callan stalked his way through the crowded bar toward them. This could not be happening. Hadn't she reached her quota for awkward moments today?

When Callan got to their booth, he didn't hesitate. He flung his large body into the seat across from them and clinked his drink to hers. "Cheers, love. Hope I'm not interrupting anything."

Her face burned. Callan didn't even try to pretend to hide his smirk.

"Dawn?" Kurt looked at her.

Callan had some nerve. As if he had *any* right to be here. And after she'd tried so hard all night to move past their terrible encounter.

She unclenched her jaw. "This is Kurt; he's an associate at the firm." She turned to Kurt and gestured. "This is Callan. He was at the firm today for a meeting."

"Okay," Kurt said slowly. "How do you two know each other?"

"We don't really know each other. We're acquaintances from a long time ago. In fact, I had forgotten his name until he reminded me." She shot Callan a saccharine smile, and Callan raised his eyebrow in response.

Kurt watched their interplay with a deeper frown. "Thanks for the drinks, buddy, but I think we're about to call it a night." Kurt wrapped his arm around Dawn's shoulders. Callan's eyes narrowed when he saw the movement and then flicked his gaze to her face. She flashed Callan a look that said *so freaking what?*

"Of course. You two kids go on ahead." Callan grabbed Dawn's drink and downed it in one swallow. She stared at him, and he tossed her a grin so carnal there was no way Kurt didn't know something was up. *Unbelievable.*

The booth was suddenly way too tight. "It's getting late," Dawn said to Kurt. "I've gotta get going. Let's go close out our tabs."

She made a show of gathering her purse and was about to slide out of the booth when Callan said, "I'd like to chat with you for a moment, Dawn. About business, of course."

Dawn glanced at Kurt. He wasn't an idiot. No client would need to talk to a first-year associate about business, especially not close to midnight in a dingy bar. But, hell, she was curious. Why was Callan here? What would he say to her? The temptation was too great. Glutton for punishment and all.

"Here, take my card." She offered her VISA to Kurt, compelled for some reason to demonstrate to Callan that Kurt was not her boyfriend and this was not a date.

Kurt brushed her card away, clearly annoyed at the situation. "Nah, I got it. I'll be right back." He leaned in closer. "You okay to stay here?" he asked under his breath.

She nodded.

He shot Callan a warning glance and left to pay the bill.

"Nice guy." Callan's lips twisted. "You seem to really get along."

God, she wanted to punch his face. "I don't give a shit what you think. Why are you here?"

"You invited me, remember? And then I come, and you are sucking face with that wanker." He jerked his thumb in Kurt's direction.

"Invited you? I never—" *Oh no.* She dug her phone from her purse. Two missed calls from an international number. She checked her texts. Sure enough, the last text was from an international number. *Not Jane.* "I didn't realize the text was from you. I thought I was texting Jane." She winced and added, "Sorry if I gave you the wrong impression."

He blinked for a moment and then huffed a short laugh. He ran a hand through his thick hair. "Well, fuck me. I made an arse of myself, didn't I?" The tension in his body dissipated, and the angry Nordic god melted away.

She smiled despite herself. "I was wondering how you found me. I'm glad I don't have to add stalker to the list."

"To the running list of my faults?" Callan asked.

She shrugged.

He stared at her and then nodded slowly. "I deserve that."

She glanced at the bar. Kurt wasn't having any luck flagging down the bartender. Now was her chance. "Why did you call me, Callan?"

He tilted his head as if he were considering his answer very carefully. "I think we have some unfinished business." His gaze heated. She shivered. The Nordic god wasn't pissed-off anymore. He was hungry instead.

"Unfinished how?" she asked, folding her arms to barricade herself against the simmering heat rising between them.

"Dawn, we need to talk. May I take you home?"

Callan raised his hands. "Just to talk. I promise."

She let out a snort. "I don't know what you could possibly have to say to me." She shook her head in disgust and leaned in, wishing her eyes could shoot laser beams. "You left me alone at the airport. Remember? With a bullshit excuse. I think that says everything."

Callan reached over the table and snagged one of her hands. And like a dummy, she let him. "I know. You're right. Please, Dawn."

She studied their intertwined fingers. Callan's hands were so much larger and stronger than her own, his skin rough and warm. Those hands could work magic like no one she'd been with before or since. A wave of desire crested over her. The temptation to be with him overwhelmed her, dueling with her pride and self-respect.

What if *she* used *him*?

With a flash of guilt, she pulled her hand away. Would she take an old lover home right after she'd made out with a potential new one? An old lover who'd spurned her? Made a fool of her? *Mathison, get a grip on yourself.*

But the truth was, any attraction she'd felt for Kurt had withered away the second she saw Callan on the barstool. Callan was the heat, the flame for her. He'd burn her right up, but she'd shine like a star while it happened.

One night wouldn't hurt, would it? Dawn shook the treacherous thought away. It was time to go.

"I don't think so," she said, annoyed at the uncertainty ringing in her voice.

Kurt sidled up to the booth and reached down for her hand. "Sorry I took so long." He obviously wanted to get her away from Callan.

She didn't know how to tell Kurt he didn't stand a chance.

"I'm going to take a rideshare home," Dawn said and cringed inwardly when Kurt's face fell. It was for the best. Dating coworkers was too messy anyway. *Riiiight, Dawn.*

The two men stood up from the booth and ordered their rides and then waited outside with her under the bar's blue awning. No one spoke. Dawn's car was the first to pull up, and she quickly gave them awkward goodbyes.

She stepped forward to get into the car. Kurt opened the door for her and muttered, "See you tomorrow."

She slid in, but before Kurt could shut the door, Callan's hand grabbed the doorframe. He leaned in close and murmured, "I'd like you to reconsider our business discussion." She glanced up at Callan, and her heart tripped. His gaze was fire incarnate. She sat on her hands to prevent herself from grabbing him by the collar and crushing her lips to his. His eyes grew hooded, as if he also felt the invisible pull and knew exactly what she wanted.

But the moment passed. Callan stepped back onto the curb, and Kurt slammed the door.

The driver pulled away, following the map app to her Chelsea apartment. She twisted her ponytail in her fingers and pulled out her phone. Her thumb hovered, frozen with indecision.

Is this how it ends? For good?
Of course it is, you ninny.
He'd hurt her, and she'd told him no.
End of story.

A distinct memory popped into her head. She was five years old, playing with her plastic kitchen while her mom cooked on the real stove. She'd been curious, dissatisfied with play toys. She'd wanted the real thing, and she'd reached up to grab the pot when her mom wasn't looking. She'd burned herself badly. Her mom had scolded her and told her she was too curious for her own good.

She stared at her hand. The skin on the back was creamy smooth. She didn't have any scars from that day. Nothing but memories.

Before she could lose her nerve, she texted her address to Callan.

Her phone buzzed. —*I'm on my way.*—

She slapped her hand over her eyes. Her curiosity and greed for more memories would be her undoing. Callan *was* the flame. He may not have physically scarred her, but he'd seared her down to her soul. And here she was, opening herself up to more pain from him.

Screw it. She sat back and stared out the window. She'd made the decision, and she'd live with the consequences. A dangerous thrill shivered her body.

She didn't know where this night would lead, but she sure as hell was going to find out.

Chapter Three

Callan focused on the driver's phone, which was mounted to the dashboard, and opened to a map app. The small blue dot wasn't moving nearly fast enough. Anticipation pulsed throughout his body while his mind reeled at the turn of events tonight. When he'd received Dawn's text earlier, he'd thought it was too good to be true. Then he'd shown up to find her snuggled with a wholesome, fresh-faced kid who was precisely the type of guy Dawn should be with. He'd sat at the bar, watching them for a few minutes, irrationally pissed. He'd ordered their drinks on a whim. A bit melodramatic, but it'd matched his mood. Then she'd made out with the tosser, and he'd become furious.

His reaction to Dawn and Kurt's chaste kiss was ridiculous. Callan had wanted to maul the guy, his body responding viscerally to the scene. An instantaneous possessiveness had taken over. This other man dared to kiss *his* woman? Like a caveman, he'd approached her with a fierce need to use whatever means necessary to get her back.

He laughed at himself. *What a hypocrite*. Who the hell was he to go storming in, claiming Dawn, when he'd tossed her aside because he couldn't get over his past? He rubbed his temples. His past wasn't something to *get over*...

"This is it," the driver said, pulling the car in front

of an elegant stone apartment building. Colorful pansies lined the walkway, and the marbled lobby shone brightly inside. Callan exited the car and paused on the sidewalk. Should he do this?

Fuck it. He bounded up the three steps to the call box, found Dawn's name, and dialed.

"Come on up. Third floor. Apartment thirty-two," she said through the speaker and buzzed him in.

Callan took a deep breath and opened the building door. He punched the lift button and then grew impatient and took the stairs instead. He raised his fist to knock on apartment door thirty-two and stopped. Was it anticipation or nerves causing his hand to shake?

Blood pounded in his ears. He didn't give a shite what it was; he needed to see her *now.*

Dawn opened the door, and Callan's heart leaped in his chest. Without a word, she backed up so he could enter, her luminous green eyes wary but curious. He stepped inside the flat and closed the door behind him. His hands itched to reach for her. He jammed them into his trouser pockets instead.

She hadn't changed out of her work clothes, but she'd slipped off her shoes. He glanced down at her delicate toes and painted pink nails. His gaze traveled up and took in her killer legs, sexy as hell hips, and perfect palm-sized breasts. Even barefoot, she was tall, almost six feet. But she wasn't a supermodel; her build was much more athletic and fit. Did she still go on daily runs? Did she remember their hot, post-run showers—and even hotter sex?

Her cheeks flushed. She'd noticed his inventory of her body, and she seemed as off-balance as he felt. Callan tore his gaze away from hers and looked around her flat, searching for any way to break the ice that wouldn't involve him pouncing on her.

She stood with her arms folded while he took a slow turn through the living area. The apartment was small but newly renovated, the furniture sparse but modern and expensive. He raised his eyebrows. "Nice place."

Dawn cleared her throat. "I'm housesitting until I can find a permanent place. The couple I've sublet from are traveling across Europe for the year. I'm weighing my options." She smoothed her ponytail.

He approached her slowly, but she backed away and went into the small kitchen. "You want a drink?" She pulled out a craft beer from the refrigerator and popped the top off with an opener.

"Thanks, I'll have one of those." She grabbed a second bottle, opened it, and set it on the granite countertop. She leaned against the range as he took a pull from his beer.

She watched him. "It's weird having you here."

"I meant what I said earlier. It's wonderful to see you." He took a step closer. Christ, he wanted her. He felt out of control, like he'd been wandering alone in a dark cave and finally found the sunlight. Only it was too late, and now he was out of his mind.

"How are your parents?" she asked. She folded her arms again, shielding herself from him.

"Good. Mum asks about you sometimes." Callan didn't add how his mum's face had fallen when he'd told her he wouldn't be seeing Dawn again. Or how he wouldn't dare tell his mum about this encounter; it would get his mum's hopes up, and he'd have to dash them once more.

Dawn pursed her lips. "She knows we don't talk." It

was a statement, not a question, and the hurt in her eyes stabbed him. Christ, he wanted to hold her, take her pain away, absorb it himself. He could handle pain; it festered inside him every day.

He changed the subject. "How is Jane?"

Dawn's lips curled slightly. "Still in Canton, Alabama. Still hanging out at the country club with Todd. I think they'll get engaged soon." She cracked a genuine grin. "I'm sure I'll be expected to wear some fluffy monstrosity of a bridesmaid's dress and throw a bachelorette party with penis cups."

He chuckled. He'd only met Jane once during a video call, but he enjoyed Dawn's stories about her. Mostly because they gave him so much insight into Dawn herself. Jane was the ying to Dawn's yang. Jane was the prototype for a spoiled Southern Belle with a heart of gold, while Dawn was a fascinating dichotomy of a competitive Type A champion and yearning dreamer. Dawn drove herself to be the best at everything, but to what end? Last summer she'd contemplated other options than practicing at a law firm. Options that would have made her more fulfilled. Happier. Guilt crashed over Callan. Last summer she'd considered other options partly because of *him*. When he'd gone away, maybe Dawn's dreams had too. He'd spent the past year hoping she'd found happiness, at least in her career. Part of him had been dismayed to see her in the office today. Not because she wouldn't make a brilliant lawyer, but because he knew her heart wasn't in it. But he'd forfeited the right to say anything about her decisions.

"I can imagine how wild Jane's party would be."

"It would be epic," Dawn agreed. An awkward silence spread between them. He would never see Dawn in her fluffy monstrosity. Wouldn't see pictures of her and Jane cavorting around God-knows-where with penis cups and veils. Wouldn't see Dawn give a teary wedding speech, or dance with her on a parquet dance floor, or watch her catch the bouquet.

Fuck, this was brutal.

Desperation seized him. He had to make her understand. This horrible awkwardness, this *sadness*, was not Dawn's fault. He owed her that much. "I never intended to hurt you," he said quietly.

She flinched and immediately turned away. "I'm not hurt." She reached out to straighten a dishtowel hanging on the oven handle. She ran her hand over the ivy pattern, refusing to look at him.

"Dawn, I made promises to you. And I had every intention of keeping them. But I," he paused, and she looked at him sharply. "I couldn't," he finished lamely.

Her brows scrunched together. "What happened that day? I thought—" She broke off and shook her head, setting her beer on the counter. She squared her shoulders and lifted her chin. "You need to tell me the truth."

"It was never about you." How could he tell her the truth when he could barely face it himself?

"Listen to me, Callan. You begged me to let you come over tonight so you could talk. So start talking."

He knew she was fed up with his mixed signals. One moment, he was all burning attraction, and the next he was, well, ditching her at the airport like a proper douchebag.

Callan swallowed thickly. *Tell her.* "I don't do relationships," he croaked.

"You don't do relationships," she repeated. She

cocked an eyebrow. "Well, I'm real glad you came over to tell me such an insightful nugget of information." She turned and wiped the already clean counter. Her frustration was palpable.

Callan grabbed Dawn's arm and spun her around to face him. She refused to meet his gaze. Her head bent and her eyes lowered; thick lashes fanned her cheeks. Had he broken her? Maybe he'd broken them both.

"I had some things happen…in the past." The words were gravel he couldn't spit out. "I told you last summer I was married before." She didn't respond. "It's been hard for me. These past few years." He placed his hand over hers, gently caressing the familiar fine bones and soft skin. He was doing a piss-poor job explaining himself, and he wouldn't blame her if she kicked him out right now. She finally raised her eyes to his, and he continued, "I wasn't prepared for a relationship. I thought you and I would have a fun summer. But then it grew into more, and I…" His jaw locked up.

"And you panicked," she finished for him, her mossy green eyes accusatory. He deserved the daggers she shot at him.

"I panicked." The excuse sounded so hollow, but how could he make her understand the depth to which his guilt ran, the incapacitating panic that gripped him whenever he allowed himself to think about his past? Even now, with his mind barely skimming the surface of what happened, his heart pounded, and the dreaded tightness squeezed his chest. He gripped her hand harder, as if he could transmit his feelings to her without words. Because the words were knives to his heart, every syllable slicing open a wound no one should ever have to endure. Making him bleed and bleed.

Dawn stared at Callan, her eyes willing him to say more. To give more.

He couldn't.

He glanced at the kitchen clock. One a.m. His flight didn't leave until tomorrow night, but he had early morning meetings, and she also had work. *Let her go. This is a mistake.* But dragging himself away from her was not an option. Not anymore.

He did the only thing he could do, the only thing his body would *let* him do. He pulled her tightly into his chest and banded his arms around her slender shoulders. His lips brushed the top of her silky head, and he breathed in her feminine scent. She hesitated but then circled her arms around his waist. Their bodies melded together. They stood in silence, their breaths in unison, and his heartbeat slowed.

She felt so *right* against him. They fit together like interlocking puzzle pieces. A calmness spread through him.

Callan rubbed his chin against her hair and murmured, "You feel so good, Dawn. I've missed you so much." Her small sigh tore his heart and fed his guilt. He was wrong to lead her on again. Tomorrow he'd fly back to London. Their relationship was doomed last summer, and it was doomed now. He was too fucked up to make a real relationship work, and she deserved more, so much more. But damn. He ached for her.

Callan raked his hands up Dawn's back and twined his fingers into her ponytail, gently pulling. She tilted her head back and stared into his eyes. Her mouth parted slightly, and he raised his thumb across her full bottom lip.

His heart raced again. Not from panic, but from

finally having her in his arms after a year of unsatisfying dreams. He couldn't stop his body's violent reaction to having her so close. He was on the verge of exploding, tension pulsating through him, and he felt a need to satiate the profound hunger he'd never satisfied. *Lift her up, take her to bed. Gently, slowly.*

Framing her face with his hands, he descended his lips to hers…

****

Dawn's breath hitched with Callan's tender kiss. The kiss undid her, breaking the tenuous seal holding her emotions in check. Her brain screamed—*he's told you nothing!*—but right now he was here, kissing her, and a powerful craving rocked her so hard she couldn't think straight.

She gripped his waist and felt the hard, corded muscles bunch and flex under her fingertips. His lips were soft and coaxing, and she opened up to him, returning his kisses and bending to him. She brought her hands up, skimming the solid planes of his chest. He deepened the kiss, and his lips turned urgent, demanding, parting her mouth with his tongue and slanting his head. He gripped the back of her head and twined her ponytail around his hand. She felt the forceful tug and reveled in the silent command to go deeper with him. To dive down to where they didn't need such pesky things as food and light and air. Only each other.

They were getting carried away, but she wanted to be carried away, swept up with the current, surfacing only to take a quick breath before plunging back to his mouth. She could drown in this man. Her body turned liquid, pliable. She barely stood upright. Thankfully, he gripped her bottom and lifted her tight against him. She

35

wrapped her legs around him and clung to him with a desperation she neither could nor wanted to control.

"Bedroom," Callan grated. Whether a command or a question, she didn't know.

"Yes," she responded in between frantic kisses. He kept her hoisted against him, his hands firm and strong. She hooked her ankles together behind his back and shimmied until her aching wetness lined up perfectly with the delicious hardness in his jeans. She pressed tighter against him, wanting to feel his hardness up and down, up and down, through her thin underwear. Was she already humping him? He staggered around the kitchen bar, across the living area, and to the bedroom where he tossed her onto the bed and stared down at her with molten heat in his eyes. *Oh, God.* Her panties practically dripped.

Dawn opened her arms, and Callan poured himself over her, bracing his body with his arms on either side of her. Somewhere along the way, she'd peeled his shirt from him, and she ran her hands along the steel smoothness of his shoulders and down his powerful biceps. He trailed hot, wet kisses across her brow and over the bridge of her nose before claiming her mouth again. Branding her. She threaded her fingers through his thick hair and spread her legs wider for him, allowing him to sink deeper between them.

Where are the condoms? She stopped short.

Was she really going to do this? Her body wanted him so much, but her mind screamed, *Stop, you idiot!* Callan was leaving tomorrow, and she had no idea if she would ever see him again. He'd given her no real explanation for his behavior last summer, and they hadn't resolved anything.

She could lie and tell herself she deserved a good lay and just wanted to get off. But if she slept with Callan tonight and never saw him again, the scars on her heart would be torn wide open. Could she piece herself back together a second time?

Dawn stilled. Callan raised his head, and a questioning look pierced through the haze of desire in his hazel eyes. She swallowed hard and shook her head. He ran the back of his hand gently against her cheekbone. "Not tonight?" he asked quietly.

"Not tonight," she whispered.

He rolled off her and onto his back beside her. He reached down and squeezed her hand. "Give me a moment," he said, his voice pained. They both stared at the ceiling. Regret and relief battled within her. She had no clue which one would win.

"I'm sorry. I—"

"No," Callan interrupted. "*I'm* the one who's sorry. I shouldn't have started this." He closed his eyes for a moment and then launched off the bed so quickly she scrambled to follow. He strode into the living room and retrieved his shirt. Dawn looked away while he buttoned it. He was leaving. *Leaving.* This was it. Regret was kicking relief's ass.

Callan headed for the apartment door, and she trailed behind him. How would he end it this time?

"It's late. I better go," he said.

Dawn nodded. Her heart splintered. She'd put a stop to their insanity tonight, but she was breaking apart as a result.

He laid his hand on the doorknob and paused. He turned around, and his gaze bored into hers. He reached out and cupped her face with his large, warm hands.

"Dawn, I want you to know you are the best thing to come along for me in quite some time." He shook his head, almost to himself. "*Any* complications we encountered were due solely because of me and my issues."

He caressed her cheek with his thumb. "I think you are amazing," he whispered.

And then he was gone.

Chapter Four

"Then he said, 'I think you are amazing.' " Dawn swiveled back and forth in the leather conference chair while she rehashed last night's encounter with Jane. She kept an eye on the empty hallway outside the conference room, ready to dive onto her computer in case anyone wandered her way. Her research assignment sat untouched on her open laptop. It was mid-morning, and she hadn't done jack-shit for work. She couldn't care less about researching the rules around proper notice to a corporate board. She couldn't concentrate on work right now. Mr. White would fire her in a heartbeat if he knew what she was doing.

"And so he's not into relationships because of his mysterious past with his ex-wife?" Jane asked dubiously.

Another work email popped up in Dawn's inbox. She minimized it. "I guess so. We started kissing before I could pin him down on that." She bit her lip.

"So, he thinks you're amazing, but he doesn't want a relationship with you because he got burned? Sounds like some bullshit."

"Like I said, we didn't get that far."

"You let him off too easy, Dawn. He probably started kissing you so you'd stop asking him questions. Typical guy." Then a muffled, "Not like you, babe," directed to Todd, who'd taken the later shift at Mac's hardware store so he could spend the morning with Jane at the country club. Their cuteness would be unbearable if Dawn didn't love them so much.

Dawn twisted her hair. "Maybe I should've had sex with him. It was so good last year."

"Hell, no. You did the right thing. Don't give him your power. It's a mindfuck."

More muffled voices sounded, and then Todd's familiar twang came on the line. "Dawn, I've been listening to ya'll bitch about this guy for a year. I heard all this last year, and now I'm hearing the same shit again. Fuck this guy. Even if he likes you, he lives an ocean away. He's got major issues. Jane's right. Don't give Callan what he wants. You have to move on and be with someone who can love you without putting you through this bullshit. Love should be easy. Being with Jane is easy. Love shouldn't be painful. Don't put up with that."

Dawn smiled at the loud smacking kiss on the other end of the line.

Jane came back on the phone. "Awww. Am I lucky or what? Todd's right. Callan has issues. I feel bad for him if he had a horrible breakup or something, but he's still shady. I mean, he's not even on social media." Jane was an open book online and thought the only people who didn't have profiles were serial killers and the Amish.

Callan's lack of a social media presence didn't bother Dawn—much—but she wished she could find some clue about his past. The friends of his she'd met last year, Will and Sarah, rarely posted, and they never posted about Callan. Dawn and Jane had scoured the Internet again this morning. They'd found a few articles discussing the rise of residential solar installations in the

UK, which either mentioned Callan's company, Green Solar, or quoted Callan himself. Still, none of the business articles mentioned his personal life.

Another email pinged Dawn's inbox. She groaned. "I should let you go. I need to get back to work."

"Buck up, buttercup. Sounds like you've got a pretty good second option walking the halls of your office. Why don't you see if he wants to have lunch?"

"I dunno. We'll see. Kurt probably hates me after last night." *He for sure hates me after last night.*

"Psh. You'd be surprised what a guy can forgive when he likes a girl," Jane scoffed. Then, muffled, "I don't have anything you need to forgive, babe. I was talking figuratively."

Dawn laughed and said goodbye. She hung up the phone and stared at her computer. She needed to buckle down and get back to work, but she couldn't wrap her brain around her assignments. Callan was a distraction, plain and simple. He'd distracted her last summer, and he was doing it again. She gritted her teeth. She'd already lost her heart; she would not lose her job because of him.

She looked up to find Bill White Sr. shuffling down the hallway with an eye on her. She waved to him through the glass. He smiled and opened the door.

"Hello, Ms. Mathison. Are you having a fine day?" The old man was the complete opposite of his son. Dawn and Kurt had nicknamed Bill White Sr. "The Leprechaun" because he was kind and small, with tufts of white hair shooting haphazardly from his head. He straight up looked like a guy who knew his way around a rainbow.

"Oh, I'm doing well. Working on a memo today," she said lightly.

"You spent last summer in Cambridge, right? How does it compare to this year?"

"Well, there wasn't much studying or working going on last summer," she admitted.

He chuckled. "I can imagine. I did the same when I was in school. In undergrad, I studied in Spain. How's your Spanish?"

Bill White Sr.'s non sequiturs were legendary, so she took the question in stride. "Decent. I took eight years of Spanish in school."

"Good to know. Good to know. Well, I'd better be off. I have a lunch meeting with my banking client about a project they are financing. One in Spain, as a matter of fact."

Callan.

"How interesting." Dawn attempted to sound nonchalant. "Have they worked with the developer before?"

"No. This is their first project together. I introduced them. I met the developer last fall through a charity. He has great vision, and I wanted to help him. He's a good man," he said pointedly.

Before she could think of a diplomatic response, Bill White Sr. said, "I will see you later, Ms. Mathison," and shuffled down the hallway and out of sight.

****

"May I get you a drink? We have wine and spirits available." The flight attendant leaned toward Callan, showcasing her blue-white porcelain teeth and ample bosom.

"No, thank you," he replied. She pursed her poufy lips and moved on. Callan turned his head to stare at the pink and yellow clouds billowing below. He wasn't in

42

the mood to flirt with the attendant and was glad his fellow row mate wore earbuds so there were no expectations of polite conversation.

Callan rubbed his temples. The weight of this solar project threatened to crush him. The local Spanish environmental consultants they'd engaged had utterly missed a significant issue, pushing the timeline for the project back by months, and landing his company in hot water with the investors.

Before catching this flight back to London, he'd had another long meeting with the bank financing his project. The bank reps were, to put it mildly, not happy with the project delays.

Bill White Sr. had been able to calm his clients down, but it was only a matter of time before the old man would be forced to advise Weston Bank to pull the funding or force a sale to another developer who could get the project done on time.

Had Callan pushed his company to the breaking point?

He remembered the day he and his small team had found out they'd won the bid to bring the solar project to the Granada region. They'd celebrated all afternoon and through the night. He shook his head. *We didn't know what we were getting into.*

He'd driven his company hard over the past year, almost maniacal in his ambition to get the project up and running. Why? He shifted in his seat and closed his eyes.

So you wouldn't have time to think about her.

And there was the real truth. After Dawn left England last summer—after he'd made a complete arse of himself—work was all he had left. This project was the result.

Now, right as everything was unraveling with his investors, Dawn popped back into his life.

Christ, what else could go wrong?

Last night he'd rekindled a flame he'd worked hard to snuff out. He'd have to douse the fire all over again.

A relationship with Dawn was not in Callan's future. It couldn't be. Hell, they didn't even live in the same country. And even if they did, he wouldn't be offering marriage or children to anyone. Not even Dawn. Building a relationship with her was pointless.

He'd told her last year about his wife, but he hadn't told her anything about what had really happened. About his part in it. About... Callan fingered the phantom ring on his left hand.

Not being with Dawn wouldn't be the biggest heartbreak of his life—not by a long shot—but it would be a regret he'd carry etched within him like an invisible tattoo.

Right next to the other regrets carved deep into his soul.

Chapter Five

Cambridge, England—Last Summer

Dawn was a heroine straight from the Scottish moors. Or so she imagined. Misty rain droplets dampened her hoodie and clung to her cheeks, dewy and fresh. In the gloomy first light of day, she carefully navigated the slick cobblestones, the glow of streetlamps reflecting upon street signs she'd already memorized. She took deep breaths of the crisp English air—so different from the oppressive humidity back home in Alabama.

When she'd left home two weeks ago, summer had already engulfed her small town, causing her hair to stick to her nape and her under boob sweat to, well, *gather*. But here, in Cambridge, England, the mornings remained chilly, and the days only warmed on certain sunny afternoons. Other days were overcast and drizzly, more suited for curling up with a warm cup of tea.

She loved it.

Dawn wove her way through the historic streets lined with tidy shops and inviting pubs. Cambridge was exciting and brimming with possibilities. She enjoyed squeezing into the tiny bathroom of her rented apartment. She enjoyed not quite knowing her way around. She enjoyed the strange mix of accents and sounds. She even enjoyed the law school lectures. After two weeks, she'd rediscovered a kernel of joy in learning for the sake of learning, a feeling she'd lost somewhere along the way in her relentless drive to be number one in her class. *Screw Mae Lin and her photographic memory.*

She entered the Cambridge Coffee House and wiped her rain boots on the entry floor mat. Careworn and cozy, the coffee shop reminded her of settling into an old book. She inhaled the welcoming aroma of roasted coffee and scanned today's clientele. An older gentleman in a tweed jacket was perched on a nearby stool, a stereotypical Cambridge professor-type. Two younger girls chatted in a corner, and a man sat at a table with his back to Dawn, typing away on his computer.

Her gaze lingered on the man at the table. She couldn't see his face, only his thick blondish-brown hair and broad shoulders. His long legs extended out from under the table, exposing the ends of his dark jeans and sneakers. Even though he was seated, she could tell he would tower over her.

Intriguing. Not many men topped her six feet.

Men might stare at Dawn, but few approached her. Jane said she had an *unapproachable look,* which basically meant resting bitch face. But Dawn had taken enough selfies to know Jane was full of shit. Dawn's height turned men off, not her face. Being just shy of six feet was great for playing D1 college basketball. But in the real world, it was male kryptonite.

Dawn made her way to the lacquered counter and ordered a coffee with cream to go, keeping the man in her peripheral vision. While she waited, she turned and pretended to casually look out the window so she could check him out from the front. She slid her gaze over him, and their eyes locked.

She froze.

This man did not belong here. His eyes were an otherworldly bright hazel and framed with ridiculous eyelashes. She soaked in his straight, thick eyebrows. His high cheekbones. His perfect nose. His broad, sensual mouth. His strong jawline covered in dark-blond stubble grown to the perfect length for maximum hotness.

And, dear Lord, he was as built from the front as he was from the back. His T-shirt strained over defined pecs and bulging biceps. He probably had abs of steel under that T-shirt, and his muscular thighs told her he could lift just about anything he wanted. Including her.

Holy hell.

Dawn had managed to stumble upon the most handsome man in Cambridge, possibly all of England, and she was staring at him with drool practically dripping from her mouth. Her heart thumped so hard she had to stop herself from clutching imaginary pearls.

At first, his face was inscrutable, but then a slow smile tugged at the corner of his beautiful lips. Panicked, Dawn swiveled back to the counter without returning his smile. *Smooth, very smooth.*

"Your coffee, miss," the barista called to her. She grabbed the hot beverage and hurried for the exit. She refused to look at Mr. Handsome, even though she could feel his gaze, hot and electric, along her back.

She stood outside the shop for a moment, hesitating, searching for divine inspiration.

What would Jane do?

Jane would march right back in there and ask for his number with such confidence he wouldn't dare deny the request.

Dawn sipped her coffee and peeked through the window. Mr. Handsome's computer sat open on the table next to his empty chair. He must have gone to get another coffee or go to the loo. She bit her lip. How could she be so confident when speaking up in class but couldn't find the courage to approach a cute guy?

Maybe it was a sign. Her first class would begin soon and, besides, she hadn't enrolled in Cambridge University's summer law program to find a man.

In a few months, the top law firms from across the US would arrive on her school's campus for fall interviews, and Dawn wanted to rack up as many offers as she could. She already had a fall clerkship lined up with a well-known judge in DC. Being the top student in this program would be another check on her already impressive résumé.

Asking a cute guy out on a date was definitely not on her agenda.

Dawn set off in the direction of the law college. She hitched her book bag higher on her shoulder. Something was off. She felt the front pocket. *Crap.* She'd set her wallet down on the counter when she'd paid and had forgotten to put it back in her bag.

She pivoted back to the coffee shop. Maybe *this* was the sign.

She entered the shop and spied her wallet on the counter. Mr. Handsome still wasn't at his table. She exhaled and hurried to the counter and grabbed her wallet, shoving it into her bag. She nodded to the barista and whirled around to leave.

And collided with a wall of muscle.

"Aaaa, shit," Dawn exclaimed. Piping hot coffee splashed down her chest, scalding her breasts and stomach. She looked up with watering eyes and saw horror on Mr. Handsome's face.

"Christ. Are you okay? I am so sorry." He set his empty cup down and pulled her to the side. The barista gave him a side-eye and handed him a cloth.

He began mopping her up, his hands fluttering clumsily around Dawn's chest. This was *exactly* like the meet-cute in that rom-com…except she was no Hollywood starlet, he was no unassuming gent, and *crap* coffee is hot. Dawn giggled nervously. "I don't suppose you have a flat right around the corner where I can go clean up, with water…and soap…and a phone?"

Mr. Handsome's brows furrowed and then relaxed. "Ah, you are American, and you just made a movie reference." His smile crinkled his eyes and made her stomach somersault. This man, with his muscles and beautiful eyes and sexy British accent, was her kind of catnip.

She ogled him with what had to be a ridiculous grin on her face until she realized her chest no longer burned but was wet and cold, her soaked T-shirt nearly transparent. She hastily pulled her hoodie tight across her chest. "Good thing I've got my jacket," she said dumbly. More students and professionals filed in, crowding the coffee shop. She scooted to the wall and bumped into a sideboard. God, she was a mess.

He stopped her from knocking over a stack of cups by grabbing her elbow. "I'm sorry again. What can I do? I'm afraid I'm not quite sure what would help in these situations." He was so adorably contrite; concern stamped across his handsome face.

His hand lingered on her elbow as they stood within inches of each other in the crowded shop. She could *smell* him, some manly scent she couldn't pinpoint, but it lured her into leaning closer to him. His beautiful eyes were a changeable mix of blue, green, and amber, and she wanted to study every fleck and swirl in them. And he *did* tower over her, making her feel dainty and girly and all things she usually never felt. She felt drunk and hyperaware all at once.

What would Jane do?

"Well, you could buy me a drink," Dawn said, striving for blasé confidence while holding her breath.

"You...want another coffee?" He eyed her cup.

"No, I, ah..." Someone jostled her from behind, and he maneuvered her out of the way, his warm hand still on her arm. She licked her lips. "I mean, a drink. A real drink. Like in a pub sometime?"

Surprise flashed across his face, but then he hesitated, casting his gaze to the side, and a cold lump of disappointment sank into her stomach. *He's probably taken. Of course he is. Look at him.*

She was about to tell him never mind when he said slowly, "Yes. A drink would be lovely. Why don't you give me your number?"

She pulled paper and a pen from her bag and wrote her information for him.

"Dawn Mathison," he read. "Wonderful to meet you. I'm Callan Marlowe." Then, with a sheepish laugh, "I never imagined I would give a poor young woman third-degree burns and walk away with a date."

"Don't worry, I think they are only first degree," she said, beaming.

He laughed again and held the door open for her as they exited into the street.

"Until next time, Ms. Mathison." He inclined his

head, and her cheeks burned.

"Goodbye, Mr. Marlowe," she responded, holding his gaze for a long moment until he smiled faintly and returned inside. She straightened her backpack and headed down the street to school. The rain had stopped, and the sun peeked out.

She blew out a long breath and grinned. This was turning into a fine day indeed.

****

Callan sat on his best friend's couch and turned the paper over and over in his hands. *Dawn Mathison.* She was a student and an American. Most likely studying here for the summer term. One of those study abroad programs Cambridge liked to host to fill their empty campus and give the professors something to do while the regular students were on holiday.

She was entirely inappropriate for him, of course. He was almost thirty. He shouldn't be playing around with undergrads. What if she's only eighteen? Her height made her seem older, but you never know... And an American? He'd never dated one, but they tended to be brash, yes? Except he rather liked her version of brashness. *She'd* asked *him* out, an instant turn on.

He'd noticed her the second she'd walked up to the counter. He always noticed pretty girls, even if he didn't usually do anything about it. But he had appreciated her long legs, sunset-colored hair, full lips, and wide green eyes. At first, she'd been cool and collected, her mouth set in a straight line. But then she'd stared at him, openly, like she couldn't help herself from drinking in every detail. He'd felt a sudden jolt stiffen him down below. He hadn't reacted to anyone that way in a while.

When she'd hurried back into the shop, he'd

intended to do something he hadn't done in a long time: tap a woman on the shoulder. He hadn't known what he would say or do once she turned around, but it sure as hell wasn't slamming into her with hot coffee.

He'd been mortified. Full stop. But then she'd smiled up at him with her beautiful lips and bright face, and he'd been...charmed.

Callan studied her name again. She was most likely only here for the summer. A thought crept in and took hold, one he couldn't shake.

I could be with this one.

"What do you have there? You've been burning a hole through it for the past half hour." Will vaulted the couch from behind and threw himself into the seat next to Callan.

Will was excitable, especially this week. He was getting married on Saturday to the love of his life. Literally. Will and Sarah met in primary school, and Callan had never known one without the other. The three of them had grown up together in Cambridge, the children of professors. Callan could have booked a hotel, but he rarely saw his friends and had jumped at the offer to stay with them during their wedding week.

"I met a girl..." Callan began but regretted saying anything when Will jumped up.

"Ho! All right, man. That's brill! Sarah," Will called out.

Sarah came running in from the kitchen, her red curls bouncing. "What is it?"

"Callan met a girl."

"Sweetie, how fabulous. Bring her to the wedding."

"Oh, I don't think—"

"Look, man, if you like this girl, you should bring

her to the wedding. It's a party, for Christ's sake. You know we don't care. We counted two places for you anyhow. We were hoping..." Will trailed off and shrugged.

Callan smiled tightly. He knew what they were hoping. It was the same thing his parents hoped for. What his other friends and family hoped for. What everyone hoped for.

Their hopes exhausted him.

Your hopes can go to hell. The words formed in Callan's mouth, pungent and bitter, but when he looked at Will's eager face and Sarah's bright eyes, he pushed the words back down to the low simmer where they belonged.

But this girl—Dawn—maybe she could be a temporary fix. A distraction. There would be no commitments, just a few weeks of fun. *No explaining past lives.*

"I only met her today, if you can call dousing hot coffee on someone an official introduction. Let me take her out before we get ahead of ourselves."

"All right, but you have five days to decide if she's wedding material. I mean, *our* wedding material." Will slapped Callan's back.

Callan laughed and inspected the paper again.

What could possibly happen in five days?

Chapter Six

"What the hell is punting?" Jane's face disappeared from the computer screen to paint another toe. Jane was primping for her date with Todd to one of Canton, Alabama's five chain restaurants.

"Punting is a big thing here. It's like canoeing down a calm river." Callan had called Dawn yesterday to invite her out. She smiled, recalling the conversation:

"Hi, this is Callan. From this morning."

"Hello, 'Callan From This Morning.' "

He'd laughed. "I wondered if you'd like to go punting tomorrow?"

"Punting? That's the boat thing, right?"

"You live in Cambridge, and you haven't been punting?"

"I've only been here a couple weeks."

"Then I'm honored to be your first...punting experience, of course..."

"Dawn, honey, you've got it bad," Jane observed.

Dawn twirled her ponytail between her fingers. "He was pretty cute on the phone. And, of course, his accent makes him hotter."

"Of course. Do you know anything about him? Did you look him up?"

"Yeah. He's not on social, but I think he owns his own company. I searched him, and a solar company called Green Solar came up. He's listed as Founder and

54

CEO. The company is based out of London, but his bio says he went to Cambridge. Maybe he's here for some alumni function. London's not far away."

"And you said he looks like he's around thirty? Impressive," said Jane. "Although Todd put himself as owner and CEO on his company's website, and he hasn't built his first house yet." Jane's boyfriend grew up working with his dad on residential home builds and planned to start his own company building homes in Canton and the surrounding towns.

"Green Solar's website lists a few dozen completed projects, so I think Callan is legit," Dawn said and then realized what she'd implied. "Not that Todd isn't," she amended quickly.

"Oh, I'm not offended. I know he'll succeed. He's great with his hands, after all." Jane wagged her eyebrows.

"You've been smitten with Todd since high school." Dawn laughed.

Jane shrugged with a grin. "Do you like your roommates?"

"They're nice. We all go to different law schools, and it's fun to hear what life is like in California and New York. Last weekend we went sightseeing together in London. They're talking about going to Manchester and Liverpool this weekend. I might go with them as long as they don't leave too early."

"Are they cutting class already? Won't they get docked?"

"Maybe, but I don't think they care. Technically, these grades don't apply toward our law school GPAs. But I still want to do well."

"Of course you do, you overachiever." Jane smiled.

"Well, it sounds like you might have other plans this weekend anyway—if things work out with this guy. Maybe he'll sweep you off your feet, and you'll never return to school." She held up her phone. "Hey, I've gotta go. Todd's here."

"Tell him I said hi." Dawn waved and shut down her computer. She leaned back against the bed's narrow headboard, and a small pang hit her. Even after two years in DC, Dawn still missed her best friend.

Dawn and Jane had spent almost every day together throughout their time in high school and college. It had been a hard decision for Dawn to choose a DC law school over Alabama's state school, not only because she was giving up the in-state tuition but because she was also giving up Jane.

Dawn wasn't quite sure how she—bookish and an overachiever—had become best friends with Canton High School's most beloved cheerleader and homecoming queen. Looking back on their freshman year, Dawn wondered if Jane had picked her on a whim. As if Jane had decided she needed more diversity in her friend group and choosing a dorky basketball player with no boobs would do the trick.

They'd clicked, though, and became inseparable. Jane loosened her up, pushed her to talk to boys, to wear makeup, and made her laugh until milk shot from her nose. Jane would doodle funny—and often raunchy—cartoons and post them to Dawn's locker or hide them in a textbook for Dawn to chuckle over later when she'd had a bad day. Jane knew how much pressure Dawn put on herself to achieve academically and on the basketball court, and she never made fun of Dawn or pressured her to blow off her studies or practice. Jane inspired Dawn to go after what she wanted, even if what she wanted wasn't something Jane fully understood. Jane, the queen bee, didn't get why Dawn wanted to leave Alabama, much less live in England for the summer.

But Dawn didn't have a Todd back home in Canton, Alabama, and, though she loved her parents and friends, she'd always sensed her future was somewhere else. Somewhere yet to be discovered.

She hopped up and dressed for bed. She didn't know what she was searching for, but the only way she would find it was by pushing herself to excel. Being the best was Dawn's comfort zone. She didn't know any other way to live. Surely all her hard work would pay off. Someday.

Jane's comment about this weekend nagged her. Dawn wasn't about to miss out on her experiences in the summer program because of an infatuation or let her grades slip because of a guy.

Maybe she was jumping into this too fast. She'd only been in Cambridge for a couple of weeks; she shouldn't get distracted. And Callan was distracting, for sure. Tall, broad, handsome, charming...and those eyes...

She sighed and turned off the bedside lamp.

You're getting ahead of yourself. You might not even like the guy.

But as she snuggled under the covers, her lips curled into a smile.

I think I'm going to like the guy.

****

Dawn bounded out of bed, dressed, and was out the door before her housemates stirred. She debated going to the coffee shop, but she didn't want to run into Callan again. Not yet. Not until she was ready to meet him this afternoon. She resigned instead to one of the on-campus cafés, which didn't have the same appeal as the Cambridge Coffee House, but at least she wouldn't be looking over her shoulder every second.

During her classes, she struggled to focus on the lectures. A soupy mix of giddiness, excitement, and nervousness churned her insides, and she had to stop herself from twisting her ponytail into knots.

Her sparse dating history hadn't prepared her for today.

The last guy she'd dated several months ago had been a skinny bartender/musician who'd considered her bougie because she liked craft coffee and yoga pants and had chided her for her ambition—all while paying his rent with his parents' money. She'd half-heartedly dated him for a couple of months before they'd ghosted each other. His absence hadn't registered one blip.

Callan, on the other hand… He registered above a ten on the Richter scale, and they hadn't even gone out yet.

Dawn shook her head and sat up straighter. Mentally, she put Callan in a box, closed the lid, and shoved him to the back of her brain. She tuned into the lecture, taking notes and reading along when the professors quoted the case law. Creating a mental box helped her compartmentalize her thoughts so she could focus on her studies. It was a trick she'd taught herself in third grade when she'd been unable to concentrate on her spelling words because of a fight with her best friend, and it still worked today.

But as soon as her classes ended, she let Callan out of his box and raced home to change. *What does one wear when one goes punting?* The weather was sunny and temperate, but it might be cooler on the water. She settled on a capped-sleeve top, jeans, and flats. Casual but cute. She left her hair in her usual ponytail because it might get windy. She took a deep breath and followed Callan's instructions to the meeting point on the River Cam.

Dozens of punts crowded the riverbank docks. Some of the broad, flat-bottomed boats were large, seating a dozen or so people; others were smaller, with seats for just two or three. Like the sun, the tourists were out in full force, hoping to cram the requisite activity into their itinerary.

For a moment, Dawn worried she wouldn't find Callan, but then she easily spotted him. How could she miss him? He stood tall and golden, waving to her from the thick of it all, one leg propped on the edge of a small punt and the other grounded on a dock. Like a hot pirate set to plunder her.

Oh jeez, she did have it bad.

She picked her way over to him. "Hi. I had no idea it would be so crowded."

He grabbed her hand and helped her into the punt, settling her onto the cushioned bench. "It does get crowded. Particularly when going down the Backs, behind the colleges, and under the bridge. But we'll head south, toward Grantchester, which isn't so busy." He stepped up onto a platform over the punt's square-cut bow and grasped a long pole similar to a gondola.

Dawn pretended she hadn't spent the better part of last night researching Callan. "Are you from around here? Have you done this before?"

Callan stuck the pole in the water and shoved away

from the dock. "Don't worry; I grew up here. I know what I'm doing." He gave her a jaunty grin and continued to push the pole hard on the shallow river bottom.

He'd also dressed casually in jeans and a T-shirt, and she watched, rapt, as his arm muscles and pecs flexed and bulged with the effort. He turned to bend and push the pole along the other side of the punt, which put Dawn in direct sightline of Callan's perfectly formed butt.

Holy shit. The local scenery couldn't match this view. She all but fanned herself.

He maneuvered the punt away from the other boats, and soon they were drifting along at a leisurely clip. He relaxed and held the pole at an angle, using it as a rudder to steer. "So, Ms. Mathison, what are you doing in Cambridge?" he asked, giving her his full attention.

"Well, Mr. Marlowe, I am in a summer program for law students. I recently finished my second year of law school in DC."

"So you aren't an undergrad," Callan stated with noticeable relief.

"Nope." Dawn cocked her head. "Were you scared I was a teenager?"

"I confess I was." He grinned.

She laughed. "I'm twenty-four, fully legal."

"Thank God." The look he gave her scrambled her insides, and she didn't quite know how to respond.

He saved her from her awkward fluster when he asked, "What do you study in the program?"

"I'm studying international and UK corporate law. Deal flow between borders, tax and trade issues, etcetera."

"So you're interested in corporate transactions?" He deftly avoided another punt passing by.

"Not really. I mean, it's interesting, but it's not the kind of law I want to practice."

Callan peered down at her. "So why are you here?"

Dawn shrugged. "It looks good on a résumé. I need any leg up I can get when I interview with law firms this fall." She paused and added, "Honestly, I've never been abroad before. I saw a pamphlet about this program in the student center, and I thought, when will I ever have a chance to do something like this again?"

"I get it." Callan nodded. "I grew up in this town, went to university here. At the time, my parents lived in a manor house not too far from town. I couldn't wait to get out of here. I moved to London. It's only a train ride away, but it felt like a different world."

"I felt the same about moving to DC. I had to get out of my small town." They floated under a stone bridge, and Dawn trailed her fingertips in the water.

"And coming here is…"

"An adventure," she finished.

"If you're looking for adventure, I should have chosen something more thrilling than a boat ride." He threw her a sexy smile.

She half-laughed and twisted her ponytail. She doubted anything could be more thrilling than being right here with him at this moment. "How about you? What do you do?"

"I own my own business. We install solar panels, mostly in residential neighborhoods, but we do some commercial work." He gave another good shove with the pole.

"How did you get into the solar business?"

"When I was graduating from university, I read an article about how the UK was poised to increase its solar capacity significantly because of some major tax incentives the government was about to pass. So I read all I could on the topic, talked to some people in the industry, and started a small business installing rooftop panels."

"I admit when I think of England, I think of clouds and rain, pretty much the opposite of sunny."

"We have more sunny days than most people think." Callan crouched as he spoke, leaning toward her, his lips dangerously within kissing distance. He reached over and pulled something out of Dawn's hair. He held up a leaf in front of her with a half-grin and flicked it away. He straightened back up and continued, "And people here are passionate about climate change. It's still a very small percentage of the total energy mix for the country, but it's enough to sustain my company. In seven years, we've grown to over twenty people."

"That's awesome. I admire anyone with an entrepreneurial spirit. It takes guts to forge a path on your own."

"Thanks." Callan blinked and turned his attention back to the water. Had *she* flustered *him?* "Would you ever start your own practice?" he asked.

Dawn shook her head. "I doubt it. I'm not quite sure what I want to do, but I know I need to get a good job." Those student loans wouldn't pay themselves.

"What made you go to law school in the first place?"

"I decided I wanted to be a lawyer when I was in middle school. My mom was into a TV show about lawyers at the time, and I would watch it with her and think to myself how I wanted to be just like them, locking up murderers and taking down corrupt corporate bigwigs in the big city. I suppose I saw it as my ticket out of my small town. So, it became my goal, my endgame, to go to law school. Now I'm there, and I need to keep working as hard as possible to stay at the top of my class. I'm ranked second right now…" She trailed off, embarrassed. She hadn't meant to brag.

His eyebrows shot up. "Second in your class? Brilliant. So you want to—how did you put it?—lock up murderers and take down bigwigs?" His lips turned up as he continued pushing the pole into the water.

She laughed. "I would love to, but I think something in a boring corporate law firm is more likely." She smiled, but inside, a familiar doubt crept in. She had so much student loan debt from going to a top-tier law school in a big city; she had to follow the money to a big law firm job. But the thought of billing two thousand hours a year, working for corporations instead of helping people… *Put it in the box. Shove it away.*

"Corporate law isn't all boring, especially for startups. My company hires lawyers for every aspect of our projects. It's more like a partnership, working together to build something. You should speak to my chief legal officer. She can tell you what it's like to work for a smaller company."

"Thanks, maybe I will. And I didn't mean to sound like working for companies is bad," Dawn said in a rush. *Crap.* Had she offended him? "I'm just not going to be practicing the type of law I thought I would when I first decided to go to law school."

Callan shrugged a broad shoulder. "No offense taken. I know what it is like to think your life is going one way and then…" He paused and averted his gaze. "It takes a detour." A flash of *something* washed over his face. Anger, sadness, loss?

Time to change the subject again. "This must have been a great place to grow up."

He nodded, the tension in his body visibly easing. "My parents were professors. They're retired now and live in Brighton."

"What are they like?"

"They are precisely what you might picture when you think of professors. My dad is forgetful, a bit of a fuddy-duddy, smokes a pipe. He taught East Asian literature. My mum is obsessed with arcane mathematics; she headed the math department for years. But she also bakes cookies and loves to garden." He smiled fondly. "Ever since my parents moved, I don't come back here nearly enough. I'm in town this week for my best mate's wedding. He's getting married on Saturday at King's College Chapel."

"How lovely." She'd seen the chapel, a beautiful and massive Gothic structure set against the pristine grounds of the sprawling campus. It wasn't like any chapel she'd been to back home.

"What about your family?" Callan asked.

"My parents are accountants, very strait-laced. They run a small firm in my hometown. I'm from Canton, Alabama, population five thousand. It's a nice place to grow up. A couple hours away from Birmingham, but still a small town."

Callan's eyes lit up. "I thought I detected an accent. You sound like that movie star from *An Alabama Homecoming*."

Dawn doubted she sounded anything like her, but she wasn't about to burst Callan's British bubble.

"Any brothers or sisters?" he asked.

"Nope. You?"

"Me neither. We're a couple of self-centered only children. Spoiled and bratty and expecting entirely too much attention. I'm not sure how this will work out." He gave her a mock frown.

She smiled back. "Just don't ask me to share anything, and we'll be fine."

"Selfish to the core. Typical only child." They grinned at each other for a moment, and then Callan said, "Hop up. I'm going to teach you how to punt." He reached over and pulled Dawn to her feet.

"Whoa," she said as the punt wobbled.

He steadied her shoulders. "You have to get your sea legs under you."

"This isn't even close to a sea, and I'm terrified I'm going to tip us over."

He traded places with her and helped her up onto the platform. "You'll do fine. And if we do end up in the river, it is summertime, after all."

Dawn pictured a soaking wet Callan emerging from the river like a sea god, and, for a second, she had a wild urge to toss him overboard.

"Easy there," Callan grabbed her forearm to steady her again. "Here, take my pole." Jane's voice popped into her mind. *Yeah, you'll take his pole.* Dawn snickered, and he threw her a suspicious look before handing over the long pole.

"So, ah, I push off the ground with this?" she asked.

"First, turn to the right, like you're standing on a surfboard." He turned her to stand with one foot in front of the other. "Now put the pole in the water and push it straight off the riverbed. When you want to steer, you hold the pole just under the water and hold it straight to go straight, turn it to the right to go right, and so forth." He sat back on the bench with his arms folded and a grin on his face.

"Okay, here we go." She lowered the pole until it hit the bottom of the river and pushed firmly, propelling the punt forward, gliding smoothly. "I'm a natural," she crowed. "And here I was so impressed with you. You really shouldn't have shown me how easy this is."

"Is that so?" Callan raised an eyebrow and then glanced behind him. "You know you are headed straight for another punt."

"Not a problem. I've got this." She held the pole in the water as he'd shown her, and she angled it to the right. The punt followed and veered around the other punt.

"Hello!" Dawn waved to the other punters. They waved back, and she turned to Callan with a smug smile. Their punt, however, didn't completely clear the other, and the bow clipped the other punt's front end. Their punt lurched hard, and Dawn toppled forward—face first directly into his broad lap.

"Are you okay?" Callan lifted her by the shoulders. Concern furrowed his brow, but once he saw she was unscathed, his lips quirked.

This was so embarrassing. And what the hell was he packing? An anaconda?

She leaned back on her knees and peered up at Callan. *Screw it.* "I think I broke my nose on your dick."

Callan laughed so hard his face turned red, making her face burn in return.

"It's your fault," Dawn accused him. She stood up as nonchalantly as possible. "Sorry guys," she called to the other punt. They were also laughing. Great.

"I better take it from here. I have to return this punt to the rental station in top condition." He steered her back to the bench, and she sat down with a huff. His hands lingered on her shoulders, and he gazed down at her. He was still chuckling, but there was also a hint of worry in his eyes. "Are you sure you are all right? I won't be able to properly make fun of you if I know you are hurt in any way."

"This is the second time we've had a highly awkward encounter," she said with consternation.

"It does seem to follow us, doesn't it? I don't know if we should take any more chances, but I'll go against my better judgment and ask you to dinner."

She flushed. "And I'll go against mine and say I'd like to have dinner with you."

They returned to the docks, and Dawn waited while Callan took care of the punt. He came back and reached for her hand. As they made their way toward the pubs, her entire awareness focused like a laser on their linked hands. She barely noticed the Gothic buildings, tightly packed storefronts, and crowded restaurants they passed.

"This is my favorite alehouse." Callan stopped in front of an establishment that looked as if it had been opened since the days of Cromwell. The pub's brick facade was old but well cared for, with a crisp new awning and picnic benches out front to welcome patrons. He opened the door for Dawn, and they wove their way through the warm and bright bar area, his hand settled firmly on the small of her back. He steered her to a corner table nestled against a wall cluttered with charming antique framed pictures and memorabilia.

They ordered a couple of beers with their fish and

chips. "Would you ever go back to Alabama?" he asked.

She thought for a moment. "I don't know. DC has so much to offer, so much opportunity. My goal is to work at a top firm, which means working in DC, New York, San Francisco. Big cities have the best law firms. But I do miss my parents, and my best friend lives back home. Luckily, DC has direct flights to Birmingham. Have you ever been to DC?"

He shook his head. "I've only been to the States a few times. My parents took me to Disney World when I was eight, which was brilliant. We went to one of the Florida beaches too. As an adult, I've traveled to New York several times, but mostly for business, and not often."

"Do you have to travel a lot for work?"

"No, our projects are all in the UK, for now. But we are considering expanding the business into different markets. We've been eyeing a few opportunities, but we want to be selective and make sure it's the right move for the company."

"Makes sense," she said and took another bite of her fish. There was a lull, and they smiled at each other.

"Dawn is a beautiful name," Callan said, taking her off guard. His smile faded as his gaze, golden in the pub's light, drifted to her lips, heating her insides.

His eyes became half-lidded, and an image blazed into Dawn's mind—of Callan leaning toward her in the boat, but instead of pulling a leaf out of her hair, he pulls her toward him—hard.

Her breath quickened, and she crossed her legs. She needed to get herself under control. Evidently, she was hornier than she thought.

Dawn tilted her head and smiled slowly.

She could squeeze some fun in between her studies, right? Perhaps Callan was just the adventure she'd been looking for.

****

Those lips, full and kissable, curled into a come-hither smile.

Callan was hooked.

It had been so long since he'd had the urge to do more than give a woman a perfunctory kiss. But right now, he wanted to jump across the table, crush Dawn against the wall, and have his way with her.

Callan sat back. His response to Dawn—needing and raw—surprised him. This afternoon was the first time he'd enjoyed himself in a very long time.

Over the past few years, ever since *the incident*, he'd had a few half-hearted hookups. To feel alive again, to forget. The first one happened a few months after Callan's life had crashed around him. He'd been piss drunk in a pub and had taken some nondescript brunette home with him. They'd fucked, and he'd cried. Not his finest moment.

Since then, he'd had several blessedly brief and unemotional trysts with women he'd met at parties, bars, and sometimes through work. Nothing serious; he made sure they understood the deal right up front. Even so, he rarely saw a woman more than three times. After then was usually when a woman began thinking she could break down his barriers and ask questions.

He was done playing that game.

Today though, he'd felt so free with Dawn. Knowing this was temporary, knowing she'd be gone at the end of summer, had somehow loosened him up. Allowed him to focus on her and simply have fun. Free

69

from any relationship bullshit.

And he was going to take advantage of it.

"It's plain and simple. My name, I mean," Dawn said, tucking a stray lock of hair behind her ear. "I like your name. Callan. It's unique."

He studied her. She was tall and feline, with lithe muscles and feminine curves. Her eyes were bright green, framed with thick dark-brown lashes. And her golden-red hair glowed like the sun. "I think Dawn suits you very well. Unless you are dying for a new name. Maybe something like Eugenia or Tuppence."

"Tuppence, oh yes." She giggled. "When I return home at the end of three months with a British accent and a new name, my parents will be so thrilled."

"Then maybe we'll stick with Dawn." He tipped his glass to her in salute. His gaze strayed back to her hair. It really was the most beautiful shade of burnt umber he'd ever seen. "Your hair is the color of a sunset or the dawning rays of sunshine." Christ, had he said such drivel out loud? He sounded like a complete fop.

Dawn's lush lips curved into a sensual smile. Her eyes locked with his, and a bolt of electricity passed between them.

Yes, she was definitely open to a temporary fling.

They finished their drinks and walked out into the cool summer night. Her flat was a few blocks away, and they strolled, hand in hand, down the streets still packed with tourists. They arrived at her house, a standard red brick home divided into several units, one of many in a row on the edge of campus. She lingered on the pathway. "Thank you for a wonderful afternoon and dinner. I had a great time," she said.

He stepped closer to her. "I should be the one

Just a Fling

thanking you. I had forgotten how much I love being on the river. And I had the best company, of course." He raised his hand and ran it lightly over her head, trailing down her silky ponytail. He threaded his fingers between the russet locks, as he'd been dying to do all night. "Dawn," he whispered.

She leaned into him, her face upturned. He wrapped his arms around her and took what she offered, seizing her soft lips with his own. She returned the kiss with a force matching his. The kisses became more urgent, and she pressed her body against his.

So damn hot. He was already painfully hard and knew she could feel him, which made him harder. He lifted one hand to her breast, outlining the curve and teasing the pebbled nipple through the soft fabric of her shirt. She moaned and ran her fingers through his hair as he twined his tongue with hers.

A loud voice jarred them. "Get a fucking room!" Callan raised his head and saw two teens across the street making faces.

Dawn stiffened and jerked her arms back. Then she laughed. "I guess we got carried away."

Callan waved the teens away. "Sod off," he yelled. The teens laughed and turned the corner. He shook his head and smiled ruefully. "Here, I'll walk you to your door." He led her down the pathway to the front porch and turned to her. "I'd like to see you again. I'm in town until Monday. Are you free tomorrow night?" He sounded desperate, but he didn't care. Hell, he *was* desperate and still stiff as a board to prove it.

"What do you have in mind?" she asked.

He knew precisely where he wanted to take her. "I'm thinking a picnic. I'll pick you up tomorrow, around

71

six o'clock. I'll bring everything we need."

"Sounds good. I had a great time, Callan. Despite my fall." She rolled her eyes.

"And I because of it," he said and immediately blocked her punch to his arm. She flashed him her middle finger before shutting the door, but he could hear her laughter on the other side.

Callan turned down the pathway with a grin and walked into the night.

His summer just got much more interesting.

Chapter Seven

Dawn had a grin on her face throughout the day on Wednesday, all through her classes, her regular run and workout, and her afternoon study time in the law library. Which, to be honest, was not nearly as productive as it should have been since she found herself re-reading the same case five times over. She couldn't help it. Her brain wouldn't let Callan stay in his box no matter how hard she tried.

Why was she so into him? She studied her attraction to him with the same rigor she normally applied to case law.

Point one. Callan was hot. Like, amazing sexy hot. Chockablock full of manly muscles and sexy eyes. She shivered as she recalled leaning into his broad chest, the feel of his biceps under her hands, her fingers threading into his thick hair. Warmth spread between her legs as she replayed their kiss and bloomed hotter when she took her fantasy further, imagining him touching her, penetrating her.

Point two. He was funny and nice and gentlemanly. Okay, so those were points two, three, and four, but the *real* point was that his personality matched his looks. Callan wasn't a dumb jock or an egomaniac. He was a normal nice guy with a sexy edge.

Point three—or five, whatever—the two of them simply *clicked*. She couldn't explain it, but when he looked at her, when he touched her, it ignited something she'd never felt before with another man. Her attraction to him both excited and terrified her. If the opportunity came tonight, she wouldn't hesitate to jump into bed with Callan. Which wasn't like her. Not one bit.

Dawn's grin faded. She worried her bottom lip and yanked on the end of her ponytail. She glanced around at the smattering of other students hunkered down in carrels, poring over thick textbooks. Were any of them also debating sex tonight with a virtual stranger instead of studying? Doubtful.

They'll all pull ahead of you in class if you aren't careful.

"Argh, shut up," she muttered and shook her head. Callan would not distract her from her purpose. She'd already identified her competition in the program, and half of them were here in this library. Her competitive drive kicked in and she finally, *firmly*, put Callan in the box where he belonged. She set her alarm for two hours and read her assignments straight through until it went off.

Once she was caught up on her classwork, she packed her book bag and walked back to her house to prepare for her date. When six o'clock rolled around, Dawn was ready, wearing the same jeans and flats from yesterday paired with a breezy button-down shirt and an army green jacket.

Callan pulled up right on time in a sporty electric car and held the door open when she approached. He leaned down and pecked her on her cheek. "Hello. You look lovely," he said and guided her into her seat. He settled into the driver's side, and the car zipped silently down the road.

"Where are we going?" Dawn asked. His sleeves were rolled up to his elbows, and she admired his forearms, muscular and tan with a layer of golden hair. What did the rest of him look like under that shirt?

"Not far. There's an estate next to where I grew up. Part of the property runs along the river. I used to play there." They left Cambridge behind and soon were in the countryside. Callan turned down a bumpy road lined with meadows and trees. Jane would be horrified to know Dawn had hopped into Callan's car without knowing exactly where she was going and without telling anyone her location. Jane listened to too many podcasts about serial killers.

Callan pulled off on the side of the road and parked. "We'll walk from here. It's not far." Loaded with a picnic basket and blanket, he led her to a stone pathway that wound through the trees and opened onto a clearing, revealing a quaint little cottage tucked next to the river.

"Oh, how beautiful," Dawn exclaimed. A gazebo covered in rambling flowers sat several yards away, overlooking the river. The setting sun painted a rosy glow over everything and made Callan look even more outrageously handsome and golden. Dawn could almost believe she was the main character from one of those adult fantasy books she loved to read. A human who'd somehow found herself in a magical fairy land. Complete with a sexy fairy prince.

"Our former neighbors still live in the manor house, just up the way. This is their guest property. But they never have guests. I called and asked if we could use it for a time." He gazed out onto the water. "It is quite striking. I had forgotten how so."

"It's wonderful. What a magical place to grow up."

She imagined a towheaded Callan running around, skipping rocks on the water, and playing pirate ship in the gazebo. She grabbed his hand. "I'm looking forward to a romantic picnic in the gazebo."

"Be prepared for the height of romance, then." He spread out a thick blanket on the gazebo floor and unpacked a feast: crackers, pâté, tiny tea sandwiches, cold salmon, berry salad, sausage rolls, fruit tarts for dessert, and a variety of wines. Napkins, plates, cutlery, glasses, and candles followed.

Dawn whistled. "Wow, this is quite a spread. I'm impressed already."

He laughed. "I admit, I didn't do this alone. My friend Sarah, the one who is getting married in a few days, is an excellent cook. She poached the salmon and made the sandwiches. I think she threw in the candles for romantic flair. She obviously doesn't believe I can woo you without significant help."

Dawn huffed. As if this guy needed any help.

They sat on the blanket and ate and talked. The sun set through the trees on the other side of the riverbank, and before long, it was nighttime, and their world was lit by the moon and candlelight.

Callan reached over and refilled her wine glass. "What were your summers like?" he asked, leaning back onto his forearms. She took a sip and turned to him, propping herself up on her elbow.

"Fun. Lots of nature and sports camps and vacation Bible schools, which are like art camps with Jesus. We never went to church, but both of my parents were raised Baptist and felt obligated to give me a dose of religion at least once a year."

He chuckled. "What about family trips? I'm

imagining something quintessentially American, like driving for days to see the Grand Canyon or touring the Alamo."

She laughed. "We did take a few big trips. We went to a resort in Cancun once, but, unfortunately, it was when I was in the seventh grade, and I was completely mortified to be there with my parents, so I didn't enjoy myself much. I was mad they wouldn't let me bring a friend on the trip. I was kind of a brat."

"Who isn't at that age?"

"So true. These days we're very close. We took a riverboat cruise down the Mississippi one summer when I was in college and had a great time. They're great people."

"Do they have high standards for you?"

"Honestly, I think they just want me to be happy. I've always been the one to push myself. In fourth grade, I cried for days because I got a B on my report card. I don't think my mother knew what to do with me." She shrugged and nibbled on a strawberry tart. "Your parents sound great, too."

Callan nodded. "My parents are wonderful." His grin was so genuine, it was endearing. "I'm fortunate."

"Once I'm settled in my career, I definitely want kids of my own. I think it would be so much fun, to be a parent and raise little humans."

He didn't respond. Instead, he stiffened and sat up, fiddling with the latch on the picnic basket. His mood had shifted.

Was he freaked out because she'd mentioned having kids? *I didn't say* our *future kids, for Pete's sake.* Dawn watched Callan for a few painful seconds, but then he turned back to her with a smile, relaxed once more.

Maybe she'd imagined the tension. She was prone to over-analysis, after all.

"Tell me something else about you. Something surprising." He moved closer to her and laid down on his side with his head propped up in his hand, mirroring her. She took in every detail of his face, the individual hairs of his short scruff, the flecks in his changeable eyes glowing in the candlelight, the proud lines of his nose and cheekbones.

"I was an all-state basketball champion in high school," she said, hoping he'd be impressed.

He didn't disappoint. He raised his eyebrows. "A champion? Very impressive. I played rugby, and our team did well, but I wasn't a standout. Did you play university level?"

"I got a scholarship and played for my college my freshman year. But I'm on the shorter side for college basketball, and college is a different game than high school. The time commitment to play division one college level is huge. I had to ask myself, was my future going to be in basketball or in applying myself fully to my coursework? Clearly, I wasn't going to be a WNBA player, so I decided to quit and dedicate myself to getting into the best law school I could."

"You know what you want. I admire you for it." Callan ran his hand down from her shoulder to her wrist. Goosebumps followed his path. "That's why you are so fit. You're an athlete," he murmured. Dawn shivered. Mainly because of him, but also because it was getting chilly. "You're cold," he observed. "Let's go inside the house. It has a fireplace." They packed up their picnic and blanket, grabbed the wine, and walked across the grass to the guesthouse.

Callan ran his hand around the door and retrieved a key. He unlocked the door and ushered her inside. He turned on the lamps and pulled firewood out from a small hidden door next to the fireplace. The cottage was cozy and well kept. She could tell someone came to air and clean the house regularly. The furniture was threadbare but expensive, and there were enough throw pillows and blankets strewn around to make a cottage-core fan go nuts.

"All done," Callan said, rising from his haunches. She crossed the room and stood beside him to watch the fire pop and crackle. "Are you warmer now?" He put his arm around her. She nodded and slid her arm around his waist. The setting, the food, the wine, the *man*—it was an explosive combination that made her reckless.

She wanted to be set ablaze.

Dawn rested her head on Callan's chest and closed her eyes, listening to the sounds of the fire and the thumping of his heart beneath her cheek. She turned her head into his chest, rubbing her nose against him and breathing in his heady scent.

He whispered, his voice strained, "Dawn." He kissed her temple and lifted her chin. She raised her gaze to his. Desire flashed in his eyes, dark and hot, and a sudden jolt of warmth bloomed between her legs. "I'm going to kiss you now," Callan said. "Thoroughly." His words sent a thrill down her back, and another warm surge made her squeeze her thighs together. She swallowed hard; anticipation and raw need coursed through her. He cupped the back of her head, brought her close to him, and kissed her.

****

When his mouth tasted hers, the sense of *rightness*

threw Callan off-balance for a moment. Then he devoured her, consumed by an explosion of blinding lust, his body instantly hard. She tugged at his shirt, and he unbuttoned hers. He pulled her down with him onto the rug next to the fireplace and not too gently. He kneaded her hips, ran his hands up her spine, and threaded his fingers in her hair. He needed to feel all of her. Now.

Dawn trailed her hands up his chest and down his back, her touch scorching him. He undid her bra clasp and threw the sensible nude contraption off to the side. *Magnificent.* He palmed her small, firm breasts and tweaked her dusky-rose nipples. She arched to him, and he bent his head to catch one in his mouth, rolling his tongue around the hard pebble. Her moan nearly broke his tenuous self-control. She jerked against him and spread her legs. He settled between her hips, their jeans rubbing against one another, tantalizing and frustrating at the same time.

"Let me..." She reached for his zipper, but he brushed her hand away. This wasn't about him right now. This was about her. About making her frenzied, soaking with need, and out of her mind with lust. Callan had a singular focus, and nothing would deter him from it, not even the torturous bulge pressing hard against the denim of his jeans.

Where had this drive come from? Sex was usually perfunctory for him, a momentary release of tension. Of course, he'd wanted to please his partners, but not with this almost delirious fervor. But maybe he'd held himself back during past sexual encounters because he'd been afraid. Subconsciously or not, he feared the kind of messy emotional entanglements great sex usually led to. But right now, he wasn't worried about any of that rubbish. Callan didn't have to hold himself back with Dawn, and the floodgates had opened. His body demanded that he satisfy her completely, utterly.

And, bloody hell, it felt exquisite.

He reached up and captured her wrists in one hand so she couldn't distract him from his mission. He leaned over her and ran his mouth over her other breast, leaving a wet trail. She squirmed her hips, and her moans turned to frustrated pants.

He reached down with his free hand and unzipped her jeans, shoving them around her ankles. She kicked them off. Her panties were also nude and damp in the middle. He stiffened even more at the decadent sight. He hooked a finger around the waistband and pulled her underwear down.

"You are absolutely beautiful." He let go of her wrists and sat up, admiring the pink folds in front of him. He spread Dawn's knees wider and lowered himself again, trailing kisses from her breast, down her taut stomach, and settling between her thighs. He lightly teased her with his finger, and she jerked her hips in response. He kissed her thighs, enjoying the way she trembled, the way her breaths came out in rapid bursts.

"Do you want me to kiss you?" Callan asked wickedly. "Here?" He slid his finger once more through her folds, careful not to touch her most sensitive spot. He wanted to hear her beg for it, to be needed in the basest way.

"Please," she responded. "Yes, please. Now."

He laughed and bent his head.

****

When his mouth met her, Dawn nearly jumped out of her skin. She was already on the verge of exploding, and he'd barely touched her. He buried his face between her legs and began to lap at her, first gently and then harder, rougher. She ached for him to touch her clit, but he avoided it, teasing her. She felt herself tightening, the tension building.

Dear Lord, he was good at this. Masterful, even. She'd had boyfriends go down on her, but not like this. Callan was *savoring* her, stroking his tongue up and down, plunging into her core and out again. He inserted one and then two fingers into her and stroked. "Oh, you're good," she moaned, deliciously full as his fingers worked her, pumping in and out. Then he covered her fully with his mouth, and his hot, wet licks put her over the edge, her orgasm ripping through her. He kept licking her through her tremors until she finally reached down and tugged on his hair. "I can't take any more." He laughed again and propped himself up, his smile so self-satisfied, she took it as a personal challenge.

"Your turn." She shoved Callan's shoulders, and he landed flat on his back. She struggled to unzip his jeans, but when she did, he sprang forth, rock hard and warm.

She straddled him and gave him a sultry, devilish smile. "Do you want me to touch you?" Her hands hovered over him, and she watched his cock twitch. "Here?" she asked, giving him a taste of his own medicine.

"Hell, yes," he groaned, raising his hips underneath her. She put her hands around him and began to pump up and down slowly. He watched her with half-closed eyes, and a small sound caught in the back of his throat. She bent down and ran her tongue across his broad tip, and he hissed.

"I think you'll like this." She shot him a feline grin

and took him into her mouth.

"I think you're right," Callan agreed, his voice hoarse. She worked her mouth and hands until he bowed up and released his tension with a yell. She rode through it with him, enjoying every jerk and shake of his body. When he was done, she sat back and gave him her own satisfied smile. His glazed eyes, his mussed hair, his flushed cheeks—*she'd* done those things to him. She wasn't a tall, gangly, overachieving dork right now. No, she was a sexy temptress who'd brought this Nordic god to his knees. And onto his back.

Callan pulled Dawn down to him and tucked her close, running a hand lazily over her thigh. "Aren't we both proud of ourselves." He chuckled.

"I blame you. The scenery, the wine, the food, the fire. Totally your fault."

"Completely. I'm a fiendish cad." He kissed her shoulder.

She ran her fingers through the golden hair on his chest. "This isn't very romantic, but everything happened so fast, and I didn't ask you. Have you been tested?"

"I have, and I'm all clear. My paperwork's back in my London flat."

"I have mine, too. In an email folder." She shook her head. "Dating in the twenty-first century, right?"

He squeezed her shoulder. "Quite. And thank you for asking."

She snuggled closer, and he held her tight. They gazed at the dancing fire for a long time. How could she be so comfortable with him? She'd be absurdly self-conscious with any other guy—worried if her makeup had smudged, if her leg hairs were prickly, or if she'd

Katherine Grace

made a weird face when she came. But not with Callan. She was oddly at ease in his arms. *I could fall for him. Face it. You're already halfway there.*

She sighed. "What time is it? I've got class tomorrow morning." She didn't want to break the spell, but she couldn't blow off her classes either.

"It's after midnight. I'd better get you home." They sat up and tossed their clothes to each other, dressing quickly. Callan locked the cottage door, took her hand in his, and led her back to the car. They packed the remains of the picnic in the trunk and drove away. Dawn looked over her shoulder, memorizing the path, the trees, the road, every detail so she could replay it in her mind later.

They pulled up to her house, and he turned to her. "The wedding is Saturday night, and I would love for you to join me."

He lifted his hand and brushed her cheek. His touch branded her. Things were moving fast. One more night with him would surely lead to sex. *And I'm totally on board with that.*

"You're sure your friends won't mind having a stranger at their wedding?"

He grinned. "They are insisting."

"Okay. Then yes. Will you text me the details?"

"I will. I'm going out for Will's stag night tomorrow, but I'll text you before then."

"Perfect," she said.

"Perfect." Callan leaned in and brushed his lips to hers. Soft and featherlight. "Until Saturday." The anticipation in his words and his kiss made Dawn throb between her legs. She wanted to hold on to him, straddle his lap, and have him fill her while she slowly rocked on top of him. She sucked in a gulp of air and grappled for

84

the door handle.

"Bye," she squeaked and slid out of the car. He watched over her as she ran to the house. She turned and waved when she opened the door. He nodded and drove off. She checked her watch. It was still early evening in Alabama, and she wanted to tell Jane she'd been right.

Dawn wasn't going to Liverpool and Manchester this weekend after all.

Chapter Eight

—What are you wearing?—

—It's late. Are you sexting me? During a stag party?—

—Yes. What are you wearing?—

—A transparent negligee, no underwear. I look amazing.—

—Aaa. You're killing me.—

—How's the party?—

—Fun. Drinking pints with old schoolmates.—

—No strippers?—

—Nah. Will wanted a low-key hang out with friends.—

—I'll strip for you ;)—

—If Will weren't my best mate…—

—Hahaha.—

—I'm excited you are coming to the wedding. We will have fun. I'll remember you offered to strip for me :).—

—I'm sure you will. I'm excited too. I'm glad I met you…so far, anyway.—

—I'm bound to do something asinine to make you regret your words. But seriously, I'm extremely happy I burned you with coffee the other day.—

—Oddly, so am I.—

—Must go. Will is on the pub table giving a heartfelt speech. I should pay attention.—

—Yes, you should. Have fun.—
—Sweet dreams, Dawn.—

****

Dawn didn't have classes on Friday, so she took the train to London to look for an outfit for the wedding. Callan told her the wedding was cocktail attire, which she certainly hadn't packed in her suitcase. She wanted to find something amazing to wear that would knock his socks off and make him drool over her the way she did him.

Last night—as she'd lounged in her fuzzy flannel pajamas texting Callan—she'd researched the names of several trendy dress shops in the city and had mapped out a route.

After a few transfers, Dawn exited the train at Knightsbridge and wound her way up to the street level. She was disoriented for a moment but quickly found her way to the first store on her list. With one glance, she knew the prices were way too high for her student bank account.

She meandered to the next store and the next, taking a few detours here and there to pop into other fashionable shops. She'd saved the best for last. A stylish little shop with dresses worn by the duchesses. She selected a few garments to try on, and a very proper salesclerk ushered her into a private changing room.

Dawn tried on the first dress, a blue satin slip that left nothing to the imagination, and her phone buzzed. It was a text from Callan.

—Hi. What are you up to?—

—I don't have class today, so I took the train to London.—

—I'm in town too. Working in the office before

heading back for wedding duty. Where are you?—

—In a store. Near Hyde Park and Harrods.—

—My office is close. Want to grab lunch?—

Dawn eyed the dresses. Hopefully, the right one was in this pile.

—Sure. I could meet you in an hour?—

—Cool. Text me when you are done, and I'll see where you are.—

She sent him a thumbs-up emoji and tried on the other dresses with lightning speed. To her relief, the final dress—a sleek green off-the-shoulder number—was the perfect fit. The price tag was four hundred pounds, double her original budget. *Screw it. Add it to your student loans.* Fiscally responsible as ever.

Dawn asked the shop to please hold the dress for her until later in the afternoon, and they happily obliged. She raced back through the other stores to buy the accessories she'd spotted earlier: slinky gold earrings, a large bangle bracelet, strappy shoes, and a patterned clutch.

Purchases in hand, Dawn texted Callan. He directed her to a restaurant across the street from where she stood, a bright French-style bistro packed with white-collar workers and daytime shoppers. She arrived first and put their names on the waiting list. Within minutes she spotted Callan walking toward her on the busy sidewalk. The sidewalk could have been twenty times more crowded, and she still would've seen him immediately. No one around him compared. He wore perfectly tailored gray slacks, a white polo shirt, and aviator sunglasses, making him look extra *GQ*ish. *Damn, he's a handsome sonofabitch.*

"It's a forty-five-minute wait," she informed him as he kissed her cheek.

"Let me check. I reserved a table." He had such a dominant presence, she almost expected them to be whisked immediately to a private table. She watched Callan talk to the hostess and saw him shake his head. He came back out looking frustrated.

"It's still a thirty-minute wait." He glanced at his watch. "Do you like Vietnamese food?" When she nodded, he said, "There's a great street vendor around the corner. We could pick up a couple of sandwiches and walk back to my office."

Perfect. She'd get to see Callan in his natural habitat. "Great, let's do it."

He took her hand in his, and they walked to the vendor's food truck and bought several Bánh mi sandwiches. Callan added three more sandwiches to the order. "Someone at the office might want one," he explained. They grabbed their order and walked toward Hyde Park.

"My office is in Mayfair. We'll cut through the park." They followed the path through the trees and past Serpentine Lake before winding their way onto the streets beyond the park's east side and into Mayfair.

Mayfair was a beautiful section of town, pristine and grand, and Dawn imagined she was in Edwardian London, wandering around Henry Higgins's 27A Wimpole Street.

Callan led her to an ornate white stone building, which housed several private equity firms, an advertising agency, and Green Solar. They rode the elevator up to the fourth floor. "Here we are." He directed her through glass doors and into a modern office space with bright white walls, warm wood floors, and pops of green and blue accent colors. The space held several glass offices, private cubicles, small meeting rooms, a larger conference room, a lounge area with comfortable seating, a foosball table, and a kick-ass espresso machine.

"Where is everyone?" she asked. The place was empty for a weekday.

"There are a few people working in the office today, but most of the team works from home unless there is a big meeting. I intend to give up this space soon since everything we do can be done online or by phone."

"The world is remote now."

"It is indeed. Location is no longer a barrier to anything."

Dawn gulped. Would their long distance be a barrier to them? *Oh, God.* She was already plotting their long-term relationship.

She smiled brightly. "Can I see your office?"

"Around this way." He led her to a nice but small corner office with three glass walls and a whiteboard wall covered in notes.

She sat at his desk. "So this is where the magic happens." She leaned back, hands behind her head. She imagined Callan pacing, jotting down a thought as it struck him, maybe brainstorming with a coworker. His shirtsleeves would be rolled up and his hair rumpled. He'd work late at night, and Dawn would bring him dinner. He'd need a stress reliever, a break from work. He'd pull her close, turn her around. She'd be wearing a skirt, he'd lift it, bend her over the table…

He raised his eyebrows. "I'd say you already know where the magic happens." He grinned when a blush crept up her neck.

She stuck her tongue out at him.

He laughed.

"Callan, you're back already?" A woman stood in the doorway, surprise on her face. Her head swiveled from Callan to Dawn and back again. "Oh, hello." She darted a questioning glance at Callan before quickly smiling. The woman came around the desk, her hand outstretched. "I'm Gemma," she said and shook Dawn's hand.

"Hi. Nice to meet you. I'm Dawn." *Does this knockout work with Callan? Like, every day?* She shook Gemma's fine-boned hand. The woman was gorgeous, petite with smooth, beautiful brown skin and long black hair so thick and lustrous, she looked like she'd stepped straight out of a hair commercial. Dawn found herself staring down at the woman. She was an ogre compared to this tiny, delicate woman.

"I'm glad you're here," Callan said to Gemma. "Dawn's a law student in DC. She's at Cambridge, studying for the summer." He turned to Dawn. "Gemma is our brilliant chief legal officer. She also heads up a nonprofit." Great. The woman's a miniature Amal Clooney.

Check yourself, Dawn chided. Just because Callan worked with an accomplished and beautiful woman, whom he clearly admired, was no reason to get huffy or jealous. *Besides, you are the one who made him all hot and bothered the other night.* Dawn had no reason to worry about Gemma or any other woman.

She'd take this relationship at face value and not look for trouble where there wasn't any.

****

"We brought sandwiches. Gemma, you should join us. We can eat in the conference room," Callan said.

He'd caught Gemma's questioning look. After the many lectures she'd given him over the years, he suspected she was thrilled, thinking he'd taken her advice to heart.

He'd have to explain things to Gemma. Dawn was just a summer fling. Nothing more.

Gemma peered inside the take-out bag. "Ooh, Bánh mi. Lovely." He led them to a conference room around the corner. They settled at the table, and Callan passed around the sandwiches. "Anyone else still here?" he asked Gemma. "I've got extras."

Gemma nodded. "Clint and Mark are on a call with Taiwan," she said, referring to one of their solar panel manufacturers. Callan took a couple of sandwiches over to the two engineers huddled over a speakerphone a few offices away. They gave him a thumbs-up in appreciation. Callan nodded and headed back to the conference room. He approached slowly, admittedly to overhear Dawn and Gemma's conversation. He wanted them to get along, and he felt, oddly, as if he were back in secondary school introducing a new girlfriend to his parents.

"I didn't realize it was so prevalent here, too," Dawn said to Gemma as he walked around the corner and sat down. "What is the organization called?"

They were discussing Gemma's nonprofit, which provided legal representation to immigrant minors brought to the UK illegally through human trafficking.

"It's called Lawyers ACT. It stands for Lawyers Against Child Trafficking. Given the recent refugee crisis, it's a terrible situation and getting worse. Our small group has represented twenty children over the past year, but there are so many more who desperately need help. We can't keep up." The lines in Gemma's forehead creased, and Callan knew it was from the responsibility she shouldered, trying to save each child. Which, undoubtedly, was impossible. But leave it to Gemma to try.

"Maybe you should team up with a larger organization?" Dawn suggested.

"We are exploring some strategic partnerships, but we want to remain dedicated to our main purpose. We are the only group focused specifically on representing children in immigration proceedings. Kids are trafficked here and either abandoned or, sometimes, they escape. The lucky ones are then placed with a decent foster family. Many children don't want to return to their home country quite often because their family members are the very people who sold them to the traffickers in the first place. Without our help, they might be sent back to their home country and face more abuse and even death."

"Trafficking is a major problem in the United States too. Organizations like yours are needed everywhere. Could you do some major fundraising and hire a full-time team?" Dawn's brows drew in concern, caught up in Gemma's passion for the cause. It was hard not to be once Gemma got going. Callan donated money to the group and gave Gemma hours off whenever she needed them. She deserved it after all she'd done for him.

Gemma nodded her head emphatically. "Absolutely. I can't run it part time on my own. It's grown beyond me from a management standpoint. But"—she slid her dark-brown gaze to Callan's—"I also love my job, and I don't want to give it up. I believe in the future we are helping to shape here at Green Solar."

"Sounds like you need to clone yourself," Dawn said.

"I certainly need something." Gemma smiled and shook her head as she pulled her long hair over her shoulder. "Enough about me. Tell me about yourself. And how you and Callan met." Gemma's smile was friendly, but he caught her sly look. She'd barrage him with questions once Dawn left.

Dawn started, "I've only been in England for a few weeks. I'm studying corporate law at Cambridge, and I met Callan…" She trailed off and raised her eyebrows at him.

"When I burned the fuck out of her with coffee at a shop in Cambridge."

"Very smooth, Callan." Gemma quirked her lips.

"It wasn't too bad because I agreed to go punting with him the next day," Dawn said.

"And did the boat capsize?" Gemma asked.

"Err…no, we avoided that romantic comedy trope." Dawn's amused gaze locked on his, and he knew she was also remembering her face-plant. He smiled and was struck again by how green her eyes were, how beautiful her smile was, how her cheeks flushed so prettily when she was happy. *They also flush when she's excited; when she's reaching her peak...* His expression must have changed because Dawn's smile faded, and her cheeks grew pink. He winked at her and chuckled when she pressed her lips together and cast him a *you-are-so-naughty* look.

Dawn and Gemma chatted throughout lunch, mainly about the differences between American and English schooling and credentials for solicitors, barristers, and lawyers. They circled back to talk about immigration hearings, and Gemma offered to let Dawn shadow her so Dawn could get real-world experience, which made

Dawn light up. Adorably.

Callan sat back and watched the two women. Dawn, coppery and green-eyed, tall and athletic. Gemma, a dark beauty, petite and delicate. They were different in appearance and personalities, but they'd clicked, making him irrationally happy.

Many people outside his intimate circle assumed Callan and Gemma were an item of some sort. Whether "friends with benefits" or something more. He'd heard comments from other men—*how can you concentrate with such a beauty around?* Callan always corrected them, although their faces never shook their skepticism.

But Callan and Gemma had never been an item, casual or otherwise. She was beautiful, indeed, in an imperious, dark way. Perhaps if he hadn't met her right after... Perhaps if she hadn't been someone he'd leaned on to help piece himself back together. Gemma knew his dirty secrets. Knew how broken he really was. And she had demons of her own...

Dawn didn't know his past, and she never would. When he was around her, the weight of his memories lifted, and the darkness inside him was banished to the back corners of his soul. He could pretend he was just a boy, standing in front of a girl, and all that rubbish. Maybe, after three years, it was time to allow himself a little bit of happiness. Allow himself to let go, if only for a little while.

His throat clenched. *Let go?* He didn't *want* to let go. Because letting go meant letting go of *her*.

Fuck. It was happening again. Sweat beaded Callan's upper lip, his chest tightened, and his breath quickened. "Excuse me," he muttered, not caring about the quizzical looks the women shot him. He needed some bloody *air*.

He raced to the restroom and shoved the door open, gasping. He clutched the edges of the sink. His knuckles whitened, and his arms shook. His lungs heaved as he fought to calm himself, to steady his pounding heart.

This hadn't happened for a long time. *I thought I was doing better.*

He raised his gaze to the mirror, and his reflection was pale and waxen. He closed his eyes and exhaled slowly over and over, counting to ten each time. After a while, the thunder in his ears quieted, and the nausea receded. He opened his eyes. Color returned to his face, and his heartbeat slowed to a normal pace.

Nothing to see here. Right, mate? He almost laughed at himself in the mirror.

He straightened up. This episode hadn't been so bad, but what if he'd crumbled in front of Dawn? He *never* wanted her to see him like this. She was only here for the summer, and he wanted to enjoy her. He wouldn't drag her into his miserable past. She would *never* know how wretched he was.

Never.

Chapter Nine

"You look smokin' hot," Jane observed as Dawn twirled in front of her laptop for Jane's critical eye. "Let me see the bag. Do you have a wrap?"

"No, but I think I'll be fine. It's supposed to be warm tonight." Dawn held up the chevron-patterned gold and green clutch.

"Love it. Your hair looks great too." Dawn flipped her barrel-curled reddish-brown locks, letting them cascade down her back. Her hair usually annoyed her when it was down around her face, but she resisted the urge to tuck it behind her ears or throw it into a ponytail.

"What underwear are you wearing? Did you go the shapewear or the sexy route?"

"Sexy, fo sho. I have no idea how this night will end." *I know how I* hope *it will end.*

"Um, lemme guess. With you sitting…on his face." Jane snickered.

"Har, har. I knew I shouldn't have told you about the other night."

"Please, girl. You couldn't wait to give me all the details."

Fair point.

Jane turned her mouth down in an exaggerated frown. "You're going to fall in love with Callan and never come back to Canton."

"Aww. We've only been on a couple of dates. But

he *is* quite princely." She grinned. "If he turns out to be a secret duke, you can come visit me in my castle."

"If he's a secret duke, you'd better introduce me to his friends. I'm still open to marrying for money, you know."

"As if Todd would ever let you marry someone else." Dawn scoffed. Jane smiled her *I'm-so-in-love* smile that would look dopey on anyone else.

"All right, I've got to go. I'll give you the details tomorrow," Dawn said.

"Make good choices!" Jane cried as Dawn closed her laptop. Still smiling, Dawn posed in front of the mirror, tossed her hair back, and planted her hands on her hips.

Jane is right. I do look hot. She imagined Callan's reaction to seeing her in something other than jeans. She wanted him speechless, salivating, and craving a repeat of the other night in the cottage. Or more. She wasn't wearing her sexiest underwear for nothing.

She frowned. Would he be back to normal today? At the end of their lunch with Gemma yesterday, he'd seemed...off. When he'd suddenly jumped up and excused himself from the conference room, he'd looked like he was about to yack all over the table. He'd been pale and sweaty, his eyes wild. And when he'd returned, he hadn't offered any excuses; he'd simply ushered her into a cab with a perfunctory peck on the cheek. He'd texted an apology last night and said he thought his sandwich had been "dodgy." Sounded like a lame excuse, but she was willing to give Callan the benefit of the doubt.

She waved goodbye to her flatmates and walked along the path leading to the massive stone chapel set majestically on a vast lawn of precision-cut grass. The grandeur of King's College Chapel was breathtaking, and she was excited to see it up close. She followed signs along the path to the back lawn, where a large white tent served as the reception area. Under the tent, rows of tables and chairs and a parquet dance floor filled the space. A small band warmed up off to the side. Fresh flowers, twining greenery, and hurricane candles decorated the entire area.

Wedding guests milled around and greeted each other with hugs and handshakes. Being the best man, Callan was tied up with pre-wedding activities and couldn't escort Dawn to the ceremony, which normally wouldn't bother her, but she felt awkward approaching this group of strangers. She smiled politely and stood to the side, grateful when ushers escorted the guests inside the chapel.

"Bride or groom's side, miss?" asked an usher.

She took his arm. "Groom's, please," she responded faintly as she craned her neck to take in the magnificent Gothic architecture and the intricate stained-glass windows. He led her to a seat in the front of the chapel where the wooden chairs faced perpendicular to the altar and handed her a wedding program. She glanced around at the other guests. A few women wore hats—or fascinators—but not many. The men wore suits, with and without ties. This early evening wedding was a more casual affair than what she'd read online when she'd researched "what to wear to an English wedding." She relaxed. As long as Callan was back to his usual self, they'd have a great time tonight.

The chapel's beautiful windows glinted in the setting sun, sprinkling drops of color onto the carved stone walls and dark wooden seats. Soft music floated in from the violinist playing in the chapel's antechamber. A side door opened, and a lanky man with dark hair stepped up to the slightly raised altar. He must be Will, the groom. Callan and two other groomsmen filed in behind Will.

The men wore smart dark blue suits with purple ties and white stephanotis boutonnieres, but Dawn could only focus on Callan, as if he alone stood in the spotlight, everyone else fading into the darkness. He towered over the other three men, and the tailored cut of his suit emphasized his broad chest and lean waist. His dark-gold hair was perfectly mussed, and his five o'clock shadow was trimmed to scruff perfection. The mere sight of him made her blush, paranoid everyone in the chapel knew the dirty deeds they'd done—and her even dirtier fantasies. She fanned herself with the wedding program.

Callan and the groom leaned close, and whatever they said to one another cracked them up. Laughing, Callan scanned the congregation and landed on Dawn. His grin spread into a dazzling smile, and he nodded at her. She smiled back, and warmth bloomed in her stomach, down her limbs, and settled between her legs. She doubled the speed of her makeshift fan.

The music signaled the beginning of the wedding ceremony, and Callan's attention went to the redheaded bride walking down the aisle. Even though Dawn didn't know the couple, she was profoundly touched by the ceremony. Will and Sarah appeared to be so in love. Will wiped the corners of his eyes as he spoke his vows, and Sarah laugh-cried when they exchanged rings. They held onto each other's hands tightly and gazed into each other's eyes with love and genuine affection.

Dawn had spent her young adult life with a singular focus—getting into a great law school—and hadn't put much thought into finding a husband or even a serious boyfriend. But as she sat there, a thread of deep longing tugged on her, threatening to unravel her at any moment.

Callan's glances and little grins melted her insides. Dawn imagined herself and Callan at the altar, professing their love before friends and family, ready to start their own adventure together. She gave herself a small shake, banishing the image before it could take hold and make her forget why she was in Cambridge in the first place. *Which is definitely not husband hunting.*

When the service ended, the photographer grabbed the wedding party for photos, so Dawn joined the guests in the tent. The tables were set with place cards, and she found her name at the head table and set down her clutch. She made her way to one of the two open bars flanking either side of the dance floor and ordered a prosecco.

She wandered back to her table, debating what to do. *Is it weird to sit down at the head table before the bridal party comes? But I don't want to mingle and introduce myself to strangers—*

"Hello. Hello? Hello?" A middle-aged woman with curly gray hair was speaking directly to her.

"Oh, pardon me. I didn't hear you."

"Are you Dawn Mathison?" the woman asked, pointing to Dawn's seat.

"Yes, I am," she responded politely.

"Oh! So lovely to meet you, dear," the woman exclaimed and pulled her into a tight hug before Dawn could react.

"Oh. Okay. Hello." She awkwardly patted the woman's back.

The woman released her and clasped her hands. "So sorry, dear. I'm just so thrilled to meet you." The woman's eyes shone, and Dawn panicked. Was this woman about to cry? The woman gazed at her as if Dawn were a lost puppy or the main character in a sappy Christmas movie.

"Nice to meet you, Ms.?" Dawn raised her eyebrows in question, but as she studied the woman, with her effusive smile and her hands clasped in delight, a suspicion rose. The woman blinked her beautiful hazel eyes a few times, and Dawn laughed. She *almost* felt sorry for Callan.

"Why, dear, I'm Eleanor Marlowe. Callan's mum!"

****

Oh no. What was Mum doing here? Callan had only mentioned Dawn to his mother because he thought his parents weren't coming to the wedding. Obviously, plans had changed. She was already smothering Dawn. Lord knew what his kooky mother was saying to her. He hurried across the tent and greeted them.

"Hello, Mum, please don't scare off my date just yet." He pulled Dawn to his side lest his mother make another grab for her. "I didn't know you were coming," he added pointedly.

His mum gave him a guileless look. "What? Will and Sarah are like my own children. I wouldn't miss their wedding for the world."

"Is that so? Because I recall you said you give expensive gifts so you don't have to sit through tedious wedding ceremonies."

Eleanor clucked disapprovingly. "Callan, really. I said no such thing."

"Hmmm," he murmured and arched his eyebrow,

which she shot right back at him. Dawn giggled beside him, and he lightly pinched her, making her jump. "Don't encourage her," he whispered in her ear. She made an unladylike snort and rolled her eyes.

"Is Dad with you?" Callan asked, looking around.

"Oh no, it's only me tonight. You know how he hates to miss his programs." She hooked her arm through Dawn's. "Dawn here will just have to keep me company, won't you, dear? You can tell me all about yourself. I'm so curious. You are studying law, I hear. Such a noble profession. I want to know more. Do you plan to return to Cambridge after this summer? You know Callan grew up here. I taught maths in the building right over there for thirty years. I adore Cambridge. You really should consider coming back."

For fuck's sake. "Mum, what would you like to drink? Dawn and I will go fetch it for you."

"Gin and tonic, dear. Run along. Dawn and I can catch up later," she said with a wink.

Brilliant.

He clasped Dawn's hand and pulled her along. "Your mother is nice." She laughed.

"She is preventing me from properly admiring my date." He stopped and held her at arm's length so he could take her in from head to toe. She was a vision. Everything about her tempted him to touch her. He wanted to thread his fingers through her curling reddish-brown hair, kiss her full red lips, skim his hands all over her body in that tight green dress, which showcased her fit figure. She'd have him in a lather by the time the night was over. "You're beautiful, Dawn," he said simply.

She cocked her head. "I'm glad you're feeling better today."

"So am I." Callan shrugged, not elaborating. Frankly, he *did* feel better, and he didn't want to think about yesterday's episode.

They went to the bar and ordered their drinks and then wove their way through the tables back to his mother, who stood chatting with Will's mum. "Your gin and tonic," he said, handing it to her with a flourish. "I regret I don't have a drink for you, Janet," he said to Will's mum.

Janet waved her hand. "No matter. We're about to be seated. Will and Sarah are set to come out soon."

"It was a lovely wedding. Thank you for having me," Dawn told her.

"Of course, lovey," she said and then exchanged a conspiratorial smile with Eleanor. *Fabulous.* He was clearly the cause du jour of the knitting circle. Thankfully Dawn didn't seem fazed by the women. Rather, he suspected she enjoyed watching him squirm.

"Oh, here they come," Janet cried as the band played Will and Sarah's entrance song. The happy couple bounded into the tent to the cheers of their guests. They made their way to the head table, greeting guests along the way. When they reached them, Callan introduced the newlyweds to Dawn.

"I'm so happy for you both. It was a beautiful ceremony," Dawn said to them.

"We're happy you could make it," Will said. "Saves us from having to trade dances with this guy." He jerked his head toward Callan.

"Yes, we are thrilled you are here," Sarah said with a bright smile.

Dawn said to Sarah, "I heard you are the one who helped Callan pack for our picnic the other day. Well done. I was highly impressed with his picnicking skills."

Sarah laughed and elbowed Callan. "You weren't supposed to tell her you had help, you ninny."

"What can I say? I'm honest to a fault." He laughed. But for a brief moment amid the wedding clamor, his throat constricted, and Sarah's smile faltered.

She knew him too well.

The wedding reception commenced with speeches. Callan stood in front of the gathering and drew a long breath. He'd mulled over what to say for days. How could he convey how much Will and Sarah meant to him? He could never repay them for seeing him through his darkest hours.

He began by ribbing Will and Sarah with childhood tales and stories from university, ending with, "I've never known a couple better suited for each other. I've never seen you fight, except for when Will shaved the hair off all of Sarah's dolls and when he stumbled into the wrong girl's dormitory after our first-year end-of-term party—"

"I pulled him out by his ear," Sarah shouted.

"She did," Will added cheerfully, and the crowd laughed.

"Yes, it was quite a night. Quite a memory." Callan paused, waiting for the laughter to die down. "I want to thank you both for so many memories. So many wonderful times. When I think back on any happiness in my life…" He paused again and swallowed. Christ, don't let him get choked up now. His gaze locked with Dawn's, and she nodded encouragingly. As if by magic, the tightness in his chest dissipated.

He continued, "You have both been there for me, more than you realize, more than I deserve." Sarah's eyes shone. He pressed on. " 'There is nothing on this earth more to be prized than true friendship.' That's a quote by Thomas Aquinas, and I think it is very apt. I'm honored to be a part of your life, to be celebrating here with you today. Here's to many more years together and a long and happy marriage. Cheers!"

Will and Sarah both jumped up and hugged him tightly. "Love you too, brother," Will whispered. Callan sat down and held Dawn's hand. He glanced at his mum, seated at the next table over, and saw her dab her eyes.

Poor Mum. She just wanted her only child to be happy. *I shouldn't have told her I had a date for the wedding.* He'd have to dash all her hopes again and tell her this *interlude* with Dawn wasn't permanent. He wouldn't be in a relationship. Wouldn't be getting married. Wouldn't be giving her any grandchildren.

He breathed in deeply. Tonight was not the night to fret over his mother. He pushed those thoughts to the back of his mind.

He took a long swallow of his cabernet. Dawn squeezed his hand, and he turned to her, soaking her in until all the bad thoughts disappeared. Her hair glowed in the candlelight, and her slow smile was like sunshine on his face. She reminded him he had better things to think about, things to *anticipate.*

While Dawn spoke to others at the table, he admired her: the way she tilted her head when listening to a story, how her lips curled when telling a joke, her graceful hand gestures when explaining something she'd read. He raised his hand and rubbed her nape. She snuggled imperceptibly closer and settled her hand on his leg.

Waiters served course after course, and the wine and conversation flowed. Throughout the long dinner, Callan ran his hand down Dawn's sleek thigh, twined his fingers with hers, and draped his arm across her shoulders. He couldn't stop touching her. She seduced him merely through a brush of her hand, a cheeky glance, a merry laugh. She could bring him to his knees. Christ, he *wanted* to get on his knees and worship every inch of her.

He was going to have her tonight. In every possible position. Thinking about sliding into her made him swell. Callan forced himself to sit back and relax. This reception was turning into the most delightful kind of torture. During the cake cutting, Dawn leaned over and asked, "When does the dancing start? I want to see if you have any moves."

"I have plenty of moves to show you." He nuzzled her ear. "On the dance floor and off."

"Promise?" *Hell yes.*

As it happened, they both had moves on the dance floor. He showed off his waltzing skills, and she *got low* during the fast songs. By the end of the night, they were both sweaty and a little tipsy, swinging each other around and stealing kisses whenever the moment struck.

In between songs, they talked and laughed with his mother and friends. After the final dance of the night, they joined the other guests to light sparklers and wave goodbye to the happy couple as they ran to their getaway car. The sparklers sizzled, and Dawn giggled in delight as the light danced across her face.

This night is perfect.

Callan pulled Dawn in for a long and proper kiss right there, and she melted into him. "Let's say our goodbyes," he said, and she nodded. They made the rounds—his mum especially effusive in her farewell—and then took a cab back to Will and Sarah's place.

"Are you sure Will and Sarah don't mind you bringing me to their house?" Dawn asked.

"They are renting a special room at a bed-and-breakfast tonight before they leave town tomorrow for their honeymoon. I am positive they don't mind."

"Well, in that case…" Dawn leaned in and slid her hand across his crotch, making his cock jump under his trousers. He gave her a low growl.

Oh. It. Is. On.

Chapter Ten

Dawn knew she was in trouble when Callan honest-to-goodness *growled* at her. "I can play that game too," he said in a deliciously dangerous voice. His hand ran along her calf, up her thigh, and under her hemline. He hitched the tight dress up to almost her ass and then cupped her between her thighs, his palm lightly massaging her. It felt too good. She was already turned on from their dancing and flirting, and now her panties were soaked. She was dying to move her hips, to grind against his warm hand, but the cab driver shot them a suspicious look.

"I cry uncle. You win," she said, pulling on his wrist. In a flash, he withdrew his hand and pulled her dress back down, giving her a sexy smirk. "Cocky bastard," she muttered under her breath.

The corners of his mouth turned up in a devilish smile. "Don't worry, I'll let you get me back."

They pulled up to the house, and Callan walked around to open her door. He wrapped his arm around her waist as the cab drove away. "You were smashing tonight," he said. "Everyone loved you."

"I had a great time. Your mother is sweet, your friends are great. The music was awesome."

"The music *was* awesome, wasn't it? My God, you drove me crazy dancing in this dress tonight." He ran his hands up and down her sides. "Brilliant choice, by the way."

"Thanks. And I take back any doubts I had about your moves. You're pretty hot yourself."

He leaned in as if to kiss her but then shook his head. "Let's go inside. As much as I love this dress, I need to tear it off of you. Right now." He swooped down and lifted her into his arms. With one hand, he unlocked the door and swept her inside.

He stalked through the small living space, toward the back of the house, and into what Dawn assumed was the guest room. He set her onto her feet and immediately slanted his mouth over hers, giving her a long, hard kiss that felt hours in the making. He turned her around and unzipped her dress, shoving it to the floor unceremoniously. With her back still to him, she heard him suck in his breath, and she smiled to herself, glad she'd opted for the sexy black lace thong and matching strapless bra instead of nude shapewear.

"Your ass is incredible," Callan murmured as he splayed his hands on her bottom, squeezing lightly. He ran one hand up her spine to her nape while he massaged her with his other hand. He held her in place by the neck as his other hand delved between her legs, lightly brushing her sex from behind and then back up to knead her bottom. The tightness in her core became more acute, bordering on painful. She began to move, needing harder contact with his fingers, but he spun her around instead.

"This pretty thing comes off." He snapped open her bra, and it fell to the floor. Her nipples puckered under his smoldering gaze, and she tore his suit jacket from his broad shoulders and followed with his shirt and pants. They both stood in their underwear, gazing at one another.

"I've been waiting all night for this," he said, reaching for her.

"All night," she agreed as Callan pulled her into his arms and lightly brushed his lips to hers. She loved how dominant he was one moment and then sweet and tender the next. She ran her fingers through his thick hair and felt the muscles in his shoulders and down his back. Every dip and bulge of his lean torso enthralled her. The man was built like a professional athlete. Someday she'd have to ask him how the hell he got a body like this but, for now, she was reaping the rewards of his hard work.

Callan cupped her breasts and nibbled her ear. His hardness pressed against her stomach. "Let's get to the naughty part," she said and dragged his underwear off.

"You read my mind completely." He tossed her onto the bed and covered her with his body. He eased her thong past her hips and down her legs, following it with his lips until her legs were free from the black lace. He pushed her knees wide and admired her for a moment, which made her feel gloriously sexy.

He reached over to his bedside table and grabbed a condom. "I had hopes we would end up here tonight," he admitted as he rolled it on.

"Whatever gave you the idea I was so easy?" she teased.

Callan gave her a half-grin, but there was something in his gaze that made her heart skip a beat. "Certainly not easy. More like a connection I haven't felt in a very long time."

Dawn's stomach flipped. What did he mean? She'd have to mull it over later because now he was kissing her so deeply, she couldn't think straight. The throbbing between her legs intensified; she was a tightly wound coil ready to spring. He dipped his finger between her folds, and she groaned at the touch. Confident and commanding, he knew exactly how to play her. He palmed her sex and slid his fingers through her slickness. She spread her legs wide, inviting more, more, more.

He positioned himself at her entrance and pushed slightly. She wrapped her legs around him to increase the pressure. "Dawn, do you want me inside you?" His voice was hoarse but playful.

"Yes. Now. I can't wait any longer." She lifted her hips and squirmed from side to side.

Callan huffed a gruff laugh and paused, teasing her. "Are you ready? Let me make sure." He reached down and circled his fingers inside her once more. His touch made her muscles clench, and she whimpered.

"God, Callan, you're killing me." His fingers weren't enough. She needed all of him. She batted his hand away and pushed her hips up harder.

"You've already slain me," he whispered. He paused and then ran his teeth down the column of her neck. Her pulse leaped wildly under his mouth.

"Callan—" she began, but his broad head made contact with her, and her breath whooshed out. He entered her in one swift thrust, and she cried his name, reveling in the delicious fullness. He pumped his hips, and she clung to his flexing biceps. He grabbed her hip with one hand and pinched her nipple with the other. She raised her knees, and he filled her completely, hitting all the right spots. He moved in and out in a relentless rhythm, twisting and grinding against her. His hand cradled her skull and gripped her hair. His face grew taut, and his gaze bore into hers. For the first time ever, her body and soul were in perfect unison. Was this what people meant by the phrase "making love"? *You've already slain me.*

She squeezed her eyes shut, breaking the spell. She tilted her head back and focused on the delicious friction between her thighs. The tension building in her body made her legs shake and her back arch. She was right on the edge and *oh, God.*

His thumb stroked her clit, and she exploded into fragments. Saw literal freaking stars. She was still tremoring when he gave one final thrust and erupted with an animalistic roar. After a few more languid thrusts, he collapsed beside her.

"Fucking hell, that was good," he groaned, dragging one arm over her and pulling her close.

She nodded against his chest. "It was pretty incredible." But incredible didn't do it justice. Mind-altering. Time-shifting. World-exploding. Like nothing she'd ever experienced before with any other guy. *You've already slain me.*

Her heart jumped into her throat. *It hasn't even been a week...* If someone had told her she'd fall for a guy in the span of six days, she would have laughed right in their face. Yet here she was, already thinking about the rest of the summer with Callan—and *maybe* even the rest of her life with him.

If she wasn't careful, she'd turn into a stage-five clinger.

But maybe Callan had feelings for her too. *You've already slain me.*

She smiled and snuggled in closer. He stroked her back. The long night of socializing, dancing, and sex caught up with her, and she drifted off to sleep with one final thought.

I want to keep this man.

****

Callan woke up early. The light outside the bedroom window was a hazy dull gray, the sun had yet to rise. He kept his arm wrapped around Dawn while she slept, her chest rising and falling slowly. His own chest tightened as he watched her. Not a good sign.

The sex last night had been great—no surprise there—but the time leading up to it had been more fun than he'd expected.

You've already slain me. He couldn't believe he'd said those words out loud. But the bigger shock?

He'd meant them.

He was developing feelings for her. Strong feelings. The kind that made a man think about the future, about *moving on.*

Callan rubbed a hand over his face. No. Don't worry about the future. Don't even *consider* a future.

Enjoy the moment.

Dawn moaned a little in her sleep, and her leg brushed along his. Callan was instantly aware of her body pressed against his, her breasts against his arm, her thighs straddling his. He ran his hand down her side, kissing her shoulder. She woke, and he made love to her again. Slowly, deeply.

Losing himself in her.

Enjoying *her.*

****

"How do you like your eggs? I can cook them any way you want. Scrambled, poached, sunny side up, over easy, over hard. What'll ya have?" She sounded like she worked in a New York diner, but she looked like a *Sports Illustrated* model. Her hair hung in wet tendrils, damp

from the shower—the very long, sexy, *hot* shower—
they'd taken together this morning. She wore his white
dress shirt from last night, which did little to cover her
long tan limbs or the shadows of her nipples beneath the
shirt. She held a spatula and stared at him. Callan
supposed he should concentrate on what she'd asked.

"Scrambled, please."

She nodded and mixed the eggs in a bowl. The bread
popped up from the toaster, so he grabbed the chocolate
hazelnut spread. She gave him a side-eye look.

"What? You don't like chocolate?" he asked.

"I'm a buttered toast kind of gal. I don't put
chocolate on my bread."

"Crazy American. How have you survived without
the brilliance of chocolate and hazelnut?"

"Do you eat like this every morning?" she asked
incredulously.

"This or a couple of pastries."

She shook her head. "How the hell do you have a
body like yours? Typical guy."

"I go to the gym almost every morning. My building
has one." He nodded to her. "You certainly keep fit, too."

She shrugged. "I never worried much about staying
in shape until I quit playing basketball. Now I run or go
to the gym in the afternoons after class. I'll probably
switch to early mornings once I get a real job. I hope I
can stay as disciplined as you."

Her appreciation flattered him. She obviously
admired what she thought was hard work. But he didn't
tell her getting up in the mornings was easy when you
hated your dreams and pushing your body to the limit felt
good when you wanted to punish yourself anyway.

"Are you going back to London today?" she asked

casually.

"Yes. I'll clean up around here a bit and then return home this afternoon. I didn't get much work done over the past week, so I need to dig into it tomorrow."

"I figured." She turned back to the stove.

He leaned on the counter next to her, watching her face. "I'd love to see you again, of course. Would you like to come down for a visit next weekend?"

She glanced over at him. With relief in her eyes? "I'd love to. We are taking a field trip to London on Thursday to observe a parliamentary debate, so I'll be down there anyway."

"Pack a bag. I'll show you the sights; take you to a nice dinner. It'll be fun." Callan tamped down the warning bells in his head. He wanted to see her again. For the brilliant sex, of course. Nothing else.

"Sounds perfect. I will." Dawn scooped the eggs onto two plates and set them down with a flourish. "Breakfast is served. I can't wait to try your chocolate culinary masterpiece."

"Oh, it'll be nothing less than life-changing." He handed her a slice of toast.

Dawn scoffed and took a bite. She raised her eyebrows. "Okay. You might be onto something with chocolate in the morning."

"Just so."

"That was the most British response I've heard from you," she snorted. "Just so. Right, old boy. Pip pip. Cheerio." Her British accent was atrocious.

"Is that how you Americans truly think we sound?" he asked, acting affronted.

"I think my accent's pretty good. Do you have any American friends?"

"Not really, no. I have American acquaintances. Business partners. But no, not any real *red-blooded American friends.*" Callan ended with a twangy Old West accent.

She winced, laughing. "Yikes. And you say *my* accent is bad? So, I guess I'm the first Yank you've been with?" She teased, but he could tell where she wanted to steer the conversation, and he dreaded it, even as he knew it was a normal conversation to have with the person you're screwing.

"Just so." Callan said it with a smile, but inside he braced himself.

"Have you had many relationships in the past?" *And there it is.* He'd anticipated this topic since he'd met her but hadn't yet decided how to respond. *She's only here for the summer. You don't have to tell her* everything.

"A few. Only one was serious." He paused. Dawn put down her fork and stared at him. She could tell he was about to reveal something big. "I was married."

"Oh." She raised her eyebrows. "What happened?"

"She...left me. It was a long time ago. Years, in fact. We were very young." Dawn nodded in understanding. After all, young marriages seldom work out. An inkling of guilt nagged him. He was purposefully misleading her. *Well, she* did *leave me, in a way. And we* were *young when we married.* It wasn't a complete lie.

He quashed his guilt. Was he supposed to lay bare all the pain in his life after a few short days? In a couple of months, Dawn would return to America, and he'd never see her again. There was no reason to have such a serious conversation with someone he'd only known for a week. Even if she felt as familiar to him as...

"What was her name?" she asked.

Callan swallowed thickly. "It doesn't matter. She's gone." He hadn't said her name aloud in a very long time and didn't know if he could. He cleared his throat and picked up the dishes from the table. "What about you? Any beefy American suitors I should be concerned about?"

"No, not at all," she said, gathering the rest from the table. "You are probably the beefiest guy I've ever been with. I usually go for the artsy types."

"Surprising. I would have thought large American footballers were more your style."

"No way. I played basketball, but I wasn't popular. The football players only dated the cheerleaders."

"Sounds like an eighties teen movie." He took the plates from her.

"Exactly. I was a total dork. Always studying, hanging out at coffee shops instead of drinking beer. My best friend, Jane, was popular, but I was on the fringes."

Callan dropped the dishes in the sink and pulled Dawn into his arms. He pictured her as a young girl, tall and awkward, with a giant set of braces. It endeared her to him even more. "You were studious and unpopular, but then you blossomed into a beautiful woman who became a high-powered lawyer. You returned to your alma mater, and the men who once mocked you fell to their knees in abject worship."

She wrapped her arms around his waist and slid her calf up his leg. He peered straight down her shirt to the valley between her breasts. She really did have the most beautiful bosom he'd ever seen.

He began to unbutton the shirt. She watched him make his way down, button by button, and then looked into his eyes, canting her head. "I like where this story is going," she said. "I have to know. How does it end?"

Callan stared into her green eyes. He knew exactly how this ended, and he felt a gut-punch of sadness. *Fuck*.

Even if he grew *attached* to Dawn, he couldn't do anything about it. He wasn't fit for anything beyond a temporary affair. He wouldn't even consider it.

He refused to make any promises—not to her and not to himself.

So he answered her with a kiss instead.

Chapter Eleven

Throughout June and into July, Dawn fell into a routine with Callan. She visited him in London on the weekends, and on Tuesdays and Thursdays, he visited her in Cambridge. He worked remotely from the Cambridge Coffee House while she went to class or studied in the library. On the rare days when the weather wasn't pouring rain or blazing hot, they'd work and study together on a blanket in Parker's Piece, a large green space in the heart of Cambridge.

Dawn lived for those days. She treasured looking up from her book to see his golden-brown hair glinting in the sun, the gentle breeze caressing her skin as he absently rubbed her arm. Callan was adorable when he muttered to himself, poring over contracts and project plans. She admired his ability to resolve conflicts and issues during business calls, his deep voice both assured and reassuring when talking to colleagues and clients. His obvious business acumen made her hot between her legs.

Apparently, she was into competence porn.

When the sun grew long over the park, they wrapped up their blanket and went back to her place to change into workout gear. Some afternoons they hit the gym, but most days, they went for a run around campus. She loved running with Callan, mostly because she smoked him.

"Damn. You are fast." Callan panted when he

caught up to her the first time they ran together.

She grinned. "I forgot to mention I was also All-State in cross country." She'd kept with his pace for a few miles but then had suggested they race the last mile, knowing she would beat him. Everything about Callan was so impossibly amazing and perfect. She'd wanted to show off and impress him, to throw him off-kilter.

His gaze swept over her appreciatively. "I can't be upset with you. I certainly enjoyed the view from behind." He planted a sweaty kiss on her lips.

She laughed and pushed him away. "You need a shower."

"How about the winner gets to take a shower with the loser?" His voice turned low, and he dragged her closer.

They returned to her place, and he *did things* to her in the cramped shower she didn't think were possible. Delicious, indecent, toe-curling things that had her biting back moans so her flatmates wouldn't hear.

The post-workout showers became a part of their routine. Dawn fought blushes when her flatmates teased her but realized she had nothing to be embarrassed about after hearing their sexcapades. Everyone was getting theirs in Cambridge.

On Saturdays, Callan took her sightseeing around London or on day jaunts to sights like Oxford and Stonehenge. On Sundays, they stayed in his flat, making love and watching movies. They cooked breakfast together, went to the grocery store in the afternoons, and spoke to his mom in the evenings.

Dawn helped Callan shop for a new dresser when he decided he needed more storage. Callan helped Dawn select a new smartphone when hers died.

Their domestic bliss was both thrilling and frightening. Callan had quickly angled his way into her life, her heart. She wanted so badly to ask him what would happen when her program ended. Would they stay in touch? Try to keep the relationship going? She'd never had a long-term boyfriend, but Callan behaved exactly as she imagined one would. The intensity in his eyes when he watched her, the way he listened to her and valued her opinions, the possessive hand on her back as he guided her through a crowd, the strength in his arms wrapping her tightly after making love.

Her fall for him wasn't candy and roses; it was jumping off a cliff and praying for survival.

She played it cool, choking back her words whenever her anxiety over their future bubbled to the surface. She pretended like they had all the time in the world. But she'd memorized the calendar and could recite precisely how many weeks, days, and minutes they had remaining.

"Ask him what he is thinking," Jane sensibly advised during their last video chat.

But Dawn didn't ask. She couldn't put her finger on it, but something about Callan made her hesitate every time she mustered the courage to talk to him about the future. He held a piece of himself back from her. And sometimes, she caught a sadness in his eyes, a melancholy buried so deep and hidden inside him she couldn't excavate it no matter how close they became.

Or maybe she was just paranoid.

Ex-wife. Dawn and Jane had scoured the Internet for any sign of his former love but found nothing. Callan had clearly been too upset to even utter her name, and he hadn't mentioned her since.

As the weeks flew by with alarming speed, Dawn's anxieties and worries echoed louder and louder in her head until they melded together into one loud question.

Was Callan still in love with his ex-wife?

****

The two-week summer holiday during July was intended to allow program students to travel throughout the UK and Europe, but Dawn used it to shadow Gemma and other volunteers through the immigration process for trafficked children. She'd initially taken Gemma up on her offer as a way of adding another highlight to her résumé. It was Gemma's idea to call the two weeks a "concentrated internship." Having such a hot topic on her CV would give Dawn a boost when applying for jobs in the fall. Mae Lin wouldn't have this on her résumé. *Suck it, Mae Lin!*

Dawn hadn't expected to become so invested in the process. She went with various volunteers to meet with the guardians and children to prepare for their cases. Some of the children were so young it broke her heart. And their stories… She couldn't shake what these kids had seen, what they'd been through.

On Dawn's final day, she observed Gemma at a closed hearing with a judge, a court-appointed guardian, a child, and the child's foster family, all working together to find the best solution for the child. And her own throat constricted when the foster family, who loved the tiny Serbian girl with the haunted eyes, cried tears of joy when they realized there was a path forward to adoption and citizenship.

"It's so different," Dawn commented to Gemma and Callan during their celebratory dinner at the Indian restaurant around the corner from Callan's flat. She took another bite of the delicious curry chicken.

"What is?" asked Gemma, sipping her merlot.

"What you did today was not adversarial. It is so different from the law firm environment."

"Only certain law is adversarial. You can still work for a firm and not fight people." Gemma's bright-brown eyes, framed by luxurious black lashes, held amusement as her delicate manicured fingers folded and refolded her napkin. Dawn noticed Gemma didn't eat much. But to be fair, Gemma's stomach in her tiny body was probably half the size of Dawn's.

Dawn picked up a large piece of naan and shrugged. "I worked for a firm during my first year of law school. The lawyers were always competing to get something over on the other guy."

"I thought you wanted to storm into court. Fight people to take down the bad guys," Callan said, replaying her words from their first date.

Her lips tugged upward. "I thought so, too. I mean, I like competition, and I like winning. But I enjoyed watching the process of working together to help someone."

"Maybe you need to consider other possibilities," offered Callan, and Gemma nodded in agreement.

Dawn regarded them ruefully. "I wish it were so simple. You don't even want to know what student loans are like in America." She'd need a six-figure job—at least—for the next thirty years to pay off her massive debt, which meant a big firm associate's salary and even bigger partner pay. She was locked in, whether she wanted it or not.

Callan put a large hand on Dawn's thigh and squeezed. He must have seen her uncertainty and wanted to reassure her. But instead of comforting her, his concern and tenderness saddened her. She couldn't stomach the thought of leaving him, and now she wasn't even excited about her career path.

You could stay. Get a loan deferment. What would Callan say if she told him she wanted to stay in England? Would the program director let her work something out with the university? Spend another year studying here? Was it possible? Should she veer so far off course?

They wrapped up dinner and said goodbye to Gemma, who promised Dawn she could help out any time. Walking back to his apartment, Callan attempted to lighten the mood. He told Dawn a silly story involving himself, Will, a pack of wild geese, and fireworks. She gave him a half-hearted chuckle. He stopped her along the pavement.

"Where are you right now?"

"I want to be with you," Dawn admitted. Her breath stopped as she watched Callan. Hoping. Willing him to respond as he did in her daydreams. *I want to be with you too, Dawn. I'm so happy you feel the same way...*

Callan's expression shuttered. The teasing glow in his eyes faded, and his smile turned bland. "But you are with me."

Her stomach churned. "I guess my head is somewhere else, but I want to focus on you." God, she was a coward. The light came back into his eyes, and he pulled her close. She clung to his jacket and buried her face into his chest, inhaling the masculine scent that would forever remind her of Callan. Tears burned Dawn's eyes, and her stomach roiled with a dread she couldn't identify. They still had over a month together before she left. Why was she feeling this crushing sadness?

"What are you worried about?"

"I'm behind on my studies." Which was true. She was behind on her reading assignments by several days. She'd been slacking on her schoolwork because of Callan—something she'd never done before—and she hated the unfamiliar feeling of falling behind. She was usually so on top of things. She squeezed her eyes tight. Great, now she had anxiety about school piled on top of her anxiety about Callan. She was a freaking mess.

"Tell you what. Let's skip the visit to Blenheim Palace tomorrow, and you can spend the weekend doing what you need to do for school."

Dawn reared back and lifted her head. Her heart twisted at the concern stamped on Callan's face, and pain stabbed her sharply in the stomach. She felt like a lovesick puppy.

"No, no. We don't have to skip it. I'll be fine."

"You aren't fine, Dawn. I can read you. Please, I want you to feel prepared, and I would be a complete arse if I convinced you to skip out on your work and added to your stress."

A giggle bubbled to the top of her throat. He *was* her stress. "It's okay."

"I've got work to do as well. We can have a workday and then a fun night. I'll treat you to a date night for a job well done."

"You promise you don't mind?" She wasn't feeling up to the trip, anyway. A day reading on the couch with Callan sounded much better than touring a castle.

"Promise." He reached up and ran his finger through her ponytail. He was obsessed with her hair, constantly stroking it, brushing his lips to it. She couldn't say she minded. "I don't care what we do as long as I'm with you," he said and brushed a featherlight kiss on her lips. His kiss made the aching in her gut grow even more.

She felt sick.

"Let's go inside," Dawn said, pulling him toward the door.

Callan frowned. "Are you sure you're feeling well?"

"I'm fine. Just tired."

It was the first night they spent together without making love. Callan simply tucked Dawn by his side and turned out the lights. He curled his body against hers, and she snuggled into his hard warmth while his face nuzzled her hair. She felt loved and protected. Cherished.

Long after his breath deepened with sleep, she replayed their conversation over and over. *I don't care what we do as long as I'm with you.* Did he mean what he said? If so, for how long? Just the summer? Nausea rose.

Did Callan want to be with her?

Chapter Twelve

There is no way Callan wants to be with me.

Dawn leaned over the toilet for the third time and emptied her already hollow stomach.

Knuckles rapped on the door. "Are you okay? Can I help?"

"No," she groaned. Callan had already seen her throw up once when she'd raced to the bathroom early in the morning. He'd held her hair and rubbed her back. How embarrassing. She didn't want him hovering over her now.

The bout was over, and Dawn wiped her mouth with toilet paper. She looked in the mirror. The blood vessels on her cheeks and around her eyes had burst, creating splotchy red dots. Her coloring was a sickly green-gray, and her hair was pulled into a not-so-sexy bun.

She looked like shit.

She grabbed some toothpaste and swished it in her mouth. Ugh. She felt awful. At least the stabbing pains in her abdomen had subsided. For now.

She opened the door. Callan stood outside with a glass of water. "I'm going to go to the market and get you some soda and biscuits. It's what my mum always fed me when I was sick."

"Don't bother, please. I just need to rest." Having him fuss over her only heightened her embarrassment.

He put his hand to her head. "You don't have a

fever. You have food poisoning." He scowled. "I don't think it was the Indian food. Otherwise, we would both be sick. What did you have for lunch yesterday?"

"Uh, a street sandwich. Rib meat." Dawn and Gemma had eaten on the go in between court sessions yesterday. Thinking about it made her stomach roil.

"Could be food poisoning, could be a bug. Get back in bed. I'll run out and get some supplies for you." Callan ushered her to bed, and she didn't have the strength to argue. He fluffed her pillow and tucked her in before standing back to survey his work. "I'll get you another pillow."

She reached out to stop him but then dropped her arm. She didn't have the heart to object. And, frankly, it was nice to have someone care for her when she was so far from home.

He tucked another pillow under her before heading out. The apartment door opened and shut, and then silence. She blinked and realized she didn't feel so bad now. She sat up. This wasn't the first time he'd left her alone in his apartment, she'd been crashing at his place for the past two weeks, but it was the first time she'd been alone with an overwhelming curiosity. She probably had a fifteen-minute window before the nausea or Callan returned.

She should snoop.

She shouldn't snoop.

She was going to snoop.

She slowly eased out of bed and glanced around. Callan's apartment was clean, with very few personal items. No pictures. If she hadn't met his friends and family at the wedding, she might think he was a serial killer.

She didn't even know what she was looking for. Maybe she should call Jane and ask her what to search.

She started with his desk drawers. She wasn't sure what she would find, but she knew exactly what she wanted to find. *Details about the ex-wife.* Did he still have memorabilia from their time together?

Nothing in the drawers. Dawn turned to the closet, a small walk-in. She entered and switched on the light. Peering through the hanging clothes and into the cubbies, she found nothing. She craned her neck to see the top shelf.

There. One banker's box. She retrieved a chair from his desk and hopped up. She brought the box down gently and glanced behind her. What would he think if he found her now? *That you are a complete psycho.*

She lifted the lid. *Bingo.* A wedding album sat right there on the top. This was too easy. She opened the cover and flipped through the pages. A young Callan, fresh-faced with no scruff, beamed in the photos beside a petite attractive woman with short dark hair. Dawn recognized Will and Sarah in the wedding party photos along with Callan's mom and, she assumed, his dad. He and his bride looked so happy. Young, yes, but very much in love. What had happened to make them end their marriage?

Dawn lifted the album and spied a stack of photos and papers. The papers appeared to be certificates, tax forms, and other official documents.

She reached for them but then paused. What was she doing? She was totally invading Callan's privacy. Guilt swamped her. How would she feel if Callan went searching through her personal papers? She quickly dropped the album back in the box and replaced the lid.

She stepped onto the chair and put the box back where she'd found it. Dawn scurried into bed and folded her hands on top of the covers. All she'd seen were a few pictures, nothing more. She hadn't *totally* violated his trust. She fingered a thread on the comforter. Jane would likely tell her she'd been well within her right—no, her *duty*—to find out all she could about Callan and his ex-wife.

And what good had it done to see those photos? To see him smiling, with his arms around another woman so tender, so full of promise, hope, and love? She flopped her head back on the pillow as the familiar tingles of nausea set in. She glanced at the clock. Fifteen minutes on the dot. Callan would be back soon. Did she regret seeing his wedding album? Not exactly. But it made her realize maybe her summer love affair was just that. An affair. Not the true love he'd experienced with his ex.

She needed a distraction. She reached over and pulled her book bag off the floor and hoisted out a book on UK public company case law. She concentrated on reading a complicated corporate conflicts case, but the words muddled together. The book landed with a thud by her side. It was already mid-morning, and the icky feeling had returned. There was no way she'd be able to catch up on her reading.

Dawn's lower abdomen clenched and knotted. Worrying over Callan and school didn't help.

The front door opened; grocery bags crinkled. Callan appeared in the bedroom doorway and strode over to the bed. He wore a vintage Star Wars T-shirt and jeans, which displayed his muscular arms, chest, and thighs. Basically, his entire body was muscle. And his beard was especially scruffy and adorable today. The combination of nerd and hotness melted Dawn's insides and *almost* made her want to make a move on him despite her nausea.

Almost.

He frowned. "You're green again."

"It's coming back. What did you get?" She nodded at the bags.

He set the bags on the bed and pulled out items. "Crackers. Sport drinks. Fizzy drinks. Ginger biscuits. Peppermint tea. Heating pad. Bananas. Applesauce. Paracetamol."

"You're like an overprepared nanny."

"I take good care of my charges." He winked. "Can I get you anything?"

"No, thank you. I don't think I can keep anything down right now." She clenched her eyes. Her mouth watered, and the wave began to rise. She lurched off the bed and ran to the toilet.

The sickness crested through her, and Callan rubbed his palm across her back soothingly. When it was over, he helped her up and wrapped an arm around her waist. She was beyond embarrassed now, but Callan didn't seem fazed. She brushed her teeth again, and he led her to the bed, tucking the covers around her once more.

He picked up her case law book and cocked an eyebrow. "Some light reading?"

She settled in and closed her eyes. Exhaustion took over. "I tried. I'm so behind. But I couldn't," she mumbled behind closed lids. A warm hand touched her forehead and then lightly stroked her cheek. He remained close, standing watch beside the bed. She hadn't been sick like this since high school, and she was so grateful not to be alone, even if she was a tiny bit mortified by it all. She drifted off to sleep, comforted knowing Callan would take care of her.

No matter what.

****

When Dawn woke, the bedroom was dim and cast in long shadows. "Callan?" she called.

"Good evening," he said from the doorway, leaning against the frame.

"Evening? What time is it?"

"About seven o'clock."

"I slept the whole day?"

"I'm afraid so. But you needed it."

She struggled to sit upright. He came forward and plucked her up, settling her back against the headboard.

"How do you feel?" he asked.

"The nausea is gone, I think. But I have a massive headache."

"You're probably dehydrated. I'm going to fix you a simple meal. We'll see if you can keep it down." He left the room and rummaged around the kitchen.

She leaned forward and saw herself in the bedroom mirror. Cripes, she looked like she'd been hit by a truck.

"I'm going to take a shower," she called.

"Be careful in there. Let me know if you need help washing your private bits," he said from the other room.

"Doubtful," she responded, and he laughed.

The shower made her feel like a new person. When she was done and towel drying her hair, he came in with a tray loaded with his purchases from the market.

"Bananas and saltines," Dawn observed. "Yum."

"Only the best for my lady."

"I can eat at the table so I don't get crumbs in your bed."

133

"I'll get you set up at the dining table."

They passed through the living room and into the smaller dining room adjacent to the kitchen. Like the rest of Callan's apartment, the room was modern but warm with a walnut and brass dining table and comfortable stone leather chairs. He set the tray down and pulled out a chair for her. She reached for a cracker and glanced across the table. He must have been working while she slept because papers were scattered across the table along with his open computer and several books. She looked at the spines.

"Are those my books?" Dawn asked, biting into a cracker. Her stomach rumbled with hunger instead of sickness, thank goodness.

"They are," he commented.

"What are you doing with my case books?"

Callan gave her a sheepish lopsided smile, and her curiosity piqued. "Well, I thought maybe I could help you." She raised her eyebrows, and he continued, "I know how stressed you are about catching up on your studies, so I took it upon myself to do a little work for you."

He went around the table and grabbed some papers and a notebook. "You left your syllabus out," he said, seating himself in a chair beside her. "And I noticed you marked what you've read so far, so I took the reading assignments you were behind on, and I summarized the cases for you."

She took the notebook from him and thumbed through pages of neat, masculine handwriting. Each page had a case cite, a paragraph summarizing the issues of the case, and bullets detailing why the case was important. Her mouth dropped. He did this for her?

"I would have typed it out for you, but my printer is out of ink. I know I am not a lawyer, but I looked up how to summarize a case, so I hope it is fairly accurate. I may have Googled the main points for some cases." His smile faltered at her silence. "I'm not sure if you can use this. I know you probably need to read the cases yourself, but I hoped this could help you catch up in the meantime."

"So you sat here all day and read case law?"

"Yes."

"And then summarized it for me?"

"Yes."

"By hand?" She stared at the notebook.

"Yes?"

"This is amazing." She looked up at him and found him watching her closely, his eyes a dark amber. He lifted a hand and brushed her cheek, tucking a strand of hair behind her ear. "Callan, I can't believe you sat here all day reading this stuff." She was floored. No guy had ever gone out of his way to do something so nice for her.

Callan shrugged, his lips curling. "It wasn't all bad. Some of them are quite interesting."

Dawn rolled her eyes. "Great, let's switch places then." She laughed and then paused. "Wait, how did you get all of this done? There are at least twenty cases here." She'd been behind in several classes.

Callan actually *blushed*. "I, ah, can read fast."

"Like how fast," Dawn asked suspiciously.

"Like photographic memory fast."

"What?" she screamed. "Why have you never told me this?"

He ran a hand through his hair, and his thick waves flopped in disarray. "It never came up. And I didn't want you to look at me like you are now."

"How am I looking at you?"

"Like a freak."

"No way. I'm amazed. And jealous. You're like Mae Lin," she accused.

"Who is Mae Lin?"

She scrunched her face. "My nemesis."

Callan laughed. "Nemesis? Sounds pretty heavy. Do tell."

Dawn sighed. "Mae Lin is the nicest person you'll ever meet," she grumbled. "But she and I are battling it out for the top spot in our law school class, and she has an unfair advantage because she has a photographic memory. Just like you."

"Ah, I see." He tilted his head. "I'm sorry to have reminded you of your nemesis."

She laid a hand on his arm, feeling the rough hairs beneath her fingers. "No, I'm sorry. I'm joking. Well, half-joking. I *am* jealous of you. And Mae Lin. School always came easy to me. I never had to try very hard to be number one. But law school is a different game." She fingered the hairs on his arm, staring at the golden skin underneath. "I actually have to apply myself. And I don't know what for."

"Like we said last night, Dawn, there is still time to choose a different path."

"I know, but I don't know what I want to do. And the time for me to decide is running out."

Callan placed a hand over hers, his face set in severe lines as he leaned toward her. "Dawn, listen to me. Life can change in a second. Believe me, I know." His eyes glazed over for a moment. Was he thinking about the end of his marriage? "Don't go down a road you don't want to. You're an achiever. So use some of that to achieve the life you want."

She nodded, and he squeezed her hand. "You're right. I'm complaining when I should be figuring out a way to get what I want." She stared at him and inched closer to him. She felt pulled, connected to him, electric currents sizzling back and forth between them. She reached her hand up and stroked his rough jaw, half expecting a spark to fly. "You are amazing," she whispered.

His eyes shuttered, and then he reached across and swooped her into his lap. She cradled his face and gazed down at him from her perch. He swept his thumb across her bottom lip and leaned in for a light kiss. She sighed against him and ran her fingers through his hair, tugging him closer.

He exhaled a low chuckle. "Are you feeling better?"

"Much." She angled for a deeper kiss, but then her stomach let out a loud growl at the same time her phone rang from the bedroom.

Callan lifted her with a slight groan, wincing as he eased her off the bulge in his lap. "Go get your phone. I'll fix you some soup."

Dawn hurried to her phone and answered the incoming video chat from Jane. "Hey."

"Where have you been all week? Are you still at Callan's?" Jane lounged in a pool chair under an umbrella, the top of her yellow bikini visible and her thick dark hair piled in a bun.

"Yeah, I'll go back to Cambridge tomorrow night."

"Let me talk to him."

"No way."

"I have to approve of him, and I've never even seen him. Let me talk to him."

"I—" A large hand reached over her shoulder and snatched the phone away.

"Hello, Jane," Callan said into the phone. Inexplicable butterflies flew in her stomach when Callan smiled at the screen.

"Why hello there, Callan. Nice to finally meet you," Jane drawled. "Have you been taking care of my girl?"

"More than you know," he said in a mischievous tone.

Dawn rolled her eyes and grabbed his hand, tilting the phone toward herself so she could see Jane. "I puked all over his apartment this weekend."

Callan grinned and jerked the phone back. "Not all over the flat. In the toilet, specifically."

"Thank goodness for small mercies. I hate to tell you, but that's what happens when she takes too many shots."

"I didn't—"

Callan cut in. "She had food poisoning. She's better now but still feeble."

"Feeble?" Dawn exploded. "You didn't think I was so feeble when I was sitting in your lap."

"Oh, did I interrupt something?" Jane snickered.

"I was about to make her some soup," he said and carried the phone with him to the kitchen. He and Jane talked in earnest as he heated chicken noodle soup in a pot. They asked each other question after question, laughing and chatting and being their charming selves. Like they both knew how important the other was to Dawn and were making every effort to get to know one another.

Dawn's heart squeezed.

"All right, love. Dinner is served," Callan said with

a flourish, setting the soup bowl and spoon down at the dining table.

"Aw, what a prince. You sure you aren't part of the royal family?" Jane joked. Then she said to Dawn, "You were right about him."

"You called me a prince?" Callan asked with a teasing glint.

"Never mind her. Jane needs to pipe down," Dawn muttered and lifted her spoon.

"Pipe down? She's always telling me to shut the fuck up," Jane said.

"And it doesn't work," Dawn said with a smile.

"So, do you approve of me?" Callan sat down beside Dawn and angled the phone so they could both see Jane.

Jane narrowed her eyes and scrunched her mouth. "On the surface, yes. But why are you not on any social media? And you need to tell us the truth about—"

Dawn yanked the phone out of his hand. "Okay, I think that's enough for tonight. Love you. I'll call you later. Byeeee." She quickly hung up on Jane's protest.

Callan raised his eyebrows. "Tell you the truth about what?" He smiled, but there was a slight edge to his question.

The air hung thick between them. Now was her chance.

But she chickened out. Again.

"Nothing. Jane is crazy."

"I like her. She cares about you very much," he said, watching as she took a sip of the soup. She felt the intensity of his gaze on her.

Dawn turned to him, her heart pounding. "She does. And I think… I think you wouldn't have done everything you did for me today if you didn't care too."

****

Callan blinked. "Of course I care about you." As much as he would care about any friend. If Sarah had been sick, he'd have cared for her the same way.

Well, he wouldn't have offered to wash Sarah's private bits. But otherwise, yes, the *exact* same way.

Dawn smiled wanly. "I care about you too, Callan." Her face was still a bit pale, but her eyes shone a bright green, and her hair was drying in dark fiery tendrils down her back. He reached for a damp curl, twining it around his fingers. The *look* she gave him… Expectant, shy, and something else he didn't want to consider.

Maybe the whole helping her out with school thing had been too much. But she'd been so distressed; he'd wanted to do something to ease her burden. He'd have done the same for Sarah. Right?

He leaned over and kissed her pert nose. Clearly, Dawn and her friend had spoken about him and his revelation concerning his marriage. This conversation was now in danger of becoming too serious. He needed to steer it back into no-commitment-fun-times-only territory. "I enjoyed applying my nursing skills for you today," he said with a salacious wag of his eyebrows.

She scrunched her nose. Adorably. "I doubt it."

He sank his hand into her silky curls. He was obsessed. He'd never seen natural hair with a color like hers. "And I did find several of the cases very interesting."

She rolled her eyes but leaned into his palm. "I don't even want to know how enthralling you found corporate case law."

"Very enthralling." He placed his other hand on her hip, pulling her forward. Her eyes dilated, and she licked her lips. "But really, my ministrations were quite selfish," he continued, his thumb making lazy circles against her hip while his other hand continued playing with her hair.

"They were?" she asked, her breath hitching. She put her hands on his thighs and widened her legs so his fit between hers. She sat on the edge of her chair, an inch away, ready to jump into his lap.

He nodded. "I wanted to make you better as soon as possible."

"Because you care about me?"

"Of course." He hoisted her onto his lap, settling her legs on either side of his waist. The apex of her thighs felt soft and warm even through his jeans, and his cock thickened. "This is where we were before Jane called, yes?"

Dawn nodded and sank into him, melding her soft breasts against his chest. He nipped at the graceful column of her neck. He'd started this to distract her, to lighten the mood, but it had backfired on him. He was consumed by a bone-aching need to devour her. A need that belied everything he told himself about their relationship.

Callan shook his head. No thoughts right now, just feel. He reached down, lifting her ass with one hand and unzipping his pants with the other. She quickly hopped up and tore her sweatpants off before straddling him again, this time sinking down on his swollen cock, one delicious inch at a time.

He groaned. She rocked forward on top of him, and he clutched her hips, pulling her back and forth in a frantic rhythm as he licked and kissed her collarbone.

"You feel so bloody good," Callan said, his voice

low and guttural. He found her clit with his thumb and pressed, stroking back and forth in time with her movements. This is how he wanted her—hot, dripping with need, and wild on his cock.

He stood, carrying her into the living room, and pulled out briefly to spin her around and bend her over the arm of the couch, face down. He clutched her hips and hauled her to him. Again and again, he pounded into her from behind. *This* is what he wanted from her. *This* is why she was here.

Her legs quivered, and she began to moan. He drove into her harder, mercilessly, giving in to the raw need of his body and pushing away the tug on his heart. She reached her peak, and her inside spasmed, gripping him. It threw him over the edge, and he shouted as tremors overtook his own body. He clenched his eyes shut and grabbed her hair, tugging her head. He collapsed over her and kissed her supple back while their breaths slowed.

Just like Sarah, eh?

He was so fucking screwed.

Chapter Thirteen

Dawn leaned against the cream and wood wall outside Professor Humphrey's office, avoiding the small groups of students meandering past her while she waited for the man in charge of the Cambridge exchange program to come striding down the hallway.

"Hello, Dawn," Professor Humphrey said when he approached her.

"Hello, Professor. Do you have a moment to talk?" He nodded and ushered her into his office. She sank into a deep leather chair opposite his pristine desk.

"How can I help you?" he asked. He folded his dark-brown hands patiently.

"I want to stay," she blurted. "I mean, is it possible to stay in the exchange program?"

He raised his eyebrows. His brown eyes were kind but keen, as if he could see through her sex-addled motives and thought to himself, *Here's another American exchange student falling for a piece of British ass.*

"We do have a full-year program during the regular term. So it isn't out of the question. May I ask why?"

She launched into the speech she'd rehearsed. "I'd like to get my JD/MBA with a focus on US and UK business relations. Staying in the program for the upcoming school term would be ideal, especially if some of the credits could transfer to my school." Professor

Humphrey started to speak, but she rushed on. "And I've been volunteering with a nonprofit in London, Lawyers ACT. Are you familiar with them?"

"I am. They are a great organization and do vital work."

"Well, I have become involved in the organization, and some of the cases I've been working on are critical. I'd like to see them through." Perhaps a slight fib, but she *would* become more involved if she stayed.

"Dawn, you are a superb student, and I certainly would have no qualms with you continuing your studies in the program. We could re-enroll you in the program without an application. I'd have to run it by the chancellor, but it shouldn't be an issue. I know your dean of school very well, so I'd be happy to speak with her about transferring credits."

"I'd be so grateful, Professor Humphrey. Thank you so much." Excitement bubbled. Another year in England—with Callan. And, she'd have the bonus of an extra year to figure out what the hell she wanted to do with her life.

But then Professor Humphrey held up his hand. "I must warn you, Dawn. I wouldn't be able to waive the program tuition. And you'd most likely still have to pay your school's tuition."

She gulped. "I know that." Though she hoped her school would be willing to defer her third year of law school so she wouldn't have to pay two tuition fees at once. Otherwise, this plan might not fly.

One step at a time. Don't think about the money.

After discussing next steps, Dawn bade Professor Humphrey a thankful goodbye and left his office. She practically skipped the entire way back to her flat. She and Callan could take things slow; they didn't need to rush their relationship. And Dawn *would* become more involved with Gemma's organization and maybe others. She'd explore what she wanted to do with her life. Without the pressure of fall on-campus job interviews.

The money didn't matter. She'd pay it off somehow. She'd have to push her fall clerkship with the judge. She hoped he would understand, maybe even offer her the clerkship next fall. Anxiety built, dampening her excitement.

Screw it. Put it all in the box.

Nothing mattered except this. She was choosing her path, doing what she wanted to do instead of what she thought she should do.

And it felt glorious.

****

"I want to become more involved." Dawn handed Gemma the stack of applications for their next case.

Gemma looked up. "You are already helping when you can on Fridays."

"I'd like to do more."

Gemma set down the papers and waited for Dawn to continue.

"I'm thinking about…staying."

Gemma cocked a dark eyebrow. "Staying?"

"Yes?"

"Hmmm."

"You don't think it's a good idea?" Dawn asked.

"Tell me more," Gemma said.

So Dawn told her about her conversation with Professor Humphrey. About her plan to stay in Cambridge over the next school year and delay her graduation from law school.

"And you want to stay because of Callan?"

"Yes… No… I don't know… Okay, yes. But I also need more time to figure my shit out. And I love working with you, Gemma. I want to help people, help these kids." She waved her hand at the files piled between them.

"Would you want to work for a nonprofit full time?"

"I would. I know they don't pay as well as a big firm, but maybe I could get a loan deferment or a grant."

Gemma nodded. "It is worth looking into. I'm happy to have the help, certainly." She narrowed her eyes and leaned back in her chair. "Does Callan know?"

"About me staying?"

Gemma nodded.

"Well, no. Not yet." Dawn glanced behind her. She and Gemma were holed up in Green Solar's office. Callan could walk in at any moment.

"Are you going to talk to him before you make a final decision?"

"I'm still working out the details." She was running into complications with the tuition deferment, course credits, and her student visa. Professor Humphrey assured Dawn he would help her with the process, but nothing was settled yet. She might need to go back to DC and then return to England if she couldn't sort everything out in time. "I don't want to bring it up to him if it's a moot point."

"What do you think he would say?" Gemma asked.

"I don't know. What do *you* think he would say?"

"I think you should talk to him. Tell him what you want and what you are planning."

"Even if Callan were out of the picture, I would still want to stay. I feel like…" She shrugged.

146

"Like what?"

"Like I might be finding myself?" Maybe it was cheesy, but Dawn did feel like a door had opened for her. Yes, she wanted Callan. Desperately. But whether Callan was a part of her life or not, she wanted to stay. For herself. To give herself time to explore and get in touch with what she wanted to do with her life.

Gemma nodded again. "I understand." She leaned forward. "No matter what, you have a place here. And I won't say anything to Callan until you speak with him."

Dawn gave Gemma a grateful smile. "Thank you. I don't want to cause a rift between you, but I appreciate you keeping my confidence."

Gemma shook her head. "I am a firm believer in people speaking their own truth. It's not my place to tell him what you are thinking or planning, just as I wouldn't betray his feelings either."

"Thanks, Gemma."

"But you should talk to him," Gemma said before picking up another file.

Dawn stared at the application in her hand, not reading the words. She would talk to Callan. Once things were closer to being settled. Once she knew she was for sure staying. She would talk to him.

She would.

Chapter Fourteen

What the fuck am I doing? Callan tightened his hands on the steering wheel. He glanced to his left at Dawn, who continued to chat about something she'd learned in class. Lately, she'd been more excited about school. More optimistic and not as concerned about the competition or grades. He was happy for her, and he normally adored engaging in conversations with her about cases and English law.

But not today. He could barely follow her conversation as he replayed the phone call that had gotten him into this mess.

"Callan, can't you take a day to help your poor mum?" his mother had pleaded. "Your dad is too old to be setting posts, and I need to get the fencing done. The rabbits are eating all my tomatoes."

"Mum, Dawn and I have plans today—"

"Oh! Bring her! You could make a trip of it. I have a roast perfect for dinner. Oh, do say you will come."

Callan had sighed. He'd turned to Dawn, who'd regarded him with raised eyebrows, a signal that he needed to do whatever his mum said.

He'd sighed again. "We'll be there by noon."

"Where will we be by noon?" Dawn asked after he'd said goodbye.

"Brighton. My mum needs help digging fence posts. It might be a two-day job. Do you mind if we go for a visit and stay for the night?"

"Not at all. I'll start packing," she'd said brightly, grabbing her overnight bag.

He'd thrown toiletries into a bag and watched Dawn out of the corner of his eye.

A half-smile had played on her lips as she'd bounced around the flat packing. She'd been obviously happy with this development.

But Callan hadn't.

Now, with each passing mile, his mood soured. Everything about this trip was wrong.

Dawn probably thought spending the weekend with his parents took their relationship to the next level. She had no idea the next level didn't exist. Ever since the weekend when she'd been ill, he'd clamped down even harder on his feelings. Quashed them without remorse. He had to. It was the only way he could survive around Dawn without driving himself crazy.

He hated Brighton. Hated the memories associated with the seaside town. He lifted a sweaty palm from the steering wheel and wiped his brow.

Flashes of the past invaded his thoughts. Twisted metal. Fire. Screams.

Callan exhaled slowly, pushing the images out of his mind.

"You okay?" Dawn asked. "You're a little pale."

"I'm fine," he said in a clipped voice. She looked taken aback by his tone. He clenched his jaw. "I'm sorry. I'm just tired from driving."

"That's okay. Do you want me to take over?"

He shook his head. "We're almost there." Indeed,

they passed a road sign reading five miles to Brighton.

He was five miles from the place where his world had disintegrated. Where his soul had died by the side of the road. Crushed by metal. Turned to ash.

He never wanted to see this fucking place again.

Unfortunately, he *did* want to see his parents. So, twice a year, he made a perfunctory trek to their cottage. He never stayed overnight. And he certainly never took a woman.

His stomach roiled. How would he pull this off without becoming a pathetic sad sack curled on his parents' floor?

Once again, he fought to keep it together around Dawn. Once again. Once again.

How many times could he do this before he broke down in front of her? They were growing closer and closer every day. His feelings for her grew no matter how hard he forced them down, his heart pulling him toward her without consent from his head. A light flickered deep within him, a light he'd thought had been destroyed—snuffed out—on that road in Brighton. On that horrible day.

But…fuck. He *did* have feelings for Dawn. Feelings he couldn't control. Feelings that were utterly misplaced, wasted, and useless. They had no future together. What the hell was he thinking?

The hairs on his arms stood on end as he turned down the road leading to his parents' home.

"Almost there," he managed to say. Dawn didn't respond. Could she tell something was off with him?

Of course she can, you wanker. You've barely said five words to her in the past hour.

"Get it together," Callan muttered.

"What did you say?"

"I said, ah, this road is better." He cleared his throat. "This road, I like it better. The trees…and such."

"Why are you being so weird?" she asked with a frown.

"I just…I don't want my mum to harass you."

Dawn folded her arms. "Harass how? She's nice."

He rolled down his window and inhaled the salty air. "She's a chatterbox, is all. But I know you can handle yourself." He forced a smile. "Feel free to change the subject if she gets too personal. She tends to want to be everyone's best friend."

"I know. I've spoken to her several times since the wedding, remember?" She placed her hand on his arm. "You don't need to worry about me." She squeezed. "But I think it's cute you're worried."

Cute. Great. His mental breakdown was cute.

His mum and dad were waiting for them outside when they pulled up to the bramble-covered cottage. His mum wore an absurdly large straw hat and wellies, and his dad had on khaki shorts with black socks. God, he loved these people.

"Oh, Callan," his mum exclaimed, folding him into a tight hug. She gave Dawn the same hug and nearly choked her to death. Dawn laughed, and his mum held onto Dawn's arms, beaming up at her face. His dad stepped forward and patted him on the back.

Callan made introductions between Dawn and his dad and then carried their bags inside the stone cottage.

His mum scooted around him and went up the stairs. "I've got the guest room all made up for you." He wouldn't be surprised if she'd littered the bed with rose petals and had Marvin Gaye songs piped in.

At the top of the landing, she turned right. Callan paused on the stairs. "Mum," he called. His throat constricted. She turned back to him, and whatever his mum saw on his face made her eyes fill with pain.

"Ah, I forgot. I made up the peach room for you." She took a sharp left. Callan followed her, not daring to make eye contact with Dawn.

He followed his mum into a cozy peach-colored bedroom. The room was small but well kept. He eyed the twin bed. They wouldn't be comfortable, but the fewer reminders he had around him, the better.

"This is wonderful, Eleanor. Thank you," Dawn said.

"Of course, dear. Come down when you're ready." She patted Callan's arm and left the room.

He dropped their bags against the wall. "Bathroom is across the hall if you need it. I'm going to see about helping my dad with the fence." A glance at Dawn's face told him he was acting strange, but he couldn't help himself. He quickly left the room and sped down the stairs, out the back door, and into the sunshine.

His heart raced. Here, perhaps, in the light of day, his memories wouldn't haunt him.

****

Dawn peered out the bedroom window. Callan chatted with his mom and dad while he dug the fencing hole. She twisted her hands. Was he anxious and on edge because she was here with his parents? Or was it something more?

She'd been excited to visit his parents. She had thought maybe the ride down would give her an opportunity to talk to Callan about her plans to stay. But then he'd been so weird on the drive...

She freshened up in the bathroom and headed toward the stairs. She paused and stared at the door on the other side of the landing. She cocked her ear. She was still alone in the house. She walked past the landing and opened the door. Inside was a large bedroom with a king-size bed and an ensuite bathroom.

She'd caught the exchange between him and Eleanor on the stairs, and now she knew what it meant. This was the room he'd stayed in with *her*. His ex-wife. There could be no other explanation.

He was so torn up about his ex. And his mother was too; she'd looked at Callan like she'd wanted to cry. What in the world had happened?

Dawn went outside and conversed with Callan's dad, an affable man with a dry humor. Callan was back to normal, shooting jokes as he dug neat holes along the garden perimeter. His mom brought a pitcher of lemonade outside, and they sat in garden chairs while Callan took a break. Sweat dripped down his face, and his T-shirt was wet around the collar and armpits.

This man was not *GQ* today. Today he was rough and sweaty—and she liked it.

"Do you need any help?" Dawn asked Callan.

"Oh no, dear. He's fine," Eleanor answered.

Callan flashed his mother a wry smile. "Thanks, Mum." He turned to Dawn. "I am fine. I should be done before dinner. I thought we could go out afterward. I'll set the poles tomorrow."

His mom pouted. "Oh, but Callan, we never see you."

His dad interjected, "Let the kids have their fun, El." Callan nodded gratefully to his dad and went back to digging. Dawn stayed seated, chatting with his parents about her family, home, and school. They told her charming stories of Callan from when he was little, and Dawn could swear he blushed a time or two.

For dinner, they ate traditional roast beef with all the trimmings, including Yorkshire pudding. They talked about Cambridge, the university and the town. After dinner, Callan showered and changed, and he and Dawn were out the door by eight o'clock.

She slid into the car. "Where are we going?"

He grinned. "I have a surprise."

"What kind of surprise?" she asked, delighted he was once again teasing and playful.

They drove to the city center and to a bar district near the ocean. He parked in front of an establishment with neon lights and blinking signs.

"Karaoke?" Dawn asked, reading the signs.

"I perhaps should have asked if you like to sing?" He grabbed her hand and helped her out of the car.

She laughed. "I'm a terrible singer, but give me a few beers, and I'll think I'm a pop star."

Callan held the door open for her and ushered her inside. "Coming right up." He ordered a bucket of beers from the bar. He also booked them a private karaoke room. At least she wouldn't embarrass herself in front of strangers.

As they drank their beers and took turns with the mic in their private room, Dawn made a discovery. Callan could sing. Like, *really* sing. His deep voice was strong and beautiful as he belted everything from nineties alternative to seventies yacht rock.

When he began to sing an old seventies love song, she got up and danced with him. They swayed together as he sang to her, and she was thankful for the darkened room because when he sang the lyrics, *You may be in love with me*, she blushed furiously.

Callan drank a couple of beers, but because he was driving, Dawn downed the other four. A comfortable warmth settled over her. She gazed into Callan's eyes. She never wanted to forget this moment. This was the real deal. Something special. Maybe even once in a lifetime.

He stared down at her, his languid smile replaced by something else she couldn't quite pinpoint. Desire, yes, but something more. He felt it too. He had to. She ran her hands up and down his chest, over the bulges and divots of his muscles. He pressed against her, hard and ready, and she ached to feel more. Would she never get enough of him?

The song ended, and the karaoke auto-played their next selection, but Callan threw down the microphone and grasped the back of her head. He descended on her with an urgent, searing kiss, and she returned it with equal urgency. Their kisses were frenetic, and they didn't speak. There wasn't time. They needed each other too much.

Her fingers made quick work of the button and zipper on his jeans as she pulled him toward the black leather couch against the back wall of their karaoke room. She spun them around and pushed Callan down on the couch. She stripped off her jeans and underwear and straddled his thighs, palming his hard length.

He grabbed her hips and guided her onto him, and she sank down slowly, her inner walls stretching over him inch by inch. Her descent was smooth, aided by her slickness, but he had to push her down harder to get himself fully seated into her. He filled her completely, and *oh, God*, it felt amazing.

Dawn leaned forward, grabbed the sofa on either side of Callan's head, and moved her hips. Small, sensual movements at first, but then harder, wilder. His fingers dug into her hips and ass as he lifted her up and hauled her back down his length. He wrapped her ponytail around his wrist, using it to guide her lips to his. His kisses were messy and frantic as he dragged his lips across hers and down her neck, biting the top of her breast peeking through her blouse.

Callan let go of her ponytail and put his hand to where their bodies joined. His thumb pressed against her bundle of nerves and stroked her in time with their movements, and her toes curled. The tightness in her core broke, and her quivering explosion radiated throughout her body. Callan followed her soon after, his shout muffled by the beginning chords of a K-pop song.

She rested her forehead against his, still joined to him. His eyes were closed, and he lazily stroked her back. "I better clean up," she whispered. He groaned and lifted her off him. As she gathered her clothes, he found some paper towels and handed them to her. They quickly righted themselves and were buttoning their jeans when a knock sounded on the door.

"More beer?" A waitress poked her head around the door. Dawn spun around and pretended to flip through the song catalog.

Callan chuckled. "No thanks. We're leaving soon." The waitress left. He strode over to her and stroked her head.

Her lips quirked. "I've never had sex in a public place."

His eyes held amusement. "I'm really just trying to

prepare you for when I take you to my secret sex club."

"Oh, you own a sex club now?" She planted her hands on her hips.

"No, I'm just a member. But they let me bring my own whips and chains."

"Just so long as it is *me* tying *you* up," she said saucily.

Callan's eyebrows raised. "I'll keep your request in mind." He wrapped his arms around her and planted a kiss on the top of her head.

"Thank you," he said after a moment.

"For what?"

He shook his head, a faint smile on his lips. "For this," he said simply. Her heart melted. He wasn't just talking about the sex.

This man needs me.

****

Dawn stared at Callan with a dazed look in her eyes. His stomach lurched like he'd tumbled out of a plane.

"Let's get moving." He extricated himself from her arms. He helped gather her purse and jacket and led her out the door toward the main bar area.

She pulled his hand. "Do you mind if I get a water first?"

"Of course not." He wove them through the crowd to the bar. He seated her on a stool and waved the bartender down. It was a typical crush for a Saturday night, but they could still see the main stage from where they sat. Dawn sipped her water and laughed at the drunken singers making a hash of various pop songs.

"You should go up there," she exclaimed, shaking his arm. "You could be discovered tonight. You'd be the next big thing."

"Christ, save me." He laughed.

"I mean it. You have an amazing voice." Her green eyes were bright and twinkling.

He smiled back at her like a sop. He knew his voice was good and had wanted to impress her tonight. Almost as much as he'd wanted to escape his parents' house.

"You aren't so bad yourself," he deflected. She screwed her nose and gave him a dubious look. His lips curled again. She may have been a little off-key, but she'd been game to try, and they'd had fun. And to have capped it off with quick and dirty sex right there in the room? Incredible.

Quick and dirty sex that made him feel…

The woman who sat before him was intelligent, sexy, funny, ambitious, and caring. A total package wrapped in a fantastic body and a beautiful face. She consumed him. All his waking thoughts and sleeping dreams were filled with reddish curls and sparkling green eyes, lithe limbs, and beautiful breasts. Laughter and savviness. Sunshine and brightness playing the foil to his darkness and shadows. Callan's need for Dawn grew each day. They only had a few more weeks together. What was he going to do when she left?

He tamped down hard, but the feelings wouldn't stop. They shot through him like hot steam forced through worn cracks in the earth. *Fling, fling, fling. Remember, she's just a fling.* The truth knocked at the back of his mind. He refused to let it in.

"These singers make me feel better about myself," Dawn said, gesturing to the group on stage. He turned to the giggling group of five twenty-something girls teetering on their high heels, their gazes fixed on the teleprompter as they clustered around the microphone.

The first bars of a familiar song began to play.

The group was horribly out of tune, but he still recognized the melody and the sing-song words. It was a ubiquitous song from one of those popular animated princess movies. A song from a lifetime ago. He swallowed. The harmless melody enveloped him like a straitjacket. Dread set in. He shut his eyes tight, but he couldn't keep out the rush of images, the onslaught of pain.

The words floated around him, reminding Callan of another little princess who used to float around him in sparkling blue dresses and crowns. Who would warble her own mixed-up and adorable version of the tune. Would laugh as her blonde ringlets bounced. The tiny voice echoed in his head like a harbinger of shame. Then came the familiar tightness in his chest, the familiar pound of his heart. *It's all my fault.* A poisoned sickness rose inside him.

Callan gasped, and Dawn's eyes widened with concern. She immediately jumped off her stool, took him by the arm, and led him to the front exit.

The fresh air hit his face, and he heaved breaths of the salty air, closing his eyes. He shook off her arm and walked to the car, gaining control of himself along the way. "You okay?" she asked.

"Yeah, I got dizzy for a second, but I'm fine now."

She frowned. He knew she didn't buy it, but she said nothing. He ushered her into the car and drove them back to his parents' home.

He should break the uncomfortable silence, but his mind was in chaos, and he couldn't string together two bloody coherent words. Fuck all.

Callan reached down and squeezed Dawn's hand.

She squeezed him back. He didn't let go.

He said nothing to his parents upon entering the house; he couldn't make small talk with them right now. He ignored his mum's look of concern and pulled Dawn up the stairs with him.

They changed and washed up and then settled into the absurdly small bed. Callan clutched Dawn tightly against him, nuzzling her hair. She stroked his arm, and they curled into each other. An urgent need for her tore through him. Not the frantic lust he'd had earlier at karaoke. This was darker, emptier. A bone-deep need to feel alive again. He quietly sank into her from behind, and their movements were slow and silent. After they'd both crested, he held her close. Scared to let go.

Chapter Fifteen

"One week. I leave in one week. What am I going to do?" Dawn lay prostrate on her bed, lamenting to Jane's virtual presence.

Jane glanced up from filing her nails. "Okay. Since *all* of our conversations for the past two *month*s have been about Callan, even a trained monkey would know you have fallen in love with him. I have two words for you: *tell him*."

"I asked Cambridge to let me stay in the program for the upcoming term."

"What? Are you serious?"

Dawn nodded.

"Then why are you wailing?" Jane asked.

"Because I don't think it is going to work out."

"What does Callan say about it?"

"Callan doesn't know."

"You've got to be kidding me."

"I never told him because it probably isn't going to work out."

Jane looked exasperated, waiting for Dawn to explain this shitshow.

"I daydream about dropping out of school because he asks me to marry him," Dawn admitted in horror. "How ridiculous am I?"

Jane smirked. "I love it. You bitch about all the girls who went to college and law school just to get their MRS degrees, and look at you now."

"Fine. I'm a hypocrite. I don't care. All I think about is Callan and how I'm leaving soon." Dawn threw her hands over her face.

"Freaking *tell* him how you feel. Even if you go back to DC, you can work something out. It's not like we live in prairie times. Seriously, look at how much we talk to each other. I swear, I talk to you more than I talk to Todd." She snorted.

Dawn sighed. "You're right. Maybe I *should* tell him…"

"Of course you should. This decision affects him too, you know. I don't get your hesitation. He's a total gentleman and super sweet to you. Y'all have incredible sex. He's taken you all over England. You've met his parents. *I've* given my approval. What else do you need?"

"I've been waiting for *him* to say something first." Dawn desperately wanted Callan to declare his feelings. No, she *needed* him to confirm he felt as strongly about her as she did for him before she'd put her own feelings on the line.

Jane cocked an eyebrow. "Well, that's not very feminist of you, Ms. Law School."

Dawn jumped up and paced around her small bedroom. "I'm worried about the marriage thing. I don't know if he's in the same place as me. I've never been close to feeling like this about someone, but he's done this before. What if…what if this is just a fling for him?"

Dawn's doubts and insecurities tied her stomach into knots. After the incident at the karaoke bar, she'd been even more perplexed by Callan's mood swings. He'd held her tight against him all night, like a child clutching a treasured lovey. The next morning, she'd crept downstairs to put on a pot of coffee and had run into Eleanor. They'd sat together at the small breakfast table, sipping their coffee. Dawn recalled his mother's statement to her: "You are pulling him back from the brink, Dawn." There was so much wrapped up in Eleanor's simple sentence. Back from the brink of what? His failed marriage?

"Dawn, take it easy. What if *because* of his marriage, he's gun-shy about expressing himself?"

"Maybe," Dawn said doubtfully.

"Maybe nothing. It's obvious he's into you. I bet if you tell him how you feel, it will give him the guts to tell you the same thing. When are you seeing him again?"

"I have a test on Thursday I can't skip." Professor Humphrey had told her skipping any more classes could put her at risk of not being able to stay in the program, even if she could work things out. Dawn had never received anything but effusive praise from her teachers and school administrators, and being put on notice rocked her. She was still on track to do well in the program, but she worried about her ranking. She was torn between her brain shouting for her to be number one in the program and her heart whispering her love life was way more important.

Her heart was winning.

"I'm going to London on Friday. This is our last weekend together."

"First of all, stop pacing around so much. You're making me dizzy. Second, woman up and tell him how you feel," Jane shouted.

Jane's bedroom door opened, and Jane's mom stood in the doorway, decked out in her usual pink twinset and white clam diggers. "Jane, honey. Who are you yelling at?"

"Dawn." Jane jerked her thumb at the screen. "She's being ridiculous about a guy, and I'm knocking some sense into her."

Jane's mom ran up to the computer and waved. "Hiya, baby girl! We miss you, honey!" Jane's mother was a native Texan and proud of it. She'd die before she'd let go of her Texas charm.

"Hi, Mrs. Turner. I miss you guys, too." Dawn waved back. "Your daughter is counseling me on the appropriate actions to further my love life."

"Honey, it's not hard. The trick is to give him a little lovin' but always leave him wanting more," Mrs. Turner spoke wisely. She was, after all, a woman who'd snagged the town doctor.

Dawn laughed and then sat back. Maybe Mrs. Turner was onto something.

Leave him wanting more.

But how?

Chapter Sixteen

Callan was utterly spent. "Once again, fucking magnificent."

"We do it pretty well, right?" Dawn rolled over on the bed to face him. Her smile was absolutely mesmerizing. He reached out to stroke her hair.

Dawn's *last weekend.* He'd been jumpy all week, unable to concentrate at work, useless at home. Now she was here with him, and time was running out. Quickly. It was Saturday afternoon, and they had only one more day together.

The simple fact was he fancied her—a lot. So what the hell was he going to do about it?

Nothing.

She scooted off the bed and dressed.

"What do you want for dinner?" he asked.

She gathered her things, packing them in the small duffel bag she always brought to his flat. He frowned. Her toothbrush. Her clothes. Her makeup. What was she doing?

Callan stood up. "Wait. Are you leaving? Now?" He was totally naked, but fuck all. She was *leaving.*

She faced him. "I haven't packed at all for my trip home, and I still need to have a final meeting with my advisor. I'm sorry, but I have to go back today."

He sputtered. "Surely it won't take you a whole day to pack?" Even to his own ears, he sounded like a whiny tosser.

She held up her hands, her eyes beseeching. "I have to leave. I want to spend tomorrow with you, but I can't. I fly home Monday morning, and there's too much to do."

Before Callan could process what was happening, Dawn was ready to go, duffel bag in hand, standing at the door, staring at him.

The words he wanted to say, *needed* to say, remained in a lump in the base of his throat, and he couldn't choke them out.

Finally, he said, "Dawn, I'll miss you. Have a safe trip home." *Have a safe trip home?* How absolutely inane could he get?

She pursed her lips and then tossed him a brilliant smile. "I'm glad I met you, Callan. Give me a call sometime." She reached up, pecked him on the cheek, and walked out the door.

He continued to stare at the closed door, his mouth gaping like a complete and utter fool.

What the fuck just happened?

****

Dawn hoped to God Mrs. Turner was right.

The look on Callan's face...

She watched the suburban houses fly by outside her train window, and a wild laugh bubbled up. He'd looked gobsmacked. Standing there naked, his mouth opening and closing like a trout. But her laughter quickly turned to panic.

What if this was it? The end?

What the hell had she done?

She'd been on the phone with her school in DC all week, trying to find a way to stay in the program, but the chances were slim. Her school confirmed she would have to pay both tuition fees if she wanted the credits to count, and they refused to budge on the issue. And there were classes they required to graduate, which Cambridge didn't offer, meaning she'd have to stay in law school longer to make up those credits. An extra hundred thousand dollars in debt was a very hard pill to swallow, and she didn't even know if she would qualify for the loan increase. She could ask her parents to co-sign the loan but…

Professor Humphrey told her the best course of action would be to go back to the States and work things out there during the month between the end of the summer program and the commencement of the fall term.

So she'd turned to Plan B and followed Mrs. Turner's advice. Leave him wanting more.

Have a safe trip home.

She was a fool.

Callan had been in love before. Real love, which had led to marriage. Maybe it hadn't worked out for him, but he'd experienced something powerful, and he knew what it felt like. If he'd felt an inkling of anything remotely the same with Dawn, wouldn't he have told her? Wouldn't he have recognized it and held onto it?

Held onto her?

He hadn't even made plans to contact her after she left England. Hadn't indicated he wanted to see her at all beyond tomorrow. This whole time…this *connection* she'd felt between them. Was it all a lie? Was she completely delusional? Tears burned her eyes. She swiped at them and turned her face so other passengers wouldn't see her misery.

She'd taken him off guard today, surprised him with her abrupt exit. Maybe he needed time to digest her absence. Maybe he needed time to put his thoughts together before he could tell her how much he felt for her. Maybe Jane was right. Maybe after his marriage crumbled, Callan had a hard time expressing emotions and needed to process his feelings. When it hit him he wouldn't see her again, he'd contact her.

Dawn stared at her phone, hoping, wishing, praying a text from Callan would cross the screen. Yes, he would contact her.

Wouldn't he?

****

Heartsick. Or just sick to her stomach. Either way, Dawn was about to throw up.

It was nearly midnight on Sunday, and Callan hadn't called. Or texted. Or emailed. Or sent a freaking carrier pigeon.

She couldn't believe it.

Why had she listened to Mrs. Turner? This was the same woman who thought people were heathens if they didn't drink sweet tea or believe in Botox. How could Dawn have walked out of Callan's life without making plans? Without securing the next step?

Because he needed to step up.

She sniffed and continued organizing her toiletries. Either way, she'd done the right thing. She'd known going into yesterday that Callan would either reveal his feelings for her or he wouldn't. She'd told herself at least she'd know where she stood.

And now she did.

And it broke her heart.

She looked at her phone. Her flight tomorrow

morning boarded at ten o'clock.

Well, crap.

She considered video chatting with Jane, but she couldn't articulate her feelings yet. Not even to Jane.

She tossed her toiletry bag into her suitcase and zipped it closed. Tomorrow's outfit, along with her purse and passport, lay neatly on the corner chair. She sat on the edge of the bed. Nothing left to do but get some sleep.

She crawled into bed. Would she break down in tears tonight or save the waterworks for the plane? Definitely the plane. If she cried now, her eyes would be all puffy tomorrow morning. But on the plane, she could hide behind large black sunglasses. It would be very European, very dramatic. Reminiscent of an old Hollywood movie. Or maybe—

"Dawn. Your hottie is here," one of her flatmates yelled from downstairs.

She bolted upright, and her heart soared.

God bless Mrs. Turner!

Chapter Seventeen

Callan. In the doorway of her bedroom. With a suitcase.

"What are you doing here?" Dawn asked, her insides giddy.

"Dawn." He dropped his suitcase and strode toward her, stopping a few inches away. "I am so sorry. I know this is short notice, but you aren't starting your next term for another four weeks, right? I thought we could go somewhere for two of those weeks. I bought tickets to Spain. Barcelona. I can work remotely for a while." He set down his suitcase and shoved a hand through his hair. "You'd like to see Spain, wouldn't you?" His eyes pleaded to her. He wanted her to save him. To jump in and say something benign like, *Oh, yes, Callan, it would be grand to see Spain. How thoughtful of you.*

But she wasn't going to save him. Not from the words that mattered. So she stood her ground silently, not giving an inch.

He must have read the resolve in her face because he cleared his throat and said, "This summer has been wonderful, and I don't want it to end. I know I've fucked things up by waiting until tonight to say this, but I want to be with you." His eyes turned soft, and he held her hands. "I want you in my life, Dawn."

Her stone face cracked. "Really?"

Callan nodded gravely. "So come away with me. I

paid for the flights. We'll rearrange your ticket home. Let's do this. For us."

"I've been working on staying here in Cambridge," Dawn blurted out.

"Are you serious?" He looked surprised but delighted, and her heart sang.

"I want to enroll for another year."

"That's brilliant. Why didn't you tell me?"

"I didn't know how you would feel. If you wanted me to stay."

He drew a breath. "All I know is, I love being with you, and I don't want it to end. But I don't want you to change things because of me, either."

She shook her head. "I'm doing this for me. I spoke to Gemma about getting more involved in her program. I want to make a difference, and I feel like this is my shot. I've been so focused on getting an associate position with a top firm and lots of money, but I don't think I'll be happy. I'm in huge debt, Callan," she admitted, "but I've been doing a ton of research, and there are ways to resolve loans even in lower-paying jobs. I'll figure it out. This is the first time in my life I'm excited about what I'm doing instead of winning just to win."

"So, are you not going home tomorrow?" He glanced at her bags.

"I have to return to DC to work all this out. But I could probably spare a week. The dean of my school is on vacation until next week anyway."

"Let's do it then. One week. You and me. Together in Spain. For us," he said, pulling her closer.

"For us." She smiled up at him. It wasn't a declaration of love, but it was more than enough. "Yes, I would love to go. We'll figure it out."

Callan wrapped his arms around her and gave her a searing kiss.

And Dawn knew she was right where she belonged.

****

Can't see through the smoke… Flames everywhere… He trips over a large piece of metal. The bumper? Shards of glass and metal litter the pavement. A crunching under his feet. The heat is intense. His eyebrows singe. A crowd forms. Medics and firefighters blast the blaze with large hoses. It's not working! Nothing is! He lunges for the mangled door. Hands grab his shoulders and jerk him back. He goes wild. Crazed. Kicking and screaming. More hands grab his arms. They won't let go, no matter how hard he fights.

Why are they saving him? Don't they know?

He is already dead.

Callan bolted upright, sweating and dizzy, acid rising in his throat. He swung his feet out of bed and stood but immediately fell to his knees. He looked around the unfamiliar room. Where was he? In the shadows, he spied his suitcase against the wall and suddenly remembered. He had to make it to the bathroom without waking Dawn. He crawled to the ensuite bathroom and closed the door. Waves of nausea crashed over him. He lurched to the toilet and vomited.

After a few bouts, the sickness subsided, but he continued to shake violently, his cheeks wet with tears. He hung his head between his knees and practiced the breathing exercises he'd read about online. He forced himself to calm down. Bloody hell. He was in the grips of a full-blown meltdown.

Panic clawed Callan's gut, tearing at him from the

inside out. What the fuck was he doing? He couldn't go on a trip. To fucking Barcelona? With the new "love of his life"? Like he's a normal person. Like he deserved happiness.

You're an unworthy sack of shit.
You don't deserve anything.

****

Dawn smiled tentatively at Callan, but he didn't notice her. She smoothed her ponytail and studied him while he drove.

Dark circles haunted his eyes. She'd felt him toss and turn into the wee morning hours and had woken to find herself clutched tightly against him. She'd wondered if he was going to make love to her again, but he'd immediately let go of her instead.

He'd been distracted throughout the drive to the airport. Something was wrong. Seriously wrong. But what could have changed between last night and now?

The airport traffic lanes were congested with cars and buses, and they slowed their approach. "Long-term parking is this way." Callan gestured. "Why don't I drop you off and meet you at the ticket counter? We can talk to the agent about rebooking your flight home."

"I can walk. I don't mind riding with you to the parking lot." An uneasiness pitched in her gut. She did not want to separate from him.

He shook his head. "I'll most likely have to park in the deck, and there are several stairwells. Your bag is heavy, so it's better if I drop you off in the departures lane before parking."

"Okay." Dawn twisted her ponytail with her fingers. His reasoning made sense, so why was she rattled?

He pulled up to the curb next to the ticket agent and

hopped out. She opened her door as he popped the trunk and retrieved her bag.

"So, I'll wait for you inside. By the ticket counter, right?" she asked.

"I'll be there soon," he promised. He gave her a tight smile, and she bit her lip. He laid his hand on her cheek and then smoothed his fingertips along her brow. She stared into his beautiful hazel eyes. His eyes were not crinkled with a smile. They were wide and haunted. A jittery pit formed in her belly. *This feels like a goodbye.*

Before she could form the right words to say, he nodded and slid back into his car. She stood on the pavement and watched him drive down the lane to long-term parking and disappear around the curve. Okay, she was being crazy. He was tired, that's all. He had arrived at her house late last night, and they'd stayed up later than they should have, *and* they'd woken up early this morning to get to the airport.

She entered the automatic doors, found her airline ticket counter, and waited.

And waited.

After thirty minutes she entered the line. She had to change her ticket soon or she'd miss her window. She texted him.

—*Everything OK?*—

No response.

She called him.

No answer.

What was going on?

Her phone buzzed and relief flooded her. "Callan," she answered. "Where are you?"

"Dawn…" He sounded off. What the hell?

"What's wrong?"

174

"I'm sorry. I can't do this. You deserve so much more than I can give you. You are a lovely person, a lovely woman. But I can't do this. I'm sorry. I—we can't do this anymore."

"What the hell?" she shouted into her phone. Nearby passengers in the queue turned to stare at her. She didn't care; the line was already dead.

She gaped at the phone in disbelief. The weeks of wondering, of not being brave enough to talk to Callan about their future, of not demanding an answer from him. What had been the point? What had she been so scared of? Her worst fear had come to pass.

"Can I help you, miss?"

Dawn raised her eyes and realized she was next in line. She walked in a stupor to the agent at the counter.

"Hello. What is your destination today?" asked a chipper middle-aged woman.

Dawn looked at her in confusion. "Well, shit. Looks like I'm going to DC."

Chapter Eighteen

New York, NY—Today

"Mr. White wants to see you." Dawn glanced up from her research memo. Kurt stood beside her cubicle, polite but distant as he had been the past couple of weeks.

"Thanks, Kurt." He started to leave, so she asked, "By the way, when's the next happy hour?"

His expression turned sheepish. "We, uh, went out a few days ago. You were already gone, so I figured..."

"I get it. No worries. But I'd love to join in next time." She hated the awkwardness between them, and she cursed Callan Marlowe for the thousandth time.

"Yeah, sure. I'll let you know," Kurt said and walked across the hallway. Dawn threw down her pen. The monotonous work and lack of camaraderie with her fellow kindercubers, especially Kurt, wore on her.

Jane had pushed her a couple more times to pursue Kurt but, honestly, it was a lost cause. She'd never be into him while Callan occupied her thoughts, and the night at the bar hung over them like a moldy blanket, tainting every interaction they'd had since.

Meanwhile, she hadn't heard a peep from Callan since that night. Well, screw him. Callan couldn't stroll back into her life, tell her she was amazing, and then disappear again. One major heartbreak was Dawn's limit. She might be hung up on him, maybe for the rest of her life, but she did have enough self-respect to not chase after him.

She yawned and stretched her arms wide. Might as well go see what Mr. White wanted. She needed a break from the research anyway.

She walked over to Mr. White's office. Debbie held a phone receiver up to her ear, but she mouthed, "He's waiting for you," and motioned for her to go in.

Dawn opened the office door and stopped short. Mr. White sat behind his oversized oak desk, and his father, Bill White Sr., sat in the opposite chair. Her curiosity rose. Bill White Sr. did not normally assign associate-level work. She sat down in the other wingback chair next to Bill White Sr. and waited.

Mr. White scowled at his father. "My father is going to Spain. He is insisting he inspect a project for his client. He is also insisting you go with him."

Dawn reeled. "Spain?" she choked out. Project for a client in Spain? It had to be Callan's solar project. She shook her head, searching her brain for the most tactful way to say *hell no*.

"You did say your Spanish was quite good," Bill White Sr. said, leaning in.

"Yes, but…" Dear God. They wanted her to go to Spain? To work on Callan's project? Her stomach dropped.

Bill White Sr. continued, "I've asked my son to clear your plate. We'll only be gone a few days." He gave her a cunning smile. "Do you have other obligations, Ms. Mathison?"

"No, but—" She sputtered.

"It's settled then." Bill White Sr. sat back with a nod of his head, satisfied.

177

"Nothing is settled," Mr. White said testily to his father. "When do you plan to leave? Have arrangements been made? What exactly is Dawn helping with besides keeping you company?" He turned to her. "Can you read contracts, conduct negotiations, or other legal business in Spanish?"

Dawn bit her lip. "Um, I'm proficient in conversational Spanish. I'm not sure about legal contracts or—"

Mr. White waved an irritated hand. "Exactly. She can't negotiate for you. Why are you taking her? Why are *you* even going?" he demanded of his father.

Bill White Sr. gave his son a dark look and stood up. "Son, that's not your name on the door. It's mine."

Dawn would have enjoyed the utter shock on Mr. White's face were she not so freaked out herself.

Bill White Sr. shuffled to her chair and put a hand on her shoulder. "We leave tomorrow. Come find me. I'll give you all the details." Then he left, shutting the door firmly behind him.

For the first time ever, Dawn and William White Jr. shared a look of mutual discomfiture.

Holy hell, this is happening.
****

The plane touched down in Spain with a loud *thud*. Dawn's heart jumped into her throat, but whether from the hard landing or the prospect of seeing Callan, she didn't know.

She glanced to her business class row mate. Bill White Sr. was groggy and disheveled, rudely awoken by the offending touchdown.

They taxied to their gate and then jostled along with the other passengers exiting the plane. Once they were in the terminal, the sights and sounds bombarded her. She was really here. In Spain. She needed a moment to collect herself.

"I have to find the ladies' room," Dawn said.

Bill White Sr. nodded, his thin white hair bobbing. "I'll wait by the baggage carousel."

She watched him shuffle off for a moment and then looked around the small airport. Spotting the restrooms, she made her way toward them and almost bumped into another woman. "*Lo siento,*" she apologized. The words did not trip off her tongue as they had in college, and doubt gnawed at her as she entered the empty bathroom.

Yesterday she'd dug out a worn Spanish dictionary from the box labeled "college" in the back of her closet. Flipping through the pages, she realized how rusty she'd become. On the plane, she'd attempted to practice by watching a superhero movie in Spanish but concentrating on a dubbed Nordic god who reminded her of Callan had been so distracting she'd given up.

She cast her gaze around the bathroom, interpreting the various posters. One was a reminder to wash hands, another a warning about suspicious persons, and a few were homemade signs promoting local concerts.

One sign caught her attention, and she didn't need her dictionary to know what it said. She'd seen a similar sign in the JFK airport. *¿Eres una víctima de la trata de personas? Are you a victim of human trafficking?*

Dawn shook her head. Ever since her experience with Gemma and Lawyers ACT last year, she was much more aware of the trafficking crisis. She followed various news feeds on the subject and read the updates from nonprofits like Gemma's. The stories were heartbreaking. She understood why Gemma wanted so passionately to help.

She stared at the sign. But Gemma actually *was* helping. She didn't just read sad articles and make online donations before moving along her merry way like Dawn did.

She sighed. Now was not the time to question her life choices. Again.

She narrowed her green eyes and stared down her reflection. "Stop procrastinating." With a nod to herself, she quickly got to work washing her hands, brushing her teeth, straightening her clothes, and redoing her ponytail.

Everything would be fine. Her Spanish would come back to her, and Callan would not be at the site. In fact, Bill White Sr. hadn't mentioned meeting with Green Solar at all. She had nothing to worry about. So why was her stomach doing flip-flops?

Because you want to see him.

Dawn pushed the bathroom door open with a huff. She did want to see Callan. Very much. But not because she wanted to fall into bed with him.

They had unfinished business. She wanted to confront him. She wanted to scream at him.

She was done wasting her time deciphering his evasive bullshit. His enigmatic past and his "I think you are amazing" line to her. All bullshit.

And she itched to tell him just that.

****

"Is this our hotel?" Dawn asked as their taxi pulled up to an ornate building with a stucco facade.

"This is us," Bill White Sr. said. "It's still early, so we'll drop off our bags and get a head start over to the project site."

"What are we looking for at the site?" She

clambered out of the taxi and joined him on the sidewalk.

The small man stood, hands on hips, his shoulders hunched. He stared up at the sky for a while, still and non-responsive.

Holy cripes, is he having a stroke?

"Mr. White?" She waved her hand in front of his face.

He blinked and turned to her. "You can call me Bill." He suddenly mobilized and toted his bag up the hotel steps with a surprising spryness.

She followed him, hauling her suitcase behind her. "Mr.—er, Bill, are we going to talk about the project first? I don't really have many details or know what to look for. I read the environmental consultant's report, but I—" She stopped when he gave her an exasperated look.

"Miss Dawn, we are in Spain now. Go check in, and we'll meet down here in twenty minutes." He disappeared around the corner.

Where was he going? Didn't he have to check in too? What an odd little man.

Dawn entered the lobby, checked in at the front desk, and rode the small rickety elevator to her room. She leaned her suitcase against the wall and looked at her smartwatch. Ten minutes to spare. She was tired from her poor sleep on the plane but also jittery and jumpy.

She paced around the room, fiddling with her ponytail. The bustle of scooters and cars outside her window was loud, the street below alive and teeming with pedestrians. But inside, the patina of musty cigarettes stained the air, and the peeling walls closed in around her, dim and cloistering.

She grabbed her purse and notebook and hurried to the elevator. The janky elevator mechanics whirled and squealed until the elevator screeched to a stop on her floor.

"Please don't let me fall to my death," she muttered. She stepped in and closed the gate behind her. The elevator had no other walls other than the gate, so the hallways and subflooring were visible as she passed between the floors on her way down to the lobby.

As the elevator rattled to the next floor, the top of a man's head became visible.

Fuuuuuuck.

The slow creak of the elevator was excruciating. *Can't this thing go any faster?* Dawn looked around wildly, searching for a place to hide in the two-foot square elevator.

Don't stop, please, please, please.

But prayers and pleading were useless. With a shaking halt, the elevator groaned to a stop.

Right in front of Callan Marlowe.

Chapter Nineteen

The look on her face says it all. Mouth turned down, brow furrowed. It was perfectly obvious Callan was the last person Dawn wanted to see. He couldn't blame her, and he wouldn't try to convince her otherwise. Her anger toward him was for the best. But why was she here?

He stepped into the cramped lift. Dawn melted into the opposite wall. "I didn't know you were fluent in Spanish," he commented, closing the metal gate in front of him.

"Excuse me?" she asked, staring straight ahead.

He punched the down button for the lobby floor. The lift jolted and began its descent. "Bill told me he was bringing another lawyer fluent in Spanish to act as a translator. I didn't realize it was you. I didn't know you were fluent."

Her cheeks turned pink. "I can hold a conversation."

"Did you know I was going to be here?"

"No, I didn't. Did you know I was coming?" she asked.

He turned toward her and kept his face neutral, even as his body tensed. He stood a mere foot away from her. She wore no makeup. Her wary eyes were tired yet alert. She'd pulled her russet hair back into her usual ponytail. She wore simple gray joggers and white kicks. Christ, she was beautiful. No filters, no Photoshop, no anything. She didn't need it. She could wear a paper bag and he'd still lust after her. She crossed her arms and pulled her jacket tighter. She shrank away from him as if he were about to accost her.

The lift landed with a thud. "No. I only knew about the fluent lawyer." He sounded annoyed and, truthfully, he was. Why *had* Bill brought her? This was Callan's project, his work site. He had to be in full control. And now he had to stand next to Dawn and pretend he wasn't affected by her? While she hated him? Callan opened the latch on the elevator gate, but before he could fold it back, her hand flew to his arm.

She lifted her chin and licked her lips. "Callan, I know this is awkward for both of us, but let's keep it professional. I'm not interested in rekindling or rehashing anything. Okay?" Her words came out in a rush.

He stared at her for a moment. *For the best...* She was right. He'd already resolved to give her up. Just because they were thrown together didn't mean he should backtrack on his resolve. And if he had to endure her hate and put on an act in front of her, so be it. He couldn't fuck her up any more than he already had.

"I feel precisely the same way," he said, much cooler than he felt. She pursed her lips and swished by him to where Bill and Gemma waited.

Callan looked straight at Bill, whose expression was the picture of innocence. *Sly bastard.*

Gemma hugged Dawn and said pointedly, "I had no idea you were coming."

"I didn't know until yesterday, and I didn't realize you guys were meeting us either," Dawn said.

Gemma raised her eyebrows at Callan, and he nodded at Bill. Bill raised his eyebrows at Gemma and blinked like an innocent babe. Dawn eyed Bill sourly.

They all looked like ridiculous characters in a telenovela.

Bill broke the silence. "Well, shall we?" With more pep in his step than Callan had ever seen before, Bill trotted out the lobby doors and down to the street.

"After you." Callan gestured to Dawn. Without even a glance in his direction, she followed Bill out the door.

"Well, this should be a fun time. Your girlfriend hates you," Gemma observed.

"*Not* my girlfriend. And yes, I do believe she hates me," Callan muttered as they walked slowly to the exit.

Gemma stepped in front of him. "Callan, you need to talk to her. You need to tell her everything. I know you have feelings for her, and she's the first one—"

Callan raised his hand, cutting her off. "Gemma, stop. It's for the best. I don't want a relationship. This"— he waved his hands around—"drama, messiness. It's exactly what I don't want." He circled around Gemma and pushed the door open. Bill waited on the curb beside a taxi. Dawn was already inside.

"We have a rental car," Callan told him.

"Today we'll take a taxi," Bill responded. Gemma hopped into the taxi, and Bill motioned for Callan to follow her.

Callan paused. "Bill, did you know about..." He threaded his fingers through his hair. "About Dawn?"

Bill gave him a blank look. "Son, you're going to have to speak up. You know I'm hard of hearing, and these streets are loud. Now, let's go."

****

The drive to the project site was beautiful—and awkward as hell.

Dawn sat in the back seat of the taxi watching the countryside fly by. The sun shone brightly on gently rolling hills covered by squat bushes and skinny trees. The landscape was greener than she'd expected, yet so different from rural Alabama.

Bill sat in the front passenger seat. He hadn't uttered a word since the taxi had wound its way out of the city and onto a narrow highway. At times though, a faint smile played across his lips, and, at one point, he rolled down his window and leaned his head over, wisps of white hair dancing wildly in the breeze.

Gemma sat in between Dawn and Callan, attempting to carry on a conversation no one wanted. "How are you liking your work, Dawn? White & Halston is an excellent firm."

"I love it. I'm very happy there." Dawn didn't hear a peep from Callan, nor did she look at his face, but she sensed his incredulity wafting toward her just the same.

"Callan tells me you have a fabulous flat in New York," Gemma said.

Dawn glanced at Bill, but his attention was not on the conversation in the car. He'd drifted off to some other time or place, his eyes closed in the wind. Still, she didn't know how much Bill knew or what he thought about her acquaintance with Gemma and Callan. Had they all discussed her before?

"I'm just housesitting." Dawn continued to gaze out the window. Maybe Gemma would take the hint.

"Dawn is weighing her options." Callan's voice cut through the car and set her on edge. Like a slideshow on fast forward, her mind raced through their night together in New York: their conversation, their *almost* hookup, and then his excuses.

She remembered Todd's words, *Love should be easy*. No matter what, she'd done the right thing by telling Callan to keep it professional.

"How close are we?" Dawn asked. They'd been in the car for almost forty minutes, and her legs were cramped. Gemma's small frame didn't take up much room, but she was hip to hip with Dawn since Callan's long legs barely fit in the back of the Renault.

"We're almost there. We're going to take the next right turn," Gemma said. Sure enough, the taxi turned off the narrow highway and onto an even narrower gravel road. The car bumped along for a while until Dawn saw something glinting in the distance.

"Are those the solar panels?" She craned her neck to see out the front windshield. Large mirrored solar panels loomed ahead, forming the beginning of a perfect semi-circle. The site was like a scene from a sci-fi movie.

"Yes. About a fifth of them are constructed," Gemma said.

"And the project will span twenty acres when it is completed?" Dawn asked, recalling what she had read in the project documents. Twenty acres seemed vast but, in reality, this project was only ten megawatts, small potatoes compared to many other large-scale solar projects around the world.

"Correct. It's the largest project we've ever done." Callan's voice sent another shockwave through her. She really needed to fortify her system somehow if she was going to make it through the next few days with him. She couldn't let the mere sound of his voice put her into such a tizzy.

Remember, we are wearing our professional hat today... "And how much longer will it take to complete the project?"

Dawn chanced a peek over Gemma's head to Callan and saw him rub his forehead. "Another two years."

A tiny prick of sympathy for Callan stung her. Bill hadn't told Dawn much about the project—or about their objectives in coming to Spain—but he had given her access to the project files. The project had already faced major zoning and environmental issues, which could have derailed the entire scheme. And then she'd read an email about another hiccup with the power agreement between Green Solar and the local utility company. Apparently, Callan and Gemma had sorted out the agreement issue while they'd been here in Spain.

She glanced at him again while his gaze was fixed on the solar panels ahead. His hair was slightly longer, his beard slightly scruffier. His time in Spain had given him a deeper tan and had turned the hair on his arms more golden. Overall, he looked more like the Nordic god than a businessman.

She frowned. She did *not* need to be comparing him to a superhero again.

"What do you think?" Gemma interrupted her thoughts.

Dawn jerked her gaze to Gemma. "Huh?"

"What do you think? About the panels?" Gemma's lips tugged at the corners. Dawn suppressed a flush. Could Gemma tell she'd been mooning over Callan?

"They're amazing. I didn't realize they would be so big. They look futuristic in person," Dawn said.

"We can get out and walk around so you can see the steam reservoirs and—" Gemma paused mid-sentence when Bill motioned to the driver to stop. He then spoke to the driver rapidly in perfect Spanish.

Dawn's jaw dropped.

The driver nodded to Bill and then turned the car around and drove back onto the highway.

"Where are we going?" Dawn asked.

"We've seen the site. Now let's go back to the city," Bill said.

"But don't we have to inspect it or something?" Dawn turned to Gemma. "Don't you have to meet with your contractors?"

Gemma shrugged. "We've met with everyone. We were set to return home today, but Bill requested we stay a few days to walk him through the project. We're on your time, one might say."

Bill turned in his seat and raised his bushy eyebrows at Dawn. She didn't know what was happening, but she'd been trained well enough not to question her boss in front of others, so she tamped down her confusion and kept her mouth shut for the forty-five-minute ride back to Granada.

When the taxi arrived at the center of the city, Callan finally spoke up. "I need to make some calls back at the hotel."

"We're going back there. I also have some business to attend to," Bill said. What business? So far, they hadn't accomplished anything but a boondoggle ride around the countryside. Bill hadn't clued her in on anything.

Gemma pulled her long dark hair over her shoulder. "Dawn, would you like to grab lunch with me?"

"Sure. I don't have anything planned this afternoon." *Since I thought we would be at the project site all day, and I have no idea what is happening.*

The taxi pulled up in front of the hotel and they

exited the car.

Dawn said, "Gemma, we passed by a little restaurant up the street with the blue awning. Do you want to meet there? I need to chat with Bill for a second."

Gemma nodded and headed down the street. Bill raised his eyebrows and waited.

"Excuse me, but I must go make those calls," Callan said to Bill without so much as a glance toward Dawn. She watched him bound up the steps and disappear through the hotel's front door.

Her irritation spiked. This whole trip was pointless. Callan didn't want her here, Bill's Spanish was better than hers, and she wasn't doing anything useful to help with the project.

She took a breath to rein in her frustration and faced Bill. "So, what are we doing? Should I be working on anything today? Are we going back to the site tomorrow? Are we billing our time today? If we are, how much and for what?"

Bill's mouth turned down. "Did you inspect the project today?"

"I don't think so." Dawn hesitated, which was clearly not the right answer because Bill's expression turned darker. "I mean, no."

"And do you think I am the kind of lawyer who is so desperate for hours that I need to falsify my billings?"

"Of course not," she said in a rush.

Bill sighed. "Miss Dawn, we are in Spain."

"Okay." Like that clarified anything.

Bill gave her a quizzical look and then pointed at her. "You need to loosen up." Without another word, he shuffled up the stairs, leaving her alone on the busy sidewalk.

Dawn blinked.
Well then.

****

"When are you going back?" Dawn asked Gemma as she popped another *croqueta de jamón* into her mouth. They sat on the patio of a small tapas restaurant, partly facing each other, partly facing one of the many tourist-packed plazas throughout the city. The midday sun was hot and bright, and the people watching was on point.

Gemma took a sip of her sangria, a slight departure from her usual red wine. "The day after tomorrow. We told Bill we could delay returning to London by just a few days. Callan has other business back home, and I have an immigration hearing for one of our kids."

"How is everything going with Lawyers ACT? I see news reports on trafficking all the time now."

"It's been exacerbated by the recent wars. Children have been separated from their parents and taken advantage of in the chaos. Several high-profile cases in the UK hit the news cycles over the holidays, and we received an influx of donations and volunteer interest. We have over fifty member lawyers now, along with caseworkers and coordinators, also donating hours. It's incredible." Gemma's velvety brown eyes opened wide in amazement.

"I'm jealous of you. Working for a company you love, building an organization you believe in. I wish I lived in London so I could help you."

Gemma crossed her slim legs and leaned in. "I thought you were going to stay and help last year."

"Plans fell through," Dawn muttered.

"Yes, I gathered." Gemma's eyes trained on hers, and Dawn shifted uncomfortably. "You could still come back."

Dawn shook her head. Last year she'd thought she could live in England whether she was with Callan or not. Now she knew better. It would tear her up to live so close to him.

Gemma tilted her delicate face. "You could help me in New York, perhaps. We've had several cases of children who have extended relatives in North America and would be better suited to live in the United States. I've referred these children to a counterpart organization in New York, but I would feel so much better having boots on the ground, as they say." She spread her hands wide. "You wouldn't have to do much. Just, with the time difference, sometimes it's hard for me to get in contact with people, so I would love to have a person in New York to help me monitor things. I want to know everything is going well for the children."

"I'd love to help," Dawn said. "I could find some time to volunteer, maybe."

"Maybe volunteering could lead to more."

Dawn sighed. "Gemma, I have to pay my loans. White & Halston offered to pay a percentage of my student loans in addition to a large starting salary. I'm stuck where I am."

"Hmm." Gemma took another sip and waited for Dawn to say more.

Dawn frowned. "You don't get it. You went to school for a fraction of the cost I did. You don't have the huge debt I have."

"I do get it, Dawn. I understand your position. But you never know what opportunities you might find when you pursue your interests. I never expected to be where I am today."

"You may be right. But until I've passed the bar, I need to put my head down and work."

"I'll send you some details and contact information. You can decide from there." Gemma tossed her long sable hair over her shoulder and sat back in her chair. "So. Callan."

Dawn floundered. "What about Callan?"

"What's going on with you two?"

Dawn twisted her napkin in her lap. "Nothing. Absolutely nothing is going on. We are keeping things strictly professional."

"You know I don't believe in gossiping about others." Gemma paused and cast her gaze to the side.

"But?"

"Last summer." Gemma looked her straight in the eyes. "I hadn't seen him so happy in a very long time."

"Well, he must not have been *so* happy." Her little laugh tasted bitter in her mouth.

Gemma poured more sangria into both their glasses. "If you want my opinion, and I realize you very well might not, I think you need to talk to him."

"What's there to say?" How much had Callan told Gemma about how he'd ended things and why? Did Gemma know the full story of what haunted him?

"I know you know he was married."

Dawn nodded. "I'm guessing there is more to the story, but he never told me anything else." Gemma stared at her. Dawn could read her expression. As much as Gemma might want to help Dawn, her loyalties were with Callan. She wouldn't divulge his secrets to Dawn. "Even if there is, it seems like he doesn't want me to know, and I can't do anything about it."

Gemma cleared her throat. "Listen, I hate others

prying into my business. So if you want to tell me to bugger off, then fine. All I mean to say is, I think you owe it to yourself to talk to him."

Dawn peeled off her jacket. The sun warmed her skin, and a light breeze tickled her nape. Gemma might mean well, but what was the point?

She raised her glass to her lips and bit into a wine and brandy-soaked apple slice. *Crap.* Ignoring Callan wasn't going to work. She had to know. She'd never be able to move on without knowing Callan's full story. It was time to demand answers.

No more secrets.

Chapter Twenty

"Can I tell you a secret?" Callan asked Gemma as he tossed the papers onto the coffee table. The setting sun cast long shadows across his hotel room. He stood up to stretch and turn on a few lights. They'd just finished reviewing a new project report from their contractors. Gemma had returned from her lunch with Dawn slightly buzzed but she'd still managed to plow through the documents. The woman was a machine.

"Go ahead," Gemma responded through a yawn.

"I don't think I'm over Dawn."

Gemma rolled her eyes. "Is that so? Because I really thought you'd moved on to having a solid relationship with your hand."

Callan aimed a throw pillow right at her head. "Sod off. I'm trying to talk to you. Bare my emotions and all that."

Gemma knocked the pillow away with a laugh. "Callan, I love you, but you really are dense sometimes. Didn't I tell you this morning to talk to her?"

"I know. Did she say anything about me at lunch?" He cringed. He sounded like a tween with a crush.

Gemma raised her eyebrows and stood up. "I told her to talk to you as well. Don't be like those inane people on *Upton Abbey* who have some grand misconception a simple conversation could have cleared up."

"First, don't make fun of *Upton Abbey*, it's my mum's favorite show. Second, you know this isn't a simple misconception."

Gemma stooped and gathered the papers. When she straightened, all the humor disappeared from her face. "You have complicated feelings, Callan, but having a conversation is simple."

"Ouch. You know how to cut straight to the heart of the matter." He jammed his hands in his pockets. "You're right. I've been playing hot and cold with Dawn since we first met."

"She told me you two decided to keep things professional."

He barked a short laugh. "I was completely distracted by the mere presence of her in that ridiculous car. I don't know if I can keep things professional with her. Not unless it's what she truly wants."

"She has to know everything to be able to make a decision."

He nodded. "It's time to let her decide for herself if she wants anything to do with me. Did she say where she was going this afternoon?" He looked out the window toward the purple sky. It would be dark soon.

"No, I only know she wanted to explore."

Callan grabbed his wallet and room key. "Then I'm exploring as well."

****

Dawn pulled her jacket back on and wrapped her arms around herself. The temperature had dropped rapidly with the setting sun, and none of the streets looked familiar. Was she getting close to the hotel, or was she off by a few streets? The map on her phone wouldn't update her location. Her signal sucked.

Dawn had spent the afternoon wandering the steep steps of the *Albaicín* quarter of the city. With narrow winding streets and whitewashed buildings, the area served as a time capsule to Granada's Moorish history. She'd perched herself on a stone wall to view the Alhambra, the famous Muslim palace. Shades of tan, orange, and pink slid down the enormous facade of the sprawling palace as the sun went down.

She'd spent the time debating how best to approach Callan. *No more secrets.*

She planned to return to the hotel and knock on his door. Demand answers. Demand the truth. Once her phone signal returned, she'd text Gemma to get his room number. Gemma wanted her to talk to him anyway—

"*Hola, chica. Hola,*" a man catcalled to Dawn as she neared a group of four men hanging out on the sidewalk. The others in the group made hissing and sucking sounds and laughed. She looked around. Cars drove by, but there weren't many pedestrians around.

She stared straight ahead and picked up her pace to skirt around them, but one of the men jumped in front of her. She ground her teeth in irritation. *Not today, assholes.*

"*¿Como estas, chica? ¿Por que tienes prisa?*" *What's up, girl? Why are you in a hurry?*

She steeled herself and moved to step around the man. He was much shorter than her, but he had a blocky boxer-type physique and could probably overpower her. Especially with three other buddies in tow.

She said sternly, "*Perdóname.*" *Excuse me.*

He blocked her path again, and his friends casually circled her. One of them, tall and lean with a set of crooked darkened teeth, asked, "*¿Es usted Británica?*

Americana?" Are you British? American?

He leaned over and reached for her hair, and she slapped his hand away. They laughed and spoke over one another. She only caught snippets. *She's spicy... I think she's Canadian... She thinks she's too good for us...*

She'd dealt with harassment before, of course, but too late she realized she might really be in a dangerous situation. She looked around again and calculated her options with rapid fire. They stood between streetlights on a darkened part of the sidewalk. Cars flew by but no one noticed them. She spotted an elderly woman walking on the opposite side of the street, but the woman was out of earshot. A restaurant's lights glowed down the next block. Could she break away from the men to run there? Maybe she could jump into the street and dodge the cars to cross over to the other side. The man in front of her grinned. How far did they plan to take this?

Dawn changed her stance and prepared to run. She'd take boxer man by surprise and sprint past him, making a run for the restaurant. She was fast, and they held cigarettes. She could outrun them.

But just as she sprang onto her toes, boxer man spun around and fell to the ground in front of her feet, knocked out cold. She blinked. Standing over the man's body was Callan, his arm outstretched and lunging for her. "Run!" he commanded, seizing her upper arm and hauling her to him.

She didn't hesitate. She tore off with him down the sidewalk, her years of competitive training kicking in. She didn't dare look back as she pumped her arms and ran in lockstep with Callan. Thank God she'd worn tennis shoes today.

She used the light from streetlights and passing cars

to keep an eye on the uneven pavement below her feet. After a few blocks, Callan grabbed her arm again. "We can stop now. They didn't follow us."

She slowed to a stop and turned around. No marauding gang in sight. She huffed a few times and put her hands on her hips. "I'm glad to see you. How did you find me?"

"I followed the scent of a bloody daft American!" Callan scowled at her. He was also breathing in heavy gulps as he loomed over her, angry and virile.

God, he was so hot. She wanted to reach up and pull him down to her in a long, hard kiss.

She turned from him instead.

"Now *that* is the most British thing you've ever said to me." She stalked down the street toward the restaurant.

Callan appeared right at her side. "I mean it, Dawn. What were you thinking, wandering alone in a strange city by yourself?"

"I was thinking I'm a tourist in a crowded city, and it's only eight thirty at night." She glanced at her watch. Whoops. Make that nine thirty. "It's not like I'm lurking in a seedy part of town at three a.m. Those guys were assholes. They probably wouldn't have done anything anyway."

He stopped her. "But what if they had?"

"I don't know, Callan. What if they had? How would you have reacted? Like a professional coworker?"

He ran a hand through his hair and scowled again. "No, damn it. Not like a coworker. I know we said this morning we'd keep things professional, but today, in the car, you drove me crazy and then, all evening, I've been searching for you. All my calls to you went straight to voicemail. I finally find you, and you're being accosted by those arses, and I snapped. So, no. Not like a coworker."

Drove him crazy? Searched for me all evening?

"Callan—"

"Dawn—"

And then, in unison. "We need to talk."

Chapter Twenty-One

He was stalling.

They'd picked up two falafel sandwiches from the restaurant, strolled to the famous Plaza Nueva in the center of the city, and parked themselves on a bench. They ate their sandwiches and watched the teens hanging around the central fountain. Dawn checked her phone. Ten fifteen p.m.

Time to get this party started.

She crumpled her sandwich wrapper and wiped her hands on a napkin. "I'm here to listen. But I'm not going to be here forever."

Callan leaned over, his forearms on his knees. He hung his head for a moment and then stared straight ahead. "Sarah introduced me to Robyn in our first year at university. Robyn was a classmate of Sarah's, and she thought we'd get along, so she brought her to a party.

"We spent the whole night talking and, from then on, we were inseparable. The four of us: me, Robyn, Will, and Sarah, we were the best of friends. And I was instantly in love.

"Everything with her was so easy. We never fought." He glanced at Dawn and half-smiled. "Well, hardly ever fought. If we did, it was over something utterly absurd like what Halloween costumes we would wear or where we would go for a holiday trip." He chuckled as if recalling something from the past.

Robyn. Dawn swallowed her jealousy. Callan spoke about Robyn as if she were the perfect match for him. Her mind flashed back to the wedding photos she'd found last summer. They'd appeared so happy, so in love.

He continued, "We were the steady, strong couple. Will and Sarah made a pact not to get married until they were thirty. Robyn and I thought it was smart of them. They needed to mature. But us? We didn't need to wait; we were in love. So, right after graduation, I took the small earnings I had from my fledgling business and bought her a tiny engagement ring. It didn't matter how small it was. She screamed and said yes immediately.

"We had a simple ceremony, moved straight to London and into a small flat. I worked out of a shared office space, and Robyn found an entry-level marketing job for a cool Internet company. We were so happy."

He paused for a long while. She looked down and noticed his knuckles were white. She put her hand over his. "What happened?"

He drew a breath. "We got pregnant."

Wait, he has a kid? Dawn's mind reeled, but she held tight to his hand as he continued.

"It was a surprise, we hadn't planned on having kids yet, but we were excited. Those nine months, I think they were the best months of my life." His eyes shone in the nighttime lights. "She was so perfect. Our little Sophie."

A pit grew in Dawn's stomach. She almost told Callan to stop talking; she didn't want to know what happened to Robyn and little Sophie after all. But she squeezed his hand and waited for him to continue.

"Sophie was a typical baby. The first few weeks were hard on both of us, but especially Robyn, of course.

Sophie was up every two to three hours, and Robyn was exhausted. She had a terrible time feeding her, Sophie wouldn't latch, she would get so agitated she wouldn't eat, and Robyn eventually got mastitis in both breasts.

"Finally, the nurse recommended we switch to formula feeding. I was relieved. I had watched Robyn break down in tears for weeks, and I'd felt so helpless. Now, I could take over some of the feedings and let Robyn sleep. I thought she would get back to normal if she slept.

"But Robyn was devastated, her reaction so extreme. I couldn't understand why. I know breast is best and all, but plenty of kids are raised on formula, including me. Robyn would sob when we gave Sophie her bottle, but then she was listless the rest of the time. Robyn began to sleep for such long stretches that I asked my mum to come and help us for a few weeks.

"After being with us for less than a day, my mum pulled me aside and said, 'You realize your wife is depressed, don't you?' And everything clicked. All the signs were there.

"That night, I told Robyn I thought she needed professional help. And she agreed. She told me ever since we'd brought the baby home from the hospital, she'd felt like she was in a well of despair she couldn't climb out of. She'd been thinking of getting help because she'd had visions of harming herself and the baby, which she knew wasn't normal.

"I was alarmed, of course, but relieved we had a plan. We found a doctor and made the appointment. He diagnosed Robyn with postpartum depression and prescribed an antidepressant for her, along with exercise and talk therapy. Within a few weeks, she was better and life got back to normal. Sophie began sleeping through the night, my mum went back home, I went back to full-time work, and Robyn seemed to be coping well.

"When Sophie was about eight months old, Robyn switched doctors. I'll never know exactly why. She told me she didn't like her doctor anymore and wanted a second opinion, but now I wonder if it's because he refused to increase her medication. In any case, she changed doctors, and her new doctor put her on a more intensive drug. And that's when everything went out of control.

"Robyn became manic. She had unpredictable mood swings. One moment she was highly productive to the point of obsessive-compulsive, and the next moment she was back to being depressed and unable to get out of bed. I begged her to return to her old doctor, but she refused.

"I noticed she was taking more pills than she should, and I lost my patience. I was so frustrated. We went through months of fighting, and I became angry. Why was she doing this to herself? To us? And Sophie, she just wanted her mum to love her. Bloody hell, how that little girl loved Robyn. Her first word was 'mama.' " His last sentence was a whisper.

He cleared his throat and gripped Dawn's hand. "Right after Sophie's second birthday, we took a trip to visit my parents. When we were there, I knocked over Robyn's makeup bag. Bottles I'd never seen before spilled out, and I realized she wasn't just taking the anxiety pills prescribed to her. She had a hidden stash of opioids, mostly OxyContin and Vicodin."

His voice shook. "God help me, I blew up on her. I demanded she get addiction treatment, and I told her if she didn't get help, I didn't know what would happen to her, to us. She asked me if I wanted a divorce. I told her no, but I didn't see how we could go on like this.

"It was a beautiful day. My mum wanted help building a portico for her garden. Robyn took Sophie to a nearby lake for a picnic and to feed the ducks.

"In the afternoon, I borrowed my dad's car and went into town to the hardware store to pick up some supplies. As I was leaving the store, I heard a fire engine, but I didn't pay any attention."

Dawn held him fast. "It's okay," she said softly, even though she knew it wasn't.

He closed his eyes. "I drove along the road back to my parents' house, and I noticed a crowd ahead. I saw smoke rising and the fire engine off to the side. I knew it had to be a terrible wreck. The road was blocked, so I got out to look. And I saw the car. *Our* car. Slammed headfirst into a tree."

He opened his eyes, and the sadness in them broke her heart. "I tried to reach them, I was crazed, but the bystanders held me back."

"Oh, Callan. I'm so sorry." What more could she say?

"Afterward, I was a mess. More than I am now, if you can imagine." His mouth twisted bitterly. "I fell apart. Most of my friends were friends Robyn and I had made together. I couldn't stand the sight of them. I only tolerated Will and Sarah. I stayed at their flat for a time, hiding from the world. And poor Gemma." He laughed without humor. "I'd just hired her. I don't know how she did it, but she kept everything running for me. I would have lost my company if it hadn't been for her. She kept the pieces together and helped me get back to work."

He sat for a time, his Adam's apple bobbing. Dawn

stroked his knuckles.

He took a deep, shaky breath. "The hardest part is, I'll never know. Did she do it on purpose? Was she high? Was it just a terrible accident? Or did I— Did I make her so upset she was distracted?" He shook his head. "I know it was my fault. If I hadn't been so angry with her, if I had handled myself a different way, with more understanding and patience, they…" Callan swallowed hard. "They would be here today." His voice caught, and a teardrop fell onto Dawn's forearm.

He covered his face with his hands and sobbed. Real, gut-wrenching, racking sobs. She'd never seen a man cry so hard, as if his sorrow was being ripped straight from his soul. Her own throat burned raw with emotion, and she laid her head on his shoulder, still clutching his hand.

After a time, Callan wiped his eyes and said with a harsh laugh, "This is likely the worst date you've ever had."

"My high school date threw up in my lap on a roller coaster. So, you're still ahead of him." She squeezed his arm.

He gave her a broken smile and wrapped his arms around her. "Thank you for listening." He exhaled and tightened his grip. "I've never told anyone the whole story in one sitting."

"Callan, have you spoken to anyone? Like a professional?"

He shook his head. "I went to someone once. It was an acquaintance of my mum's. It didn't help."

There was no way one visit to a therapist was enough to heal the level of trauma he clearly had, but she didn't push him. Not today.

"Do you have a picture of Sophie?" Dawn asked.

He pulled out his phone, scrolled for a moment, and then handed it to her. A toddler with hazel eyes and blonde ringlets smiled at her. Then Dawn noticed the little girl's ice-blue dress and princess crown.

Dawn's eyes prickled with unshed tears. "She's dressed like a princess."

He nodded. "She loved that princess movie. I think she watched it fifty times a day." He chuckled sadly. "When that song came on at karaoke, all I heard was her little voice."

So much made sense now. "She's beautiful. She looks like you."

He stared at the screen for a moment. "Robyn had dark hair and brown eyes, so everyone said Sophie looked like me. But I think she had Robyn's smile. They had the same dimples."

"How does it feel? Talking about what happened, sharing pictures? Does it help?"

Callan wiped a hand across his face again, his eyes following a group of tourists taking pictures near the large fountain. "I think it does. Maybe I need to try seeing someone again." He slanted her a look. "The irony is not lost on me that I begged Robyn to get help, but I won't do it for myself." He turned to her. "I am relieved you know. I'm sure you were confused. I didn't give you a very good explanation or a reason to trust me."

"I admit I did some sleuthing on my own. I searched your name, but I couldn't find anything about you or your wife." She hesitated. "I didn't find your name connected to an obituary."

"There's an easy explanation. She didn't take my

last name. Her name was Robyn Andrews. Second, the paper misspelled my name, and I didn't bother correcting them. I didn't care. The fewer people who knew, the fewer people who would send their condolences. Robyn didn't have much family."

They sat silently together for a while before Dawn spoke. "What happens now?"

Callan sighed and closed his eyes. When he opened them, he searched her face. His brows knitted together. "Dawn, you are the first person I've felt anything for in four years. When you're around, I want to touch you. And when you're not around, I *really* want to touch you. And talk to you. And simply be with you." He smiled faintly. "I realized today, not for the first time, I've been a complete wanker, and I needed to respect you enough to tell you everything. If you decide you don't want to have anything to do with me, or if you decide all you want from me is friendship, I'll abide by it. But you had to know the truth first."

"What do you want?" she asked.

Even in the darkness, his beautiful eyes pierced her. "I want to feel alive again."

****

Callan traced his fingers down Dawn's soft cheek. "I already feel more alive than I have in weeks. I didn't realize how much I needed to share this with you."

"It's almost like you should have done this a year ago." She raised one eyebrow.

"I fucked up everything. I'm sorry." He looked into her eyes and willed her to believe him. She had to. This could be a new beginning for them.

"I understand." Her soft words exploded in his heart. "But seriously. Now what?"

"I'd like to see you. Have a relationship with you if you'll put up with me."

She pulled away. "Callan, I know you are feeling a lot of relief right now. You've carried such a horrible weight for so long. But just talking to me won't fix your panic attacks. It doesn't fix the guilt you still feel, the grief."

He knew exactly what he wanted, but was she willing to give it to him? "Dawn, the panic attacks intensified last year because of our relationship, because I had feelings for you. Normally, those kinds of feelings lead to marriage and kids." He grabbed both of her hands. "I want to be absolutely honest with you tonight. I'm not in a place where I can think about marriage or kids, and I don't know if I ever will be." He saw the confusion creep into her features, and he rushed on, "I want to be with you. I want to see you as much as possible, but I can't promise anything but myself to you. Not right now."

Dawn bit her lip. "So, you want to see me and have a relationship but…"

"It's all I can commit to now. I don't know if it is enough for you, but it is all I can do."

"How would this work? We're an ocean away from each other."

Relief flooded him. She was at least receptive to the idea.

"I can come to New York once a month, maybe twice. I'll fly you to London. Or Spain while this project is still going on. We can make it work for as long as we want." If this relationship had any hope of working, she needed to realize it would just be the two of them, no commitments and no promises. Last year, he'd fucked up by hiding that from her.

She sighed. "So, essentially, you want a fling."

He shook his head. "A fling implies no strings at all. I can't promise you traditional marriage, but I can promise you will be the only woman I think of, the only woman I want to be with, the only woman I give myself to."

She narrowed her eyes and canted her head. "Okay. Let's try it. We'll be with each other for now. No commitments except for one. You're with me and I'm with you. No one else."

Callan framed Dawn's face with his hands. "No one else. That I can promise you."

Her wide smile pierced him straight to his soul. Everything was out in the open, they were on the same page, and they could begin anew.

He leaned down and pressed his lips to hers. The kiss was chaste, but he savored it.

He wrapped his arms around her. She wore a thin jacket, and the night air was chilly. "Let's go back to the hotel, you must be cold."

She jumped up and rubbed her hands up and down her arms. "I hadn't noticed, but I'm freezing now."

He drew her into him, tucking her by his side. Her body molded to his, and he kissed the top of her head. "Let's get going."

They walked the half-mile back to the hotel without saying much. He supposed she was thinking about what she'd agreed to. She wouldn't regret it—he'd make sure of that. He would make her happy, even without the promise of a ring. They would have fun together; he'd take her to places she'd never been before. She'd always wanted an adventure, and he was going to give it to her.

Hell, he'd make love to her at the base of the Sphinx if it gave her a thrill.

They entered the hotel and rode the rickety lift up to Dawn's floor.

At her door, Callan paused and ran a hand down her silky hair. "I'd like to take you out tomorrow night on a proper date."

She unlocked her door and stepped inside the doorway, gazing up at him with a smile. "A proper date sounds wonderful. Although I don't know if any date will ever beat our punting experience."

He grinned. "I know. I enjoyed your navigation skills immensely."

She laughed softly. A light, musical sound.

"Goodnight, Dawn," he said and kissed her cheek. He backed away to let her close the door. After everything he'd laid on her tonight, she needed some time alone. He wasn't going to press his luck.

"Goodnight, Callan." She closed the door gently, and he walked down the short hallway toward the lift.

As he reached for the metal door, he heard footfalls on the carpet behind him. He turned around in time to catch Dawn before she slammed into him.

Without a word, she reached up, clutched his jacket, and pulled him down to her soft, upturned mouth.

He'd be damned if he would question this. He crashed hard on her mouth, tunneling his fingers into her long hair as he stifled a moan.

She lost her footing, so he looped an arm around her and lifted her up to him. Without letting go, he backed her into the wall, and she wrapped her legs around his middle and clung to his shoulders.

She smelled of sunshine and fresh rain, and he

closed his eyes so all the world around him was simply her. Only her. *Always her.*

He flicked his tongue along her lips, and she opened to him. He cupped her nape with one hand and placed the other hand on the wall next to her head, supporting them both.

Dawn's little pants and moans undid him. He could tell she felt the same desperation he did, the same need to take from each other and make the other whole.

To his left, he heard the crunching motors of the lift spring to life. He lifted his mouth from hers, and she raised her glassy gaze to his.

"I don't want to stop," she said.

"We aren't. I'm taking you back to your room to make proper love to you."

"That sounds heavenly." She unwrapped her legs and slid down the wall. They walked the short distance back to her room, arm in arm.

When she took his hand to pull him inside, he stopped. "Dawn, love, tell me this is what you really want. Because I don't think I'll be able to stop myself once we start."

She gazed up at him through her thick lashes. His entire body tensed, ready to devour her at the word *go*.

"I need you, Callan. And I think you need me."

Go.

****

Callan swept Dawn into his arms and slammed the door shut behind them. Cradling her against his chest, he walked over to the bed and set her down. His movements were slow and gentle, but his eyes scorched her as they raked down her body.

In the hallway, they'd attacked each other with a

desperate urgency, but now he paused. She understood he meant to take his time tonight. His expression was calculating, as if he had *plans* for her.

He didn't know she had plans for him, too.

"Take off your jacket," he said. She complied. He lifted a hand, pulled her ponytail holder out, and then ran his hand through the length of her hair, watching her locks fall softly around her shoulders.

He traced her eyebrows and cheekbones and rubbed the pad of his thumb across her lower lip. She opened her mouth and sucked his thumb lightly. He groaned, and she smiled, knowing he remembered how good they were together.

"Take off your shirt," she commanded, leaning back on her forearms.

Callan slowly unbuttoned his shirt and shrugged it off with a wicked smile. "You're the best audience." He stood before her in his low-slung jeans, which showed off his hard, rippling abs and insane V-line.

"Amazing. I'll never get over how awesome your body is. And now the jeans." Dawn cocked her head, enjoying the show.

He raised an eyebrow. "Tit for tat. I'll need your shirt and bra first."

"No problem there." She quickly threw both to the side and nodded at him. "Get on with it."

He laughed. "So demanding. I want to admire you first. I didn't get to see this when we were in New York." He crooked his finger. "Come here."

She sat up straight on the end of the bed, gazing up at him. She moved to run her hands up the hard planes of his chest, but he caught them.

"Not yet," he said.

He reached down and stroked a breast. The slight touch made her breath catch, and she closed her eyes as he continued to pet her; first one breast and then the other. He finally covered a breast with his hand and massaged it, tweaking her nipple. She moaned, and he did the same to the other breast.

His hands slid down to her waist, and she opened her eyes in time to see his head descend to her chest. His mouth covered one nipple, lapping and sucking, and she closed her eyes again and threw her head back. His tongue was rough and perfect, and he lavished her with attention until the ache between her legs was too much to ignore.

"I need to touch you." She tugged his hair. He lifted his head, and she stood up, trailing her finger down his stomach and over the hard ridges of his abs. She worked his belt impatiently and tugged it free. She unbuttoned his pants, and soon they were off, his cock jutting hard at her waist.

Dawn pulled on the button of her jeans, but Callan brushed her hands away to undo it for her. He slowed down, taking his time. She twitched with impatience. Adrenaline from their conversation tonight fueled her, and she needed him all around and inside her.

Earlier, on the bench in front of the fountain, she'd made a decision. She wanted him, and he wanted her. He might protest the idea of the two of them being a permanent couple, but his actions spoke differently. So, she'd play along. Be the cool girl, up for a fling or whatever non-committal, non-permanent bullshit he'd sold himself on.

She'd *show* him how much they belonged together.

When Callan finally peeled off her underwear and

jeans, she reached for him, taking his hard silky length into her hands. His breath left in a *whoosh* as she continued to work him. She felt him grow even longer and harder, and her hands stroked the head and down the thick shaft.

He made a sound in the back of his throat and opened his eyes. "I'm going to have to stop you now or I won't make it another minute." He pulled her hands away and dropped to his knees, planting light kisses down the length of her leg and back up to the apex of her thighs.

She watched him, rapt, and when he buried his face into her folds, her legs became weak and she sat on the bed again, spreading herself wide. He grabbed her hips in his hands and lapped at her until she exploded into his mouth.

"Oh, I'd forgotten how well you do that," she groaned.

"It's not over yet," he replied, covering her with his body. He radiated heat and strength all around her, and she marveled at how freeing it felt to be caged within his arms.

Their eyes locked, and he thrust into her. Something painful jabbed her chest, and recognition flashed. Did he recognize it too? With each hard pump of his hips, his expression turned more passionate. Fiercer. He stared down at her and there, within his eyes, was proof she'd made the right decision. She reached up and placed a hand on his bearded cheek. He closed his eyes and kissed her hand as he quickened his pace.

She closed her own eyes and chased after her release as pressure built from the rhythm of his body. A thousand tingles crested over her and she yelled out, clutching him hard to her.

She kept her hold as he followed her over the edge and, finally, he lay spent on top of her, lazily stroking her hair with his big hands.

His breath deepened, and his body relaxed into sleep. She stared up at the ceiling and held him even tighter.

He loves me.

Chapter Twenty-Two

Dawn woke with a start. Daylight poured in through the faded paisley curtains. She bolted upright, panic gripping her. It felt late. Was she supposed to be somewhere right now?

She snatched her phone from the nightstand. Nine o'clock, and no messages. Still, she was technically on a work trip, and it was ingrained in her to always be on duty.

She glanced around. Where was Callan? A piece of stationery lay on the pillow beside her. She quickly read the note:

I need to do some work, and I didn't want to wake you. Bill wants to meet at the site this morning at eleven. Text me when you find this, or I'll give you a ring so you don't oversleep.

Thank you for last night. I can't wait for many more.
—C

She stared at the paper in her hands, the handwriting so familiar. She recalled last year when he'd summarized the cases for her. She smiled and ran a finger over his neat pen strokes.

She snorted and shook her head. *You've got it bad.*
But he does too. He just doesn't know it.

She bit her lip and debated for a while before sending him a quick text.

—I'm up. I had fun too, and I'm already looking

forward to another round ;)—

After a minute, he responded.

—Meet you downstairs at 10:15. I'll try to keep my hands off you.—

She smiled and eased herself out of bed, sore from the night before. She went into the small bathroom and turned on the water for the shower. Cold water sputtered from the low showerhead.

She waited for the hot water to kick in and debated her dilemma. She'd made Callan believe she was all in for this go-with-the-flow no-commitment relationship. After all, *she'd* jumped *him* last night. He probably thought she was the best kind of cake he could eat.

But she wasn't all in. Either he was going to love her or not. Commit to her, or not. And she wanted it all: career, love, marriage, children. The works.

The water finally turned warm, and she ducked under the stream. She scrubbed herself roughly. Callan was not only geographically undesirable, he was also the very definition of emotionally unavailable.

I'm an idiot. Forget that we don't live on the same continent. We might as well not even be on the same planet.

Dawn had to be honest with herself. Did she want Callan so much because he was a challenge?

No. She'd never felt like this around any man.

Certainly, she was attracted to him physically. Whenever he walked into a room, she turned to him like a beacon, her body as aware of his as her own. But their connection went way beyond simple lust and passion.

She loved Callan's affable British humor. She loved how much he cared for his friends and family. She admired how hard he worked and how he'd built his company from nothing while, at the same time, giving Gemma the support she needed for her cause.

Most of all, Dawn loved how Callan treated her. He may not know it, but he looked at her with wonder, as if she were a rare treasure. He burned for her, and she for him. They were a perfect match. They just needed to get over a few hurdles.

She turned off the shower. No, he wasn't attractive because he was a challenge to her. She wanted Callan *despite* the challenge.

****

When Dawn arrived in the lobby, she came face-to-face with Mr. White.

Junior.

"Wh-what are you doing here?" she sputtered. Her eyes darted past him to the three other men in gray suits standing by the front entrance.

"Our clients from Weston Bank want to inspect the project themselves." He leaned closer so only she could hear him, his nose hair twitching. "They received more bad news from an environmental survey. I'd like to get your take on the issues you found."

Her take? She was so screwed.

"Uh. We didn't get to see much yesterday. I was hoping we would learn more today."

Mr. White pursed his lips, which made him look even more like an aging trout. "Then I suppose we will learn together."

"Where's Bill?" She winced when Mr. White raised his brows.

"*Bill* is joining us in a moment."

"What about Cal-Mr. Marlowe and Ms. Chadwick?"

His stare bore into her. "I just rang Mr. Marlowe to

tell him we would be joining him at the project site."

"Son." Bill appeared behind her, saving her from Mr. White's inquisition.

Mr. White wasted no time with pleasantries. "We need to talk." He pulled his father aside and spoke in a low voice. "I emailed, called, texted. What the hell is going on? I tried to stall them, but they weren't satisfied with my answers and, frankly, I don't blame them. The reports are looking worse and worse. This is a first-time project for Green Solar, and Weston Bank should have never invested in it."

He dropped his voice lower; she strained to hear him. "Another opportunity has presented itself. If Weston pulls their money out now, they might be able to recoup it on another deal in Nevada."

Bill bristled. "This project is still on target."

"Barely. The water runoff is creating issues downstream, and there's a potential this could get mired in litigation. If that happens, they'll be on the hook for years. If Weston pulls out now, they could save millions."

"The project is still viable. They can't pull out according to their contract."

"They can pull out if we argue criminal negligence."

"Criminal? There's nothing criminal happening here."

"Except for your blinding loyalty to someone who is *not* your client," Mr. White hissed. He took a breath and said, "This project is being run into the ground by a company in way over its head."

Dawn's mind raced. Was this true?

"I refuse to advise Weston, which is *my* client, to pull out. They knew this was a long-term investment, and we have not encountered any issues other similar projects don't have," Bill said.

"Dad, Weston Bank is a client of the firm. And I do think the way Green Solar has mismanaged this project borders on criminal."

From the corner of her eye, she saw Mr. White place a hand on his father's shoulder. "I know you feel a connection to this project. Is it because this is where you met Mom?"

He waited a moment, but Bill said nothing. Mr. White sighed. "Dad, building a solar farm in Granada, Spain, won't bring back Mom. It won't make you young again. It won't erase the years of billable hours or whatever the hell else you are chasing. Look, whatever it is you want, I'll help you find it but, please, not like this." Any ounce of humanity Mr. White had was in that one sentence, and Dawn almost felt sorry for him.

"I will not tell Weston to pull the funds," Bill said stubbornly. "And, let me remind you, they are *my* client. *My* name is on the engagement letter, so you won't be advising them to do anything, you hear me?"

Bill passed her with a nod and went over to greet the men in suits.

Mr. White clenched his jaw when he caught her staring. Before she could turn away, he strode over to her. "When you return to New York, I need you to comb through every file we have on this project. If there are any discrepancies, no matter how slight, you tell me immediately. Understand?"

She needed to tread carefully. Mr. White was still her direct boss, and she still needed to pay her loans. "Should I loop in your dad if I find anything?"

"No. Come to me first. I'll be the one to present him

with any relevant information." He looked her straight in the eye. "That's an order."

"Got it," she said, but he was already walking away.

She hoped to God there was nothing to find in those files.

****

"And when do you expect it to be remedied?" the financier from Weston Bank asked Callan.

"Immediately. We've installed double pumps for good measure."

The men in suits all nodded as they continued to walk the perimeter of the site. They'd grilled him over the past two hours, mostly with questions regarding the environmental report.

It was true Green Solar had encountered some issues, but they'd resolved most of them, and it would be smooth sailing from here on.

Callan turned to catch Dawn's eye, but she avoided him. She was probably freaked out her boss had shown up unannounced. He wished he could kiss her and tell her not to worry.

At first, Callan had been annoyed when he'd discovered William White Jr. and Weston Bank were at the hotel. It felt like a big "gotcha" setup, but now he was glad they were here. He'd been able to address every concern in detail and have them see first-hand the steps Green Solar had taken to fix each issue.

He felt lighter than ever. First, his big talk with Dawn last night, and now this. He was unburdened, completely free.

No more secrets waiting to be discovered. No more worrying about when the bottom would fall out.

He glanced at Gemma. She grinned and dodged a

mud puddle. Her steps were lighter too, and he knew she was also relieved.

He was going to get a big *I told you so* from her.

"Well, Callan, I have to say you've answered all my questions," a representative from Weston said. "You've done a fine job considering the problems you encountered in the beginning."

"Thank you. I believe phase two of the project will go smoothly, and we will be operational in two years, as we estimated in our original projections."

Bill and the Weston men gave him a round of friendly nods and handshakes.

William White Jr. stood to the side with a slight scowl. Well, fuck him. He was a miserable bugger. He didn't hold the purse strings, anyway.

The group walked back to the row of rental cars, carefully avoiding the project workers and the busy work site.

One by one, they removed their hard hats and work boots, though Callan was reluctant for Dawn to take hers off. She looked adorable, traipsing around the muddy site in construction gear. He'd discovered something new about himself today.

He had a thing for sexy construction workers.

He felt a jab in his side and looked down at Gemma.

"Let's not dawdle, shall we," she said pointedly.

He threw her a grin. "Right you are."

"I reckon things went well last night?" she murmured.

He didn't respond and could almost feel her *I told you so* beat him over the head.

"Would anyone like a ride?" Callan asked the small group, hoping Dawn would volunteer. But she shrank back instead, obviously being careful in front of her bosses. Sleeping with her client's business partner might get her fired. He'd be discreet, for her sake.

"No, thank you, we all have our cars," William White Jr. said in a clipped tone.

Callan pasted a smile on his face. He'd kill the bastard with friendliness. "Brilliant. I appreciate everyone coming here to see our work. We are very excited about this project, and it is nice to know our partners share in our excitement."

"Let's hold off our excitement for when the panels are fully operational. A lot can happen in two years." William White Jr. said.

Bill jumped in. "We'll come and inspect the project again when you begin Phase Three. This was very helpful for my clients. Thank you for taking the time to walk us through the project."

Callan and Gemma returned to their car.

"White Jr. is going to be a problem," Gemma said quietly.

Callan slid the key into the ignition and paused. "I know."

"He wants to derail us." She buckled her seat belt.

Callan cocked an eyebrow. "He's not going to."

Nothing could derail him now that everything in his life was finally on track.

****

"They're gone," Bill said to Dawn. "Had to catch a flight to Madrid tonight to make their flight back to New York tomorrow morning."

She and Bill sat side by side on a worn settee in the hotel lobby. The tension drained from her body with Mr. White gone. She wouldn't think about her special assignment and what she might find in those files.

"How do you think today went?" she asked.

"I think the bank is satisfied their investment is in good hands."

"So, the project will still go forward?"

He eyed her critically. "Any reason why it wouldn't?"

"No. Of course not." She swallowed, and they sat silent for several minutes. With a glance, she realized the little man's eyes were closed. She cleared her throat. "Now what?"

Bill raised his bushy white eyebrows and opened his papery eyelids, blinking a few times. "Now we go home." He jumped up, startling her. "I'll talk to the travel agent and ask her to get us a direct flight into JFK. Maybe tomorrow. Maybe the next day."

"Okay. Is there anything you need me to do in the meantime?"

He glanced at his watch. "You should go find Callan. I suspect you might not see him for a while."

Her mouth fell open as he gave her a distracted nod and walked out the revolving doors.

Is he off to find a pot of gold? She shook her head. How much did he know about her and Callan? Was this whole trip a setup?

Regardless, Bill was right. She didn't have much time left in Spain, and she didn't want to waste it.

She put the files, the project, Mr. White, and Bill all in her box. She'd unpack everything when she got home, but for now, she pushed it all to the side.

For now, she only needed Callan.

Chapter Twenty-Three

"Well, that's some shit," Jane said over the video chat.

"No kidding," Dawn responded from her regular conference room hiding place. She'd returned from Spain last night and had dragged herself into the office today. She'd spent the afternoon catching Jane up on the recent developments with Callan.

"So you're a friend with benefits?" Jane's sable eyebrow rose in skepticism.

"No, we are in a relationship."

"But you aren't his girlfriend. You'll never be married. You won't have kids. And your relationship won't go anywhere."

"I am going to concentrate on my career. I don't need a heavy relationship right now. We will see each other when we can. It will be fine."

Jane's other eyebrow rose to meet the first one.

Dawn sighed. "Fine. I like him. A lot. And I don't know what is going to happen."

"You're still in love with him." Jane's expression turned to pity.

"Fine. Yes. I'm still in love with him." Dawn covered her face with her hands. "I am terrified. This isn't going to work."

"He lives a world away."

"I know."

"He is emotionally fucked up."

"I know."

"His dick must be really good." Jane snorted.

Dawn laughed. "You are awful."

Jane shrugged and bent down to paint another toenail. Jane had predicted tonight was "The Night" Todd would propose, and she'd been spray-tanned, plucked, and waxed within an inch of her life so she'd be social media ready for the big announcement. A twinge of jealousy hit Dawn. Why couldn't her life be as straightforward as Jane's?

Because you are the nitwit who fell for an emotionally unavailable Brit.

"Dawn, just see how it goes. You don't need to understand everything right now. I know you like to have all your next steps lined up. But maybe it will be good for you to go with the flow. Maybe a messy relationship is what you need to shake up your life."

Dawn scowled. "Why do I need to shake up my life?"

Jane glanced up from her toes. "You hate your job."

"So? Everyone here hates their job." Well, except for Kurt.

"You've never had a real boyfriend. Last year with Callan was the closest you've ever come to a steady relationship."

"I've been focused on other things."

"All I'm saying is, it might be good for you to not have your whole life planned out."

"You're planning your life with Todd. You know you are going to get married. How are we different?" Dawn demanded.

Jane paused from painting her nails and tilted her

head. "Because we are different. I'm happy here in Canton. I've never wanted to leave. We hang out with my parents almost every day. Todd's got a job at Mac's hardware store, and they're going to go in together on some home builds. I'm going to be a small-town soccer mom, and I can't wait. Living my life in love with Todd and our families is all I've ever wanted. But you're different. You've always wanted more. You want to be the best at everything. To be the most successful, to go to law school, to have an amazing career, to live in New York. I don't think a local Canton guy would ever satisfy you."

Jane continued, "So now you have this handsome, successful, complicated British guy lusting after you, and it's screwing up your life plans. All I'm saying is, win or lose, it might be a good thing to go with the flow and see what happens." Jane gave her a half-smile. "You know I love you, babe. I just want you to be happy."

"I know," Dawn said. And she did. Jane always told her the truth, no matter how hard it was to hear.

"Listen, I need to go. Todd's going to be here soon."

"Hey, thank you for listening to my drama. Good luck tonight. And text me when it happens."

Jane squealed. "I will. Byeeee!" She blew Dawn a kiss and disconnected from the chat.

Dawn closed her laptop, packed her belongings, and made her way to her cubicle. She needed to get a jump on the new assignments piling up in her inbox, but her entire headspace—her entire being—was preoccupied by one thing: Callan. *Go with the flow, go with the flow.* Callan's face floated in front of her as she walked down the carpeted hallway. She couldn't stop thinking about him. Their last night together in Spain had been amazing.

They hadn't talked about his past or their future. They'd simply enjoyed each other, lived in the moment. Ate tapas at a delicious restaurant, toured the city, made love in the hotel. She entered the kindercubes, and her phone buzzed. She dumped her things onto her desk and pulled it out. Callan had texted her a NSFW meme. She sat in her chair and giggled.

"What's so funny?" Natalie asked from the nearby cube.

Dawn put the phone face down on her desk. There was no way she could share this with Natalie. She'd think Dawn was a complete perv. "Nothing. It's something silly my friend sent."

Natalie shrugged and returned to her computer. Dawn sent Callan a smiling emoji and put her phone away. She was mooning over him like a fangirl, her heart all warm and fuzzy because of a dirty joke. She docked her laptop into her monitor station and opened her email. With modern technology, it didn't matter that they weren't in the same hemisphere. They'd made plans for regular video chats every Saturday and Sunday. At least once a month, he would fly to New York to visit her and conduct business meetings, and she'd book trips to visit him in London or Spain. They could call and text each other at any time. He'd told her to reach out to him no matter the time of day—or night. "I would never mind being woken up by you," he'd told her.

She glossed her hand down her ponytail. Was Callan as knotted up about her as she was about him? She replayed their interactions from the past week. She was convinced he loved her; he just didn't know it. Would he ever know it? Would he ever admit it to himself and let himself love again?

Go with the flow, go with the flow. She repeated her new mantra and straightened. No use worrying over Callan right now. She'd be patient, not get paranoid, take her time, and see how things worked out.

Easier said than done.

****

October came, and so did the day of the bar results. Dawn and her six counterparts dashed around the White & Halston office like crazed ferrets while they waited for the results to be released online at eleven a.m. Even Kurt couldn't manage a smile when a senior associate wished him good luck in the copy room. Natalie, her fingers covered in Band-Aids, had heard a rumor the results would be released an hour early, so they'd glued themselves to their computers at nine forty-five a.m. but groaned when the clock hit 10:05 with no results posted. "Goddammit, Natalie!" Matt shouted. Natalie continued to chew on her thumb.

Dawn's phone rang. "Any news?" Callan asked. He was currently working from her couch. He'd flown into town for another meeting with the investor bank and also to support her today. Unfortunately, he was scheduled to go to dinner tonight with Mr. White, Gemma, Bill, and a rep from the bank to celebrate the start of Phase Two and the release of the next round of funds. So she'd be alone tonight, drinking by herself, either in celebration or abject despair.

"No," she agonized. "Natalie was wrong about the early release of the results." She held herself back from shooting Natalie a dirty look.

"Chin up. I'll collect you early, and we'll have a toast this afternoon before I head out to dinner. I'll try to make it short tonight."

"I appreciate it, but you don't have to. You have your own celebrating to do." Entering Phase Two of the project was a major milestone for him and the company.

"I'll treat you to a romantic dinner tomorrow." His low voice promised more than just dinner.

"You're so sweet." She cupped her mouth over the phone. "Listen, I need to go, but I'll call you as soon as I know."

"Good luck, love."

She smiled and put her phone away. Things between them were going well. Really well. Operation Go With The Flow was working.

What wasn't working was her job. She flat-out hated it. Hated the contracts and the memos and sitting in boring depositions with corporate officers. Like the other associates, she wanted desperately to pass the bar, but only as a point of pride. She dreaded being sworn in as a lawyer. The thought made her panic. But if not law, then what?

She daydreamed about Callan proposing to her and whisking her off to London. But then disgust washed over her. She wouldn't use their relationship as a get-out-of-jail-free card just because she hated her job. She had to stand on her own and figure this out herself.

The clock ticked in slow motion but, finally, it hit 10:45 a.m. Dawn and the kindercubers hunkered down in front of their computers, frantically refreshing the New York State Bar's website page. The clock ticked 10:52. Then 10:57. Natalie practically fisted her own mouth.

At 11:01, a round of yells went down the line. "Ah!" Dawn screamed. There was her name with a PASS under it. Judging by the other screams, the others had passed as well. They sprang up and hugged each other, jumping up and down. A round of applause came from staff members and the senior lawyers. Even Mr. White came out of his office to join the party, and the sonofabitch actually *smiled*.

Her phone rang. "You are killing me!" Callan shouted on the other end.

"I passed!" she screamed and laughed at his cheers. "I have to go, but I'll see you after lunch." It was a tradition at White & Halston for the passing associates to celebrate at lunch and then take the remainder of the day off. No White & Halston associate had ever not passed the bar, but it was inferred that anyone who didn't pass would have to stay behind and work before being sacked at the end of the day.

"Have fun. I'm so proud of you."

She couldn't wait to see Callan, but she first wanted to celebrate with her fellow associates. They'd been through the trenches together, and this was a great opportunity to bond with them and maybe bury the awkwardness between her and Kurt.

They milled around, talking to others at the firm who regaled them with their own bar result stories. Dawn texted her parents and Jane with the good news.

Jane texted back—*Congrats. Can't wait to have a hottie lawyer as my maid of honor!*—

Jane had been right about Todd's proposal. She'd said yes, of course, and had immediately texted Dawn a picture of her ring with the comment *—Next June ;)—* Since then, Jane had sent Dawn at least one maid of honor dress option a day, each one more hideous than the last, to the point where she suspected Jane might be trolling her.

When lunchtime approached, Dawn gathered her things and went to meet the group at the Mexican restaurant they'd chosen. On her way to the elevator, she passed by Bill's office.

He called out to her. "Miss Dawn." She stopped in his doorway and beamed a smile. "Congratulations," he said.

"Thank you very much, Bill. I'm so relieved."

"Oh, you knew you would pass. You're a smart cookie."

She grinned and turned to leave when he said, "Come with us tonight. We'll celebrate your entry into the New York Bar."

"Excuse me?"

"Come with us. Mr. Callan can bring you."

Her eyebrows raised in surprise. "Oh, I don't think so," she stammered. Did he know Callan was at her apartment? She couldn't be Callan's date for a meeting with her boss and clients. She'd just passed the bar; she didn't want to have her license revoked for professional misconduct on the same day.

"I insist. You have been a part of this project team, as well. I'll add you to the reservation," he said and then waved her away.

She called Callan and told him about the turn of events. "I guess you are joining us, then. I'll act professional," he promised. She couldn't think of a worse way to spend a Friday evening than acting professional in front of her boss with her lover seated across the table.

She tried not to worry about the dinner for the rest of the day. She had a great time at lunch, and Kurt was friendly again, to her relief. In fact, he and Olivia were an item now, which lessened Dawn's guilt considerably. She walked out of the restaurant on a high: she'd passed the bar, she had her friend back, and Callan was with her. What more did she need?

Callan picked her up from the restaurant in a ride share and took her for a celebratory ice cream since she'd had several margaritas and didn't want to be sloshed at dinner. They returned to the apartment, made love, and then took a shower together, which brought back memories of their showers in Cambridge, which led to another session in bed.

When the time came for them to leave for dinner, she insisted they take separate cars. And thank God, because Mr. White appeared outside the restaurant right as she exited her ride.

He scowled at her. "My father told me he'd invited you."

He'd become even more ornery ever since she'd told him she hadn't found anything of interest in the Granada solar project files. Which, thankfully, was completely true. She hadn't bothered to tell Callan about Mr. White's request to dig through his project because she didn't want to stress him out. And because she didn't want to hear him tell her again how she should quit and find another job she enjoyed.

They were spared from small talk when Gemma and Callan approached the restaurant.

Bill and the lead investor from Weston Bank arrived, and, after the initial greetings, they went inside the swanky restaurant and were ushered to a large round table. Dawn sat between Bill and Gemma and did not make eye contact with Callan. Bill embarrassed her by calling for a toast to celebrate her bar results, and the others saluted her. The group talked business; Dawn half-listened to the conversation about site permits and power agreements. She made it to the end of dinner without any awkwardness with Callan or Mr. White. The man from Weston Bank told Callan and Gemma how pleased he and the bank were with their progress and made a show of officially releasing the funds with a final toast. Dawn's heart exploded with pride for Callan.

When dinner was over, Bill and the investor said their goodbyes. Mr. White pulled Callan aside to discuss a few outstanding questions. Gemma took the opportunity to lead Dawn to the bar. "Have a drink with me. We haven't had a chance to catch up properly." Callan winked at Dawn as she walked away.

"So things are going well," Gemma commented after she ordered her merlot.

Dawn grinned. "I'm not complaining."

"Congratulations again on passing the bar. Now that you have your license, I'd love to continue our conversation about your help with some cases here."

"I would love to if I can find the time. You sent me the information a while ago, but send it again, and I'll get on it."

Gemma nodded. "I hope so. You could really do some good over here."

"You know I'm not thrilled with my job, so I appreciate you pushing me, but I'll have to see if I can make the time. I think my workload is about to increase exponentially."

Gemma shook her head. "It's hard to work the hours when you don't feel inspired. I was like you when I first graduated. I worked for a couple of years at a firm I hated. I was so lucky to fall in with Callan. I applied for the job at his company on a lark. I had no idea what I was getting into."

"Callan told me a little bit about what happened back then—how you helped him."

Gemma's smile turned pensive. "I'm glad he is opening up to you. It's good for him."

"Yes. Although I wish he would talk to a professional."

"So do I. But it's something he has to want to do." She cocked her head. "But I think being with you might make him want to give it a try."

"I—" Shouts interrupted Dawn's reply.

"Oh my God!" Gemma cried, looking over Dawn's shoulder.

Dawn spun around. Callan was sprawled out on the floor of the restaurant, his head at an odd angle. Mr. White knelt beside him and shouted, "Call an ambulance!"

Dawn and Gemma jumped from their seats and raced over. Callan was passed out cold. The restaurant manager swooped in and placed a towel under Callan's head. Others gathered around. "Back up," barked Mr. White. "Give him some room."

Callan's eyes fluttered. He opened them and looked around, disoriented. "What happened?"

"You fainted. Here, easy," said Mr. White, holding Callan's arm as he struggled to sit up.

"We're calling an ambulance," the manager said.

Callan waved his hand. "I don't need an ambulance. I'm fine."

Gemma knelt beside him. "Are you okay?"

His gaze searched the crowd of bystanders until it landed on Dawn. He reached his arm out, and Gemma moved aside to let Dawn in close to him. Dawn helped Callan to his feet, and Mr. White pursed his lips.

"What happened?" she whispered.

"I haven't a fucking clue," he muttered.

Mr. White braced a hand on Callan's shoulder. "Are you sure you're all right?"

"Yes, I'm fine." Callan turned to the small crowd. "I'm fine." He leaned on Dawn, and she wrapped her arm around his waist. Mr. White eyed them. He was no fool.

"Can I do anything for you?" Mr. White asked Callan.

Callan shook his head. "I feel much better now. I apologize for the scare."

"We should call our rides," Dawn said. Mr. White, having assessed there was nothing more to be done for Callan, bid them all a brusque good night and left.

"I'm sorry, Dawn," Callan said. Color returned to his face, and he was able to stand without leaning on her.

"I'll deal with Mr. White on Monday. I'm just glad you are okay." She squeezed his hand. "Let's go home."

****

"I'm coming over tomorrow to check on you," Gemma said to Callan outside the restaurant. Her expression brooked no objections.

Their cars arrived, and he nodded. "Text me when," he said and ushered Dawn into their ride.

They rode back to Dawn's flat in silence, only speaking to give the driver instructions about where to pull over. Callan slanted a look at Dawn as they rode the lift to her floor. She stared at the buttons; her mouth set in a grim line. When the lift dinged, she reached out and grabbed his hand. They walked down the hall and into her flat. Dawn faced him, her expression more serious than he'd ever seen.

"Did you have a panic attack?" she asked bluntly.

He swallowed. "I-I'm not sure."

"What do you remember?"

He shoved his hands into his pockets. "I was talking to White Jr. Saw you and Gemma at the bar. I remember my hands going numb, and then my tongue. And then waking up on the floor."

"Were you triggered by something? What were you talking about?"

"I can't even remember." He racked his brain, but it was like swimming through mud. The images of those last few moments were soundless, muddled. Words floated away from him, just out of reach.

"Has this happened to you before?"

He nodded. "Right after the accident I had a few episodes. But I haven't had anything like this in years." He pressed his fingers to his temples. Why couldn't he remember? But nothing came. Despair threatened to overwhelm him, creeping up his spine like an infection. He'd been doing so well these past few months. Would he never shake this weakness?

Whatever flashed across his face prompted Dawn to make a small sound and throw her arms around him. He cradled her head to his chest and laid his cheek against her silky hair. Her warmth radiated and washed over him. Calming him.

"You need to see someone, Callan," she whispered.

He'd known it would eventually come to this, but he hadn't thought it would be this weekend. He wrapped his arms even tighter around Dawn's slender shoulders. Things had to change, but the idea of talking to a stranger, rehashing what happened, attempting to make sense of something so senseless; it was something he'd purposefully avoided for years. Bile churned in his stomach.

But he would do it. For his parents. For Will and Sarah. For Gemma. For his business. For himself. For Dawn. *For us.*

"I'll research therapists when I return home."

She exhaled, the tension draining from her body. She cared so goddamn much about him.

Did he even deserve it?

Chapter Twenty-Four

"Dawn. A word." Mr. White snapped his fingers and pointed to his office. Abbey and Hannah swiveled their heads, both with identical looks of worry on their faces, along with relief he hadn't barked at them. Dawn would have laughed if she hadn't felt like hurling into her wastebasket.

She'd dreaded coming in today. She'd pulled the covers over her head when her alarm had gone off. Mr. White knew about her and Callan. He had to after Friday's episode. What would he say about it? Nothing good.

When Callan left for the airport yesterday, he'd apologized again for putting Dawn in this pickle with her boss, guilt etched into his face. She'd assured him she could handle Mr. White and any fallout. She'd sounded braver and more confident than she'd felt.

But something good had come out of it all: Callan's commitment to finding a therapist. If she got sacked today, so be it. She and Callan would survive.

Your career is over before it even started.

She was going to hurl up her latte. She popped an antacid and walked into Mr. White's office, imagining Abbey and Hannah saluting her farewell while a distant bugle played the first notes of *Taps*.

"Yes?" she squeaked. Then, clearing her throat, "Yes, Mr. White?"

He gestured for her to come in. "Close the door and sit."

Dawn sank into the wingback chair facing his large mahogany desk. Pictures of his dad, wife, and kids peppered the bookshelf behind him in between stacks of papers and legal treatises. She stared at a photo of him on a boat, grinning with his wife and college-age kids. The smiling face in the picture did not match the ogre seated across from her.

Mr. White looked at her hard, his eyes especially bulbous today. "Do you have something to tell me?"

She inhaled. God, this was worse than the time she'd been caught sneaking out—with Jane, of course—in tenth grade. She opened her mouth but paused when he held up his hand.

"And think very carefully before you respond," he warned.

"Yes, sir." She licked her lips. "Callan Marlowe and I are dating." There. It was done. She braced for the sacking.

He leaned back and folded his arms. "Does my father know about this?"

"No. I don't think so. Maybe? I'm not sure." She cringed.

He narrowed his eyes. "When did it start?"

She shifted. *Fuuuuuck.* "We've known each other for some time."

"How long?" he hammered.

"We met last summer in Cambridge and reconnected in Spain. He had no idea I worked here, and I had no idea he was involved with the firm or its clients."

His gaze bore into her. "But you did know when you went to Spain."

"Yes." She was so dumb. She should have told Mr. White immediately that she knew Callan. She should never have gone to Spain. Why had she been such an idiot?

"You realize this is a grave conflict of interest for Weston Bank." It was a statement, not a question.

"I'm so sorry. At the time of our business trip, we weren't involved. Also, I didn't think I was in a position to say no to your father. I thought we'd keep everything professional, but then we saw each other and—"

Mr. White's mouth turned down. "I should get HR in here. I should be writing you up." He leaned forward. "I should be reporting you to the bar."

She cast her gaze down, not knowing what to say. Her career had just disintegrated into a giant ball of flames.

"But…" He sighed. "I'm not."

Her head shot up. "You're not?"

He tapped his pen on a stack of papers. "No, I'm not. Even though you went to Spain with *Bill*." She flushed at his sarcasm. "You haven't provided substantial legal counsel on the project. Not that you could," he muttered. "We will build an ethical wall, and you won't touch any of the matter files going forward. Mr. Marlowe is not a client of the firm." He shot her a piercing look. "This would be a different story if he were an actual client."

"Thank you, Mr. White. Of course." Her gaze flew to the photo on the boat. Maybe he wasn't such an evil man after all.

"Did you really not find anything in those files?" Before she could reply, he added, "I'm going to have Matt take a second look."

"I promise you, I did not. My career is very

important to me, and I would never jeopardize my position here, or my future, by lying to you." She gulped when his eyebrows shot up. "I mean, lying about my work product," she added.

"Matt is still going to review those files. But I believe you, Dawn. You are one of the sharpest associates we've had in our entry class. You work hard, and your work product is excellent. I'm willing to give you a second chance."

She gaped at him. This man had never before uttered a word of praise to her or given any indication he even liked her. "Thank you so much," she responded.

He kept tapping his pen, mulling something over. Finally, he said, "What's going on with him?"

"What do you mean?" She knew what he meant.

"Friday night."

"He passed out," she hedged.

"Yes, I know he passed out," he said, exasperated. "It's not the first time I've seen Callan have an issue."

"Oh?" She schooled her face into a blank mask, trying hard not to reveal anything.

"There was a meeting a few months ago. He had to excuse himself. He seems unwell."

"I think he is fine. Maybe he has low blood sugar."

"Doubtful. Maybe the stress of this project is getting to him. Maybe he's unfit to lead it." He scowled, drumming his pen.

"It's not that," she said without thinking. She pressed her lips together.

"What do you mean?"

"Nothing."

Mr. White sighed. "Dawn, I'm not the evil guy here." She glanced at the photo. "I am a lawyer trying to protect his client. A client who has over fifty open matters with the firm and accounts for ten percent of our total revenue. I have no personal issue with Callan Marlowe. I think he's a swell guy. But my dad, for some reason, pushed Weston Bank—and I don't care what he says, Weston Bank is a client of the firm's and not just my father's client—to use their fund program for Callan's project. He said it was a great investment even though the bank has never funded a foreign project, and Callan has never built a foreign project. Now, I'm dealing with two parties who don't know what the hell they are doing." His face and neck turned the color of beets. "If the developer is unwell, I need to know. Green Solar is a small operation. It's basically Callan, Gemma, and a few engineers and contractors. If he can't pull it off, I need to stop this madness before Weston Bank sues us for negligent representation."

He was getting really worked up now. "I've got an octogenarian advising the client, a baby lawyer—who is sleeping with the developer—billing on the file, and a developer who is in way over his head."

"He's not over his head," she protested.

"Then what is he?" he asked, waiting.

She hesitated. His bulging eyes bore into her.

She cracked.

"He has panic attacks," she blurted. "But not because of work," she added hastily. "Look, that is all I am going to say. I can't betray his trust, but I promise you his attacks are not work-related."

Mr. White stared at her.

She couldn't shut up. "He's going to get professional help. I promise he'll be fine." She was dumb to make a promise so beyond her control, but what else could she do? She couldn't let Callan lose the project. Not when it meant so much to him. Not when it was one of the reasons he was able to get out of bed every day.

Mr. White looked dubious. "That's all." He dismissed her with a nod and returned to the papers on his desk.

At the abrupt command, Dawn vaulted out of the chair and scurried to the door, closing it quietly behind her. Abbey and Hannah weren't at their kindercubes, so she was able to take a moment at her workstation to process the conversation. A different kind of nausea roiled around inside her. Callan would not be happy if he knew she'd revealed anything personal to Mr. White. Should she tell him? No, the odds of Callan finding out were low. Mr. White was a lawyer, used to keeping confidences. Surely he wouldn't say anything.

She twisted her ponytail and shook off her uneasiness. *Get to work and don't think about it.* She put her worries in a box and refreshed her computer.

If only the box would stay shut.

****

Mr. White never mentioned Callan or the project to her again. The uneasy pit in Dawn's stomach lessened with each passing week. Because of the ethical wall between her and the project, she and Callan did not talk about any details related to the project. They agreed it was best for Dawn to remain in New York and not meet Callan in Spain whenever he was there, which happened to be about every other week. Instead, Callan came to visit her in New York in between work trips. She'd gladly pushed the project to the back of her mind. All she cared about was that Callan seemed cheerful and upbeat, and they were happy together.

Well, that wasn't all she cared about.

The crisp fall air of October turned into the colder bite of November, and Dawn and Callan were cuddled under a blanket on her sofa, watching a movie with a bowl of popcorn between them. Operation Go With The Flow continued to yield positive results. Dawn could've created an infographic detailing the exact correlation between their growing bliss and her avoidance of any mention of their relationship or future together.

And therein lay the problem.

Because she was in love with Callan. Desperately, whole-heartedly in love with him. Her mind churned every time she was close to him, searching for a crack in his facade, looking for any insight into how he really felt about her. If he'd ever considered a real future with her. They were together but in limbo. It drove her nuts. He, on the other hand, was perfectly content. Or seemed to be on the surface. She couldn't chip away beyond it. His thick wall of affable confidence created an impenetrable barricade. She'd have to tunnel under to find a way in.

Or blow the damn wall up.

"I'm going home to Alabama for Thanksgiving," she said. Callan's hand paused next to hers in the popcorn bowl.

"Oh?" he said casually.

"Yeah." She paused the movie and faced him. "Want to know what a turducken tastes like?"

His mouth quirked. "What the hell is a turducken?"

"A chicken inside a duck inside a turkey."

He cackled. "And does your family go huntin' for the birds themselves?" he said in his terrible American accent.

"My parents are accountants. We aren't *The Bayou*

Brothers."

"What's *The Bayou Brothers*?"

She rolled her eyes. "Callan. Do you want to go with me or not?"

"Which days are you going?" He grabbed his phone.

"It's the last week of the month, and I'm thinking Wednesday through Sunday."

He scrolled through his calendar. "Sure, I can make those days work." He grinned, and her stomach flipped. This was a breakthrough. A huge breakthrough. Going home with her, meeting her family. It meant something.

"Great," she said, keeping her voice cool and collected.

"Maybe we can work on your résumé while we're there," he said. He grabbed the remote off her lap and unpaused the movie. She flipped her ponytail over her shoulder, annoyed. He'd been bugging her about her job lately, ever since she'd been sworn into the New York State Bar. *You aren't happy. You hate your job. You work for that wanker. You should talk to Gemma again.* On and on.

She gritted her teeth. He had no right to pester her about her career. Yes, she hated her job. Yes, she wanted to do something different. No, she didn't know what else she wanted to do or how to get off the train she was already on.

She'd loved shadowing Gemma last year in London. And, for a hot minute back then, she'd considered completely changing her future: work with Gemma, live in England, be with Callan. But that hadn't happened. So she'd licked her wounds and recommitted herself to life as a lawyer at a top firm.

And now Callan was forcing her to rethink

everything. Again.

As much as she wanted to work for the nonprofit, she didn't see a path forward down that road. Dawn hadn't called Gemma's contact in New York. She didn't have time to consider volunteering right now. Ever since she'd passed the bar, the partners had piled on the work. She barely had time every day to eat a quick lunch, and she spent most of her nights at the office. Her firm allotted hours toward pro bono work, but she had to get a handle on her real work before she could commit to outside case work. And if she quit her job, she'd need full-time employment—and a full-time salary. She'd researched staff roles at other nonprofits and organizations, but the salaries were a fraction of what she made now.

Gemma was lucky to be debt-free and working for a company that gave her a living wage and plenty of time off to run her organization. Dawn had to figure out what the hell she was doing with her life before she had the luxury of developing an outside passion or cause. It wasn't fair to compare herself to Gemma. Or for Callan to compare her to Gemma.

She reached for the remote and paused mid-car chase. Callan turned to her, and annoyance flashed across his face. Which only upped her annoyance level.

"Have you found a therapist?" Dawn asked. *Let's see how he deals with his inaction being scrutinized under the microscope.*

The muscle in Callan's jaw twitched. "I've been so busy with travel and work and visiting *you* that I haven't found time to pin down a regular therapist. But I will. Soon." He reached for the remote. She held it at arm's length. How dare he use her as an excuse?

"Maybe when we go to Alabama, we can research therapists for you," she said testily.

His eyes narrowed. "You're pissed because I mentioned your job."

"No, I'm pissed because you are pestering me about something that is *not* an issue. Yet you actually *have* an issue, but you won't deal with it."

His body tensed. "First, hating your job *is* an issue. I'm only encouraging you to find something that makes you happy. Because I *want* you to be happy. Second, I promised I would find a therapist, and I will."

"You've broken promises before." Bitterness coated her tongue.

Silence hung in the air between them.

"Are you going to throw that in my face every time we have a fight?" His hazel eyes narrowed.

"No, but I'm throwing it in your face now. How can I trust you to do what you say you'll do?"

"You can trust me."

"I need to see it."

"I told you I would, and I will," he ground out.

"It's hard for me to believe you. After last year."

His mouth set in a flat line. "I thought we were past this."

"So did I." She got up from the couch and stormed across the living room. She was angry at him and angry at herself. He'd agreed to go home with her for Thanksgiving. Now she was screwing it up. But he'd annoyed her to the point she couldn't stop herself.

Callan jumped up too. "So that's it. You just walk away?" His face shifted from incredulous to angry.

"I don't have anything to say to you tonight. I'm going to bed. You can sleep on the couch."

Operation Go With The Flow was done. She wasn't over last year, and she didn't trust him with her heart. She loved him, yes, but the bottom could drop out from beneath her at any moment.

His eyebrows shot down, and he prowled toward her. "Like hell I'm going to sleep on the couch."

"Go away," she said when he blocked her path to the bedroom. He crowded her, backing her up against the wall. She crossed her arms in mutiny. His face turned darker.

God, he was hot when he was angry.

"This is a ridiculous fight," he growled.

"I'm tired," she said, trying not to respond to him. Electricity vibrated between them. If he leaned in just a bit more, her breasts would brush his shirt. His delicious scent surrounded her. She pretended she wasn't affected. Like she didn't burn for him.

"You are being stubborn and pissy." He caged her on either side with his arms. He leaned forward and brushed his lips against her cheek.

Dawn pushed against Callan's chest, but he didn't budge. "I don't want you."

"I think you're lying." His voice was low but not from anger.

She *was* lying, goddammit. "Stop."

"Okay." Callan backed away, leaving her alone up against the wall. Her body protested.

"You're giving up?" She was deranged. An absolute crazy person.

He smirked. "You wanted to be left alone."

"You're such an asshole," she shot at him. They stared at each other in silence.

Finally, he spoke. "You know you can trust me,

Dawn. And I'll do everything I can to keep earning your trust."

She looked into his eyes. They were no longer dark and passionate but open and beseeching. *He* believed what he said. But would he follow through on his promises? This man held her heart in his hands. Would he tend to it, keep it warm and safe? Or would he mutilate it beyond recognition?

"You scare me," she whispered.

He went to her instantly and cradled her face. "Dawn, you have no reason to be scared. This is real. We are real. And I'm not running. We are together. Taking things day by day. You realize we are both fighting over things we think will help the other person. That's a good thing. It means we care about each other." He kissed her nose. "I can't wait to go to Alabama with you."

She wrapped her hands around his forearms. "Thank you. I can't wait for you to go with me."

"Everything else will fall into place, love. You'll see," he said, circling a stray lock behind her ear.

Dawn gazed up, searching his face. Did Callan know his eyes told her what his words would not? Intensity, vulnerability, passion—and love. Right there, plain as day. So she would love him back, be patient, and trust him. He was right. It would all work out.

She leaned into his touch. "Yes." The word barely escaped her lips before he swooped her up and rocked her world in the bedroom.

Chapter Twenty-Five

Three days. Just three more days until Callan flew back to New York. He'd have a quick meeting with a potential new business partner, and then he and Dawn would fly to Birmingham, Alabama. They'd rent a car and drive the two hours to Canton, where he'd meet her family. And Jane, too. They'd stay at her parents' home. Celebrate Thanksgiving with them. Eat some *turducken* and sleep in Dawn's childhood bed. He'd answer questions about himself. Field questions about them as a couple. Maybe her dad would pull him aside and ask him what his intentions were with his daughter.

Callan grinned. By God, he was looking forward to meeting her family, to being grilled by her dad. He waited for his chest to tighten, for his heartbeat to pound in his ears. For panic to set in.

Nothing happened.

He exhaled a long breath and swung the ax down, splintering the wood before him.

"Callan, dear. Can you trim the wires once you are finished with the wood?" his mum called.

"Yes, Mum," he replied, propping another piece of firewood on the block. He visited his parents more often these days and enjoyed helping them with tasks around their property. Chopping firewood, trimming hedges, cutting new fencing wire to keep the rabbits out of her garden. Winter was coming, and the little vermin would eat anything left.

Whoosh. The ax swung down, a solid hit. He set the split wood aside and grabbed another log. Anticipating the next chop. Each swing brought clarity. He felt lighter. Freer. Happier.

He was going to meet Dawn's family. *Whoosh.* And he wasn't panicking. *Whoosh.* He'd driven to his parents' house this morning. *Whoosh.* And he'd been fine. *Whoosh.* He hadn't had any issues since the night he'd passed out. *Whoosh.* The darkness in him had faded away.

Bloody hell, he was finally better.

And he'd done it without the help of a professional. He hadn't meant to delay finding a doctor. Just with work, and life, and travel, and Dawn…

Dawn.

She was the reason he was better. Not some stranger in an office. *She* chased the darkness away. Banished the memories, the pain, and the suffering. And the guilt. The terrible, crushing, mangled, twisted guilt.

She brought him hope.

Whoosh.

"Goodness me, you've almost chopped through three cords! We'll have firewood for the entire winter."

His mum beamed at him, and he grinned back. "Happy to help."

"Your father's back thanks you."

"I'll start on the fencing after these last few," he said, gesturing to the small pile of reminding logs.

His mum lingered, pulling her ridiculous appliqued sweater tighter against a strong gust of November wind.

"Yes, Mum?" He glanced at her. She was brimming with something to say.

"I spoke to Janet the other night."

He waited with eyebrows raised. He could imagine what Will's mum and his mum had spoken about.

"She says Will says you've been by to visit more."

"We met at a pub last week. Good to catch up with him." He nodded. *Whoosh.*

"He told his mum you seemed well." Her voice became more sing-songy.

"Good." *Whoosh.*

"Happy," she trilled.

"Good." He threw the pieces onto the pile.

"Oh, Callan! Tell me how she is. Tell me everything!" His mum bounced up and down, her gray curls bouncing right along with her.

He set the ax aside and faced her, his hands braced on his hips. He laughed.

And he told his mum everything.

****

The morning of his flight, Callan woke up at four a.m. and couldn't go back to sleep. He was jittery and full of energy, so he went early to the airport. On the plane, Callan made a decision. He was done playing games with Dawn. She deserved to have him fully, completely. No conditions; no artificial limits set on their relationship. She'd been jerked around enough by him while he dicked around with his feelings. He knew better now.

She was his beginning and his end, his sunrise and sunset. He felt like a warrior banishing the darkness, and she was the siren calling him into the light. She kept his pain at bay, chaining his guilt. He could no longer deny the power she held over him. And he wouldn't deny himself anymore. The truth blasted through his walls.

He loved her. Powerfully, consumingly, achingly.

Dawn was his second chance. A gift. He refused to squander her. Did he deserve her? Hell no. But he was done keeping his emotions in check, keeping a wall between them because of his past. His past was a nightmare, a tangled web of gutted failure and burned dreams. Dawn was a lush fever dream by comparison. But she was real. Tangible. And he intended to claim the precious gift the fates had given him.

Finally—*finally*—his life was worth something. Worthy of her love. Because she did love him. He was sure of it. He had sensed it for a long time but had buried it deep inside, along with his other crap.

He pictured them walking along her family's property in Alabama. He had no idea what her parents' home looked like but, in his mind, they walked along a pecan-strewn grove, the November sunlight waning, casting long shadows.

He turns to her, pulls her into the path of a sunlit ray. Her hair glints coppery fire, and her cheeks are rosy from the chill and, perhaps, from the heat between them. She thinks he is moving in for a kiss, angling for an impromptu romp amid the trees. Instead, he whispers into the delicate shell of her ear, "I love you so much, Dawn." Her eyelids flutter with unshed tears of hope and love...

He turned his head to the window and watched the ocean below, tiny waves glinting in the morning sunrise. His lips curved. He'd never been prone to fantasies and daydreams, but he'd played this fantasy out in his mind over and over until it was perfect. Until he knew just what to say to her and how to say it. He wouldn't blurt it out the second he saw her today. He'd wait for the right

time, in her hometown. The anticipation made him grin.
She had no idea what was coming.

Chapter Twenty-Six

Exhaustion set in, but it couldn't quell Callan's excitement. After he landed, he took a taxi straight to his afternoon meeting in Midtown with another developer who wanted to partner with Green Solar on future projects. The opportunities they mapped out together were sound, and they made plans for next steps. Things were snapping into place. Green Solar's Granada Project was on track, their residential service business—their bread and butter—clicked along at a brisk pace, and now new opportunities were coming into focus.

I'm the king of the world! He laughed to himself.

Okay, maybe he was past the point of exhaustion. He shook hands with his new business partner and glanced at his watch. He needed to grab his bag from the hostess closet, take a taxi to Dawn's place, and then head back to the airport to catch their Birmingham flight. He bid the developer goodbye and went to hunt down the hostess who'd offered to keep his rolling bag. He caught her eye, and she motioned for him to wait a moment while she ducked to the back.

He tapped his foot and leaned over to view the street. Plenty of cabs drove along Forty-second Street, and Chelsea wasn't too far away. But with mid-afternoon traffic—

"Callan," a voice said next to his shoulder.

He turned around. *Great.* William White Jr. stood a

foot away. Embarrassment washed over Callan as he recalled the last time he'd seen White Jr. He forced a smile and shook the bastard's hand. "Hello, William."

"Was that Max Drover?" White Jr. asked.

Nosy bugger. "Yes, it was."

"You two comparing notes?"

"Comparing opportunities," Callan responded shortly but cursed himself the second he said it. White Jr.'s eyeballs bulged like a fish. Fuck, this guy was about to launch into something, and Callan needed to leave.

The hostess, with perfect timing, came around with his bag. "I must be off," Callan said.

"One moment." White Jr. grabbed his arm. The fucker was on thin ice now. But for Dawn's sake and the project's, he sucked it up and waited for White Jr. to say what he wanted to say.

"Are you taking on more projects?" White Jr. asked.

Callan remained cool. "I don't reckon it is a concern of yours."

"I have a concern if your company overextends itself."

"If we take on more projects, we'll adjust to accommodate the increased capacity. I assure you we are well positioned to scale up if needed."

"You've put the Granada project back on track, I'll give you that. But I believe it's only because you've devoted so much time and personal attention to overseeing it. We'll need assurances your attention won't slip."

Callan clenched his jaw. "William, I appreciate the concern, but you needn't worry." He moved to skirt around him, but White Jr. continued to block the way.

"I've already overlooked a lot with this project.

Your lack of experience, for example. And your relationship with my associate." White Jr.'s neck reddened; his mouth set in a grim line.

"And yet everything is running smoothly," Callan said through gritted teeth.

"But it might not if your attention becomes divided. We'll need you to disclose what other projects may consume your resources. Taking on more could result in a material change, which could impact the viability of the project going forward."

"Fine, I'll amend our disclosure documents if and when it becomes necessary," he replied. He gripped the handle of his roller suitcase and started again for the exit.

"And I'll need assurances of your mental fitness."

Callan stopped mid-gait. "Excuse me?" He turned around slowly.

White Jr. puffed up. "Dawn told me everything. About your panic attacks. She says you are getting help for them, and I'm glad. But I'll need you to submit a doctor's report stating you are of sound mind. Now that I am aware of this information, I must protect my client, you understand."

"Excuse me?" Callan repeated. There was no way Dawn would have told White Jr. about his…issues. Why would she?

"Or else I'll have my client shut down funding, and you'll be forced into a sale."

Rage tore through Callan. "My mental state is not an issue up for debate or monitoring. Especially not from you."

White Jr. didn't back down. "And I want quarterly monitoring."

"You are in no position to demand such a thing.

Plenty of people have anxiety, depression, and panic attacks. No judge would force a person to comply with quarterly monitoring for a business deal. That's outrageous."

White Jr. shrugged. "True, we could fight it out in court. In the meantime, I'll have my client withdraw their funding. Put the money to better use in Nevada, California, or New Mexico. They don't need to invest in Spain, it was a flawed scheme to begin with."

"You never liked the deal, so now this is your trump card?"

"I will take this project away from Green Solar if you don't comply."

"This is blackmail. I could have you disbarred."

"Doubtful," White Jr. said. "You'd have to prove I acted with malice. And I'm not acting with malice, Callan. I am legitimately concerned for my client to be contractually bound to someone who may be experiencing a mental impairment which would be a valid cause to void all contracts entered into by the parties."

Callan's head spun, and his fucking heart pounded. He clenched his jaw. He would not give this sonofabitch the satisfaction of seeing him break apart.

"Take it up with my lawyers, wanker," Callan said and shoved his way around White Jr. He bolted out the door with his suitcase and waved down a taxi.

He settled into the car and looked down. His hands were shaking. How could Dawn do this to him? Without warning him? She should have at least *told* him she'd discussed him with her boss.

He felt completely sideswiped. Betrayed. Could White Jr. make those demands? He'd never heard of such a thing. But there was so much money on the line…maybe he could. He had to call Gemma and get her on this now.

He ran a hand through his hair. Panic clawed his gut. If this project got pulled, he'd lose everything. The company was so leveraged. He'd be ruined.

Did Dawn realize what she'd done?

****

Dawn placed her travel bag with her suitcase by the door and sat at her kitchen bar. Callan had said he'd text when he was on the way, but she hadn't heard from him yet. She glanced at the time. If he didn't come soon, they'd be in jeopardy of missing their flight.

The doorknob turned, and she jumped up with relief. She bounded to the door, ready to give him a big kiss.

But what she saw made her stop in her tracks.

Callan, his face dark and seething with anger.

She'd always thought Callan was hot when he was angry. But not now. Now his face was twisted into a cruel expression that made her retreat a step as he slammed the door behind him.

What the hell happened?

He stalked toward her, anger radiating from him. Directed at her.

"What—" she began, but he cut her off.

"You told that fucker about my issues? My personal issues? Why?" He towered over her but then backed away from her. As if he didn't trust himself.

"I—what?" Her mind scrambled. What was he talking about? Then it hit her full force.

"White!" he exploded, and she cringed.

"Did you see him today?" she squeaked.

"The fucker cornered me after my meeting. Told me

all about the conversation you had with him. That you'd told him about my panic attacks. About what happened to me and my *personal issues*." His lips curled with sarcasm. She started to protest, and he turned from her, disgust etched on his face. "How could you?" he asked darkly.

"I-I didn't tell him much—" God, where to begin? How could she make him understand?

"He wants me to subject myself to quarterly psych evals, or he is going to accuse me of being mentally unstable."

"What?" This couldn't be happening.

"Yeah. He is using this as a way to get me to sell the project. Probably already has another developer he'd rather work with. If I don't comply, he'll have his client pull funding and sue me for the money. Basically, fuck me over."

"I didn't know he would try to use it against you."

His jaw ticked.

She swallowed. "I was only trying to make him understand. He asked me to hunt for anything I could find that would kill the project. When I didn't find anything, he hinted you were unfit. After what he saw that night—"

He raged again. "The arsehole tried to kill my project, and you *helped* him?"

"No! I would have gone to you and Bill if I had found anything. But I didn't, so I thought it was best to leave it alone, not to mention it. I didn't want to stress you out any more than you already were."

He glowered. "Dawn, you crossed a major line in telling him anything about me."

"I know! I thought I was helping. He cornered me in

his office. I didn't know what to do." She approached him, but he backed away.

"All that fucking talk a couple of weeks ago about trust," he spat, shaking his head.

"I swear to you, I didn't intend to betray your trust. I swear it!" Tears welled in her eyes, and she swiped at them with the back of her hand.

"I've been so worried—*so fucking worried*—about earning your trust. That you were going to leave me if I couldn't get over my fucking issues. Well, what about your bloody issues?"

"Mine?" she stammered.

"Yeah. You tell me to face my issues but what about yours? You are working in a job you hate because you can't let go of being the best at everything. So you only do what you think you can win at instead of trying something new and possibly failing. You can't face yourself any more than me."

"That's hardly the same, Callan."

"And you're in love with me," he sneered. Her stomach dropped. "How sad is that? Loving someone who can't love you back, who is going to leave you when this *thing* has run its course."

Tears poured down her face. "You're right. I'm hopeless."

"Maybe it's already run its course. Maybe it's over. I don't know what I was thinking."

Anger—burning hot anger—rose inside her. "How dare you," she seethed, her voice low. "Run away, Callan. That's what you do best, isn't it?" He flinched, but she continued, wanting to hurt him as much as he'd hurt her. "Don't stay and fight for us. Just run away when you can't handle things. Maybe I shouldn't have told him anything, but he was going to try to screw you over no matter what. I thought I was *helping* you, you jerk!"

"What did you tell him? *Poor Callan. His wife and kid are dead, and he can't face it*?"

"I didn't tell him anything about Robyn and Sophie."

He snarled. "Don't say their names."

"Don't say their names. Don't think about them. Pretend they never existed. Is that how you are getting through life?"

"Fuck you," he said, his eyes bleak and hurt. She didn't care.

"No, asshole. Fuck. You. You say this is over? Fine. It's over. I'm tired of being jerked around by you. I'm tired of you not getting help for yourself. I'm tired of you denying the happiness you could have that is right in front of your dumb face!" She stomped her foot in frustration.

"With you?" he taunted.

She straightened her shoulders and lifted her chin. "Yes. With me. I know my value, Callan. I know how well we work together. I know I make you feel things you haven't felt in a long time. But you are too chicken shit to admit it to yourself."

"I was—" he growled, but she cut him off.

"You were probably searching for a way to get out of going home with me. This is so typical of you. Get scared. Find an excuse. Run away."

"You think I'm a coward?"

"When it comes to you and me? Yes. You lack courage."

"And you're so brave?" His sneer was intolerable. Her hand itched to slap it off his face.

"Braver than you. I was going to change my life last year to be with you. I risked my job for you. I *was* going to take a chance. I convinced myself that if we only spent more time together, you'd finally see the light."

His eyes narrowed. "Sorry to disappoint you, love."

This time it was her turn to be disgusted. "Just go, Callan. I don't know what you want from me anymore."

"Nothing," he ground, turning away from her. "Absolutely nothing."

She looked away as he left her apartment. She heard his footfalls stomping down the hallway. The ping of the elevator.

And then she crumpled to the floor.

Chapter Twenty-Seven

"Gemma, I'm not interested in talking to you about him." It wasn't much of a greeting, but Dawn wasn't in the mood to talk to anyone about He Who Shall Not Be Named.

She sipped her coffee and scrolled through her Monday morning inbox. There was a lot of work to wrap up this week before her flight home for Christmas. She was looking forward to visiting her family and Jane after backing out on her trip last month for Thanksgiving. She hadn't been able to stomach going home four weeks ago.

Now she felt nothing. Absolutely nothing.

"Oh, I'm not calling about him," Gemma said. Dawn half-listened. Gemma continued, "I'm calling because the nonprofit we work with in New York was awarded a massive grant. The director told me they are adding a salaried position. For someone with three years of experience to help expand the program. I told her I knew the perfect person."

Dawn leaned forward. "But I don't have three years of experience."

"Sure you do. You've had a year at White & Halston—"

"More like five months—"

"And you clerked for a judge for another year—"

"Like three months—"

"And you shadowed me all last summer—"

"For two weeks and then some Fridays here and there—"

"Which is practically like having three years' worth of experience," Gemma ended triumphantly.

"Gemma—"

"Dawn, this is not about Callan. This is about you. And the kids. I know you can do the job. This isn't rocket science; you can use Lawyers ACT as a blueprint. This is about recommending someone I trust while giving you an out."

Trust… Dawn's heart lurched at the word.

"An out?" she croaked.

"Dawn, I see so much of myself in you. A drive to succeed, but then pounding out hours without any fulfillment. You might not make the same money you would as an associate in a law firm, but the salary is highly competitive for a nonprofit. This group has the backing of some very high-net-worth individuals. Names you would know, Dawn. This could be a gateway to other opportunities if you get to know the right people."

"I'm not—"

"Dawn, go talk to the director. Even if nothing comes of it, she's a great person to know."

Dawn paused. "Gemma, thank you. I don't know what to say. After what I did to put Green Solar's project in jeopardy—"

Gemma cut in. "Dawn, you didn't put the project in jeopardy. White Jr. is a blithering idiot. He wanted to get under Callan's skin. We smoothed everything out."

Dawn blinked. "Oh. You did?" She hadn't heard any discussions around the matter and had been too rattled to approach Mr. White or Bill about it.

"The project is fine," Gemma said. Her lilting

British accent was smooth and soothing, meant to reassure Dawn and make her feel better.

Except it didn't make her feel better at all.

Blood roared in her ears.

So all was well, yet Callan hadn't bothered to contact her? Everything was hunky dory, but he hadn't cared enough about her to try to make *them* right again?

Screw him.

"Got it. Send me the info, and I'll contact her today," Dawn said tightly.

She ended the call and sat back in her chair, staring at the closed door to her office. Now that they were practicing lawyers, she and the other first-year associates had graduated from kindercubes and into their own offices. No more fish in a bowl. A new crop of law clerks had taken their place. The cycle continued.

But Dawn wanted off this train. And Gemma might just have handed her the ticket.

An email popped up from Gemma with the name and number of the nonprofit director, along with the job description. She read it quickly. It was perfect for her, exactly what she'd dreamed of. Gratitude squeezed her heart. If she got this job, she'd gladly ship a gift basket to Gemma from across the ocean.

Getting to know Gemma was the one good thing to come from her relationship with Callan. Gemma had texted her a few times over the past month to see how she was doing. But she hadn't pried or made excuses for Callan. Which Dawn appreciated. Because she was done excusing Callan.

She'd wallowed in her misery over the Thanksgiving weekend, crying her eyes out over and over, and replaying their fight a million times in her head. She'd emerged on the other side with no tears left, her heart made of stone.

She hadn't cried since.

Screw him.

It was her new mantra.

Dawn read the job description again, and excitement bubbled.

She picked up her phone and dialed the director's number.

****

"Wait a minute. I thought you were going to kiss me," the woman said.

"Oh, I hadn't forgotten," the man replied, pulling her in for a passionate kiss.

Dawn and Jane both sighed.

"You girls are too funny," Todd said from the entryway of the Turners' living room, where Jane and Dawn sat curled up in their Christmas pajamas, watching the end of their favorite Christmas rom-com.

"You are not invited to our movie marathon, so stop bothering us." Jane threw a piece of popcorn at her fiancé's head.

Todd easily blocked the shot and scoffed. "I'm not bothering anyone. Y'all watch the same movies every year."

"It doesn't matter. You aren't invited." Jane and Todd played this game a lot. Jane pretended to be annoyed by Todd while he pretended to be exasperated.

"Yeah, Todd, go away." Dawn liked to get in on the fun too.

"Maybe I'll join you for the next one," he threatened.

"Noooooo!" came their replies, and he laughed. He

leaned over and pulled Jane up by the lapels of her flannel Christmas pajamas. She threw her arms around him and kissed him heartily. Todd let her go with a dazed look on his face. Dawn didn't blame him. Even with her dark hair piled in a messy bun, her horn-rimmed glasses, and her fuzzy PJs and socks, Jane was still a knockout.

Todd gave Dawn a conspiratorial smile, and she smiled back. They were living in Jane's world, and they both knew it.

"All right, babe. I'm done helping your dad clear out the garage. I'm heading home. I'll be over in the morning, and my family will be here by lunchtime."

"All right, babe. Love you." Jane kissed Todd one last time. "Merry Christmas Eve," she whispered.

Todd squeezed her tight and kissed her nose. "Merry Christmas Eve." He let her go and waved to Dawn. "You ladies enjoy your movies."

"Merry Christmas Eve to you, too," Dawn called as he left the room.

Jane watched him leave and sighed. "I can't wait to marry the big lug."

A sharp twinge of longing pinched Dawn. *Screw him.* "Just six more months," she said, swallowing the small lump in her throat.

Jane studied Dawn. "What's going on with you? You haven't said much about Callan after your breakup."

"Not much to say." Dawn tightened her ponytail and jumped up off the plush couch. "I need a refill." She grabbed her wineglass.

Jane followed her into the Turners' white craftsman kitchen. Jane's mom had set out snacks and drinks for them, like she'd done every year since they were in high school. Only now the drinks were wine and alcoholic seltzers instead of hot cocoa and sodas. Dawn poured herself a generous glass of cabernet.

Jane grabbed the bottle and topped off her own glass, taking a healthy gulp before speaking. "If you don't want to talk about Callan, then tell me what is going on with your job."

"I'm quitting." Shock and delight crossed Jane's face, and Dawn grinned. She'd been waiting for the perfect moment to break her big news.

"What? Finally." Jane plopped onto one of the counter stools.

Dawn sat on the next stool. "What do you mean 'finally'? I've only been there a few months."

"Even one day of hating what you do is one day too many."

Dawn raised an eyebrow. "Says the girl who doesn't work."

"Actually, I *am* getting a job." Jane sniffed, pretending to be affronted. Dawn knew Jane didn't give a shit about what anyone thought. "I'm going to work part time at the Little Flowers Daycare."

"That's awesome but—"

"But what?" Jane asked.

"You have a master's degree in early childhood education. Wouldn't that qualify you for a full-time teaching position? Maybe someplace more prestigious than Little Flowers?"

Jane cocked an eyebrow. "Girl, I don't plan on working for long if Todd and I are going to start a family."

"Wait. Are you pregnant?" Dawn glanced at Jane's lithe form. It was hard to tell if there was a bump underneath Jane's boxy pajamas embellished with kitty cats wearing Santa hats.

"No, no, no. But I plan to be pregnant by this time next year. I want to have all my kids before I'm thirty so I can be a young mom."

"How many do you plan on having?"

"Three," Jane answered with a nod that said she had made up her mind, so it was practically a done deal.

"Three in five years. You're crazy."

"You know Todd's aunts are twins? We're hoping it runs in the family."

"Wow," Dawn said, stunned. "Kids."

Well, what did she expect? She was at an age now where everyone around her would get married and have kids. This might be the last year she and Jane would hang out on Christmas Eve to watch a marathon of British Christmas movies that, God help her, reminded her of Callan.

Callan. He'd already experienced unconditional parental love, and he never intended on experiencing it again. She'd been a fool to think she could change him or make him realize he was in love with her. He didn't want to have a future with her.

Screw him.

"So back to your job," Jane prompted, breaking her from her thoughts.

Dawn told Jane about her conversations with the nonprofit director. Turned out Gemma was right. They had received grant funding, and the new salary was enough for Dawn to make it work. She'd have to downsize a bit, tighten her purse strings, but it was doable.

But the best part was the work itself. Not only could she run her own cases, but she'd work side by side with the director to expand the program and help scale the organization. Gemma was a mentor to the director, so the woman had barely reviewed Dawn's résumé before offering her the job on Gemma's recommendation.

"It literally all happened this week," Dawn said.

"Wow, Dawn. I am so happy for you." Jane jumped out of her seat and gave Dawn a big hug.

Dawn grinned. "Thanks. I'm really excited. I can't believe this is happening. I'm a little scared. Actually, I'm a lot scared."

"You'll do great. Just like always," Jane said with full confidence. Dawn could kiss her for it.

"Thanks. And you'll do great at the daycare," Dawn added.

Jane snorted. "Probably not, but I'll do everything I can to not be a bad influence."

"Cheers to not being a bad influence on toddlers," Dawn declared, and they clinked glasses.

"Did Gemma say anything about Callan?" Jane ventured.

"No. She knows I don't want to discuss him. I'm glad I'm leaving the firm so I don't have to run into him ever again or hear about his boring project." Dawn picked at some peppermint bark on the plate in front of her.

"I know you are sad about how things ended with him."

Dawn shrugged. "It was doomed from the beginning. Operation Go With The Flow failed."

Jane rolled her eyes. "But it didn't."

"What do you mean?"

"It didn't fail at all. I encouraged you to take a chance and go with the flow because you needed to shake up your life. Win or lose, remember? Maybe you lost Callan but look at what you are winning." Jane's sparkling blue eyes danced.

"What am I winning?" Dawn didn't feel much like a winner where he was concerned.

"Dawn, you dummy. You just landed yourself a kick-ass job doing something you love. Maybe you were never meant to be with Callan. Maybe you were only supposed to meet him so you'd meet Gemma and land exactly where you are now."

"Huh. Maybe you're right." Maybe Callan had just been a stepping stone along the path. Maybe he had never been the destination.

"Of course I'm right. I'm always right," Jane said, lifting her glass again.

Dawn laughed and joined her. They'd be sloshed before they even pushed play on the next movie. But who cared? It was so good to be with her best friend, who believed in her no matter what.

"When do you start?" Jane asked.

Dawn screwed up her face. "I have to tell White & Halston soon. They want me to start after the first of the year."

"Get it over with. Like a Band-Aid. Do it the second you get back."

Dawn nodded. She was looking forward to seeing Mr. White's face when she told him she was leaving. She hadn't confronted him about how he'd twisted their conversation to Callan. She didn't know if she ever would.

At the end of the day, it'd been her mistake to tell Mr. White anything about Callan. And Callan's mistake to not listen to her. To not fight for what they had.

Or what she thought they'd had.

Screw him.

The asshole was nothing but a goddamn stepping stone.

****

Callan took another sip of whiskey and ignored his phone for the third time. He'd call his mum back later. The rain pelted against the glass windows of his flat, obscuring the city lights and holiday cheer outside.

His Christmases had been shitty for the past four years. He should be used to it by now.

He squeezed his eyes shut, blocking out the memories assaulting his mind. Memories of happier times when cracker surprises and paper crowns led to giggles, laughter, and kisses.

And love. So much love.

His heart pounded, and his self-loathing rose with the pressure in his veins.

Someone knocked on the door. Dear God, had his mum jumped on the train because he wouldn't answer his phone?

"Hello in there! Callan!"

He opened the door. Will and Sarah stood in the hallway, bundled in winter coats and scarves, their arms laden with an assortment of brown bags.

Callan stepped aside to let them in. "What are you doing here?" he asked. They set down the bags and took turns giving him a hug.

"We knew you were alone today, so we thought we'd swing by. See how you're doing," Will said. He hung his coat on the front hook and unloaded the bags on the dining room table while Sarah ran around the flat and turned on the lights. Callan walked over to the table.

Spread before him were dishes loaded with turkey, roasted potatoes, pigs in blankets, brussels sprouts, Christmas pudding, and other tasty fare.

"You've outdone yourself, Sarah," Callan said.

"Will helped me. He's been learning his way around the kitchen quite well."

"That so?" Callan murmured. He knew why his friends were here. Knew they could tell as well as he that he'd lost so much fucking ground. He pulled himself together during the day, plowing through work and putting one foot in front of the other. But nighttime was a different story.

At night he sat alone in the darkness, his heart a pile of charred ash.

Callan stuffed his hands into his pockets. "Not sure I can eat all of this."

"I'll get the plates," Sarah said, already searching his kitchen cabinets.

"Shouldn't you be with your families today?"

"We've spent the entire day with Sarah's family. Eight hours with her cousins is enough," Will joked.

Sarah entered the room and set the plates and cutlery. "Oh, rubbish," she scoffed. "Besides, Callan, you're family too."

His heart squeezed.

They made small talk as they dished their food and sat down to eat. Callan attempted to keep up with the light conversation, but he couldn't bear it.

"I fucked everything up. Royally," he blurted.

Will and Sarah paused. Sarah laid down her fork and gave him an encouraging look. It was all he needed to launch into everything, including his horrible fight with Dawn.

"I'm a first-class arsehole. Dawn hadn't told White Jr. anything about my family. She'd tried to protect me. Gemma spoke to White Jr. and was able to smooth things over by sweetening the pot with better terms. It had all been a ploy on White Jr.'s part to get the bank into a better risk position."

"What a twat," Sarah said.

"But I fell for it." He swallowed. "And lost Dawn in the process."

"Have you tried calling her? Saying you're sorry?" Sarah asked.

Callan shook his head. He couldn't count the number of times he'd picked up his phone to call or text her: —*I'm sorry... Please forgive me... I miss you...*—

—*I love you.*—

But he'd deleted every message.

He didn't fucking deserve her. He'd always known it, but he'd convinced himself he'd make it up to her, treat her so well she'd accept his broken shell of a soul.

But then he'd taken her love and mocked her. Ground it to dust beneath his heel.

She'd accused him of always running away. She didn't realize he'd saved her by leaving. Saved her from him. From his darkness and misery. From the anguish pulsing in every fiber of his being.

She'd called him a coward, and she'd been right. He was scared. Fucking terrified. He'd opened his heart before and had *almost* done it again. And look what happened. He'd screwed himself up even more and taken her down in the process.

No more.

"I don't think an 'I'm sorry' is going to cut it now." Callan rubbed his chest, commanding his heart to slow down.

"You need help, mate," Will said bluntly.

Sarah nodded.

Callan jumped up, grabbed his tumbler, and paced into his living room. What he needed was to expend some of this energy before his heart exploded. He took another drink of the amber liquid. Maybe he could numb himself enough this time to forget.

Please forget.

Will and Sarah followed him into the room, their eyes watchful and concerned.

Callan suddenly turned to them, desperate. "Jesus, will this never end? This pain and racking guilt. Dawn...Robyn...Sophie... How many people can I ruin in one lifetime?"

Sarah made a small sound in her throat and ran to his side. "Oh, darling, you didn't ruin them."

But he shook her off. Would he add Dawn to the list of names he couldn't bear to utter?

Her words haunted him.

Don't say their names. Don't think about them. Pretend they never existed. Is that how you are getting through life?

"She's right about everything. I pretend they never existed. I push them away so I can get through life. I'm a coward who runs away." *Fuck.* He was going to weep in front of his friends.

Will strode over and placed a hand on his shoulder. "Tell me what you need, brother. We're here for you."

Callan set the crystal tumbler down and walked into his bedroom. He went to the closet and turned on the light. Without giving himself time to think, he hauled the bankers box down from the top shelf and carried it into the living room.

He tossed the lid aside. With a shaky breath, he pulled out the wedding album. "Can you…will you please look at this with me?"

"Of course," Sarah cried. She and Will sat down on either side of Callan on the couch.

Tears welled in Callan's eyes, but he forced himself to turn the pages, to study the photos he hadn't looked at in four years.

Slowly, the tears turned to laughter as they relived that day and their antics leading up to the wedding. They spent over an hour with the album, joking about Robyn's crazy penchant for all things royal and the rambling speech Callan's dad made after he'd imbibed too much wine.

Callan set the album aside and returned to the box, sifting through papers until he found a second album.

Sophie's First Year

He ran his fingers gently over the cover. "Robyn made this album. She worked on the computer for days to get the layout just right."

"Can we see it?" Sarah asked. Callan nodded and sat back down between them.

From Robyn's first sonogram to Sophie's first birthday, it was all there. This had been his life. They'd been real.

A sob tore from his throat.

Sarah placed a gentle hand on his back. "Darling, you need to get help. You've been living with guilt and pain for too long."

He thought back on all the times he'd promised Dawn he'd get help.

"I promised Dawn I would. But I broke every

promise I ever made to her." Callan took a breath. "I don't deserve her, but I owe it to her to follow through on at least one promise."

Even if she'd never know.

Chapter Twenty-Eight

Dawn gave White & Halston's HR director her resignation letter the day she returned to the office after Christmas. The firm's halls were quiet. Except for a few transactional lawyers pushing through some year-end deals, most lawyers and staff had taken time off between Christmas and New Year's.

Thankfully, Mr. White and Bill were vacationing together with their families and weren't in the office. She wrote emails to them both—one sincere and one not—detailing how much she appreciated her time at the firm under their guidance, etcetera, etcetera. Mr. White sent her a polite but short reply, stating how sorry he was to see her go and that they would connect when he returned.

Bill didn't respond. Or maybe he just didn't know how to work a computer.

The only other attorneys in the office were her six counterparts. Each one working hard to bill as many hours as possible before the year officially ended. But when Dawn told them her news, they insisted on a Friday night happy hour at their favorite Mexican restaurant.

The seven of them sat shoulder to shoulder, crushed into a tight booth. Olivia and Kurt cuddled together next to Abbey and Hannah. Natalie, Dawn, and Matt sat across from them. Pitchers of margaritas, glasses rimmed with salt, and buckets of chips were delivered to their table, round after round, as they talked and laughed.

Dawn looked around the booth with a pang. These people had become her good friends, and she would miss them.

"Cheers to Dawn!" Kurt said, raising his glass. Olivia giggled. Kurt had already cheered her too many times to count, and they were all on the edge of tipsy.

"Cheers," they shouted and clinked glasses.

Dawn laughed. "I can't believe I'm leaving you guys."

"I know. We'll miss you," Abbey said.

"I'm happy for you, Dawn," Olivia said. "Hopefully you'll be happier than you are at the firm."

"I'm not unhappy," Dawn replied. A round of snorts rose from the group. "What? I'm not," she insisted.

"Dawn," Kurt said, "you are totally miserable. Everyone can tell."

Dawn looked around the table. "What? But we're all miserable. That's what being a first-year lawyer is."

Kurt took a swig of his margarita. "I'm not miserable."

"Yeah, but you work for Mr. Gandry." Dawn rolled her eyes.

"I'm not miserable," Matt said with a shrug.

"Me neither," Abbey said.

Olivia grinned at Kurt. "I like my job." Kurt winked back at her.

Hannah nodded.

"Me too," Natalie chimed in.

Dawn glanced down at Natalie's fingers. They were no longer mangled. The skin around her nail beds was smooth and pink.

"But we all hated it a couple months ago," Dawn said incredulously.

"I was super stressed about passing the bar. But I've always liked the work," Natalie said.

"But we hate Mr. White. He's a terror," Dawn said.

Hannah smiled. "He's a little curmudgeonly."

"What alternate universe bullshit am I in?" Dawn sputtered.

Kurt laughed. "Dawn, you are the one who says how boring everything is. How you hate the work. We don't feel the same way. We like practicing at White & Halston."

Dawn gaped at her friends. "This whole time I thought we all hated it."

"Nope. Just you," Matt said.

"When you look at the partners at the firm, do you ever think you might want to be one of them someday?" Abbey asked.

"Hell no," Dawn replied immediately.

Abbey laughed. "There you go. See, I do want to be a partner someday." She shrugged. "I think you are doing the right thing. Everyone should do what they love. Life is too short to be miserable."

Dawn sipped her margarita, and the group moved on to picking apart the new kindercube law clerks. Taking bets on which ones would crack under Mr. White. Like they were all in on the joke.

Well, the joke was on her. She'd busted her butt and landed herself a job she hated, thinking everyone around her was experiencing the same misery. She thought she had to grin and bear it because that was the price she paid for being at a prestigious firm, for being on the path to success and accolades.

She'd thought being successful was the ultimate end goal. Then, she'd thought being with Callan would make her happy and fulfilled. But she'd ignored herself in the process.

Callan. He'd be so proud if he knew she was leaving. Had Gemma already told him? Would he care?

As much as she steeled herself against Callan, she still thought about him. All the freaking time.

Screw him. He's not the destination.

Her destination was the future. And there was no looking back.

****

Everything from Dawn's office fit into one box. She'd never brought in coffee cups from home or hung her diplomas on the walls. Compared to Natalie who'd ordered rugs, planters, picture frames, and colorful office supplies, Dawn's office was a barren wasteland. That should've been a sign right from the start.

Dawn had already said goodbye to everyone in the office. All except for two people.

She ventured down the hallway to Mr. White's office. She'd been avoiding him since he'd returned from the holidays, and he hadn't sought her out. But she had to face him now.

"He's free," Debbie said, waving her in with a smile.

Dawn inhaled deeply and knocked.

"Enter," he called.

She swallowed and walked into his office, stopping in front of his desk.

"I've come to say goodbye, Mr. White. It's been a pleasure working with you," she said.

He looked up. "Have a seat, Dawn."

She slid into the chair and waited.

He put his pen down and sat back. "I'm sorry to see you go. I had high hopes for you at our firm. But I understand wanting to take a new direction."

"You do?"

"Of course I do," he said with a scowl. Her gaze drifted to the photo of him grinning on the boat.

She cleared her throat. "I want to thank you for giving me this opportunity. White & Halston is a great firm."

His lips drew back into a semblance of a smile. "Even though you are leaving us after only six months?"

She shifted in her seat and started to speak, but he cut her off with a wave of his hand. "Again, I understand. I suppose Ms. Chadwick helped you get the position?"

"Oh. You know about her work with trafficked minors?"

Mr. White smirked. "I was asked to attend a fundraiser for Lawyers ACT in London last fall." His scowl deepened. "I sent my father instead."

"Oh." Something clicked in the back of Dawn's mind, but she couldn't quite grasp it. "I worked with Gemma in London last summer. This is her partner organization here in the city."

"Yes, I know." It seemed he knew a lot.

"Oh," she said like a dummy again. He didn't speak, so she rose from her seat. "Well, thank you again," she said awkwardly.

"Dawn." He sighed. "I never meant to hurt your relationship. I'm sorry."

"Oh." She blinked. Had this man ever told anyone he was sorry? "It's okay," she muttered, not knowing what else to say.

"No, it's not okay. I don't know if my conversation with Callan is the reason you are leaving the firm but, if it is, I regret it." He stood up and reached out his hand.

She took it and they shook hands. "I wish you the best."

"Thank you." This was so weird.

He dropped her hand and sat back down. She supposed she was dismissed. She turned to the door.

"Let me know if you ever want to partner with us on pro bono work," he said.

She turned. "Really? I mean, of course. Yes. We could use the extra help."

He smiled. "Goodbye, Dawn. I think you'll make a fine advocate for those kids."

"Thank you, Mr. White," she said and left his office, stunned.

"Everything okay?" Debbie asked.

"Yeah. All good. Thanks for everything, Debbie," she said and walked back to her office. She grabbed her box and purse and walked toward the elevator. Along the way, she popped her head into Bill's office.

He wasn't there. *Crap*. She'd missed her chance to say goodbye to him. She'd have to give him a call tomorrow.

She turned and almost knocked over a small figure with her box.

"Watch where you swing that thing, Miss Dawn," Bill sputtered.

She immediately put the box down. "Sorry, Bill. Did I hit you?"

"You about took my head off," he said, but his eyes twinkled.

"I came to say goodbye."

"Hopefully not forever, Miss Dawn."

She glanced down the empty hallway. There was something nagging at her. "Bill, how did you know about me and Callan?" she asked.

Bill cocked his head. "What is there to know?"

"Bill, come out with it!" She hadn't meant to yell at the old man, but for God's sake.

"All right, Miss Dawn. Yes, I suspected you were his lady love. So I thought I would help things along."

"How in the world did you know?"

"I met Callan last fall when I was seated beside him at a charity function in London. I liked the young man, thought he was smart and had great ambitions. We talked about Spain, about the project he wanted to do. He told me he was looking for investors." He cleared his throat. "Mr. Marlowe may have had too many spirits that night. Well, maybe we both did. I told him about my wife, how I'd met her abroad while studying. He told me about this lovely woman he'd met over the summer. How she was the one who got away because he had behaved poorly. She was a law student, top of her class at a school in DC." He leaned in. "He showed me your picture on his phone."

Her mind raced to connect the dots. "But he never mentioned you to me."

"He may not remember that part of the conversation. He was well into his cups by then," he said sheepishly.

"So you hired me because you knew about us?"

Bill looked affronted. "Certainly not. My law firm is not a matchmaking service. Besides, I have nothing to do with hiring."

"Well, so then how did you know it was me?" She was so confused.

"I pieced it together when you started working here." He tapped his head with his forefinger. "And I never forget a face."

"So you're telling me you had no idea who I was when I was hired, but you put two and two together when you met me? I just happened to be your investor client's solar developer's ex-girlfriend? And you figured it out and what? You decided to throw us together in Spain?" The whole scenario was ludicrous. Bill's skills were wasted on corporate law, he should be writing for the show *Match Me*.

He nodded his head. "That's about right."

Dawn covered her face with her hands. "This is crazy. What a coincidence." How could the world be so big yet so small at the same time? For Bill, a lawyer from New York, to be seated next to Callan at a random function in London. And then for Dawn to work at Bill's firm…it was too much.

"But is it?" Bill interrupted her thoughts.

"What do you mean?" she asked.

"*Is* it such a coincidence? Just a random act in the cosmos?" He leaned in closer. "Do you believe in fate, Miss Dawn?"

"Fate?"

"Fate." He nodded.

"I don't believe in fate," Dawn responded stiffly.

He winked at her. "You should, Miss Dawn. You should."

She stared at him as he toddled off down the hallway, still processing what he'd told her.

OMG. Maybe he was a leprechaun after all.

Chapter Twenty-Nine

A lot had changed since Christmas, but one thing had stayed the same. *He* had not contacted Dawn. Not even once. And she would burn in hellfire before she broke down and called him. She recalled his face during their last fight, his sneering, twisted face. *And you're in love with me. How sad is that?* He'd mocked her. She'd let him humiliate her over and over.

Never again.

"All right, ladies, turn to me and smile." Jane's wedding photographer snapped Dawn back to reality. The photographer took a moment to change cameras and dab at the sweat pouring down her face. She then motioned to Dawn and the other four bridesmaids to stand on either side of Jane under the boughs of a large oak tree. A heatwave had blanketed lower Alabama in ninety-five-degree temperatures, and everyone was trying to maintain their cool, literally and figuratively.

Dawn attempted to stay as Zen as possible so her makeup wouldn't slide off her face before the wedding. The other bridesmaids were also panting. Jane, of course, was impermeable to the stifling heat. Instead of sweat droplets, her skin glowed as if she were the star of a skincare commercial.

Jane and her mother had bickered about having an outdoor wedding in the middle of June in Alabama, but Jane had won the argument. Dawn shielded her eyes against the lowering sun. With any luck, it would cool off in time for the reception.

Dawn shifted to a different position, per the photographer's instructions. She smiled and laughed along with the others, even though she had no idea what Jane had said to make everyone crack up. Jane glanced at her and then wrapped her arm around Dawn's waist. "You okay?" she asked.

Dawn responded with a nod and a smile. The last thing she wanted to do was dampen Jane's wedding day happiness.

Jane hugged her and grinned. "Everything is going to work out."

"You're done, ladies. I'm going to call for the boys," the photographer announced. Dawn and the other bridesmaids surrounded Jane and shuttled her back to their waiting area, careful to shield her so Todd wouldn't get a pre-wedding glimpse of his beautiful bride.

Mrs. Turner and the catering staff waited for them under a tent with glasses of tangy cold lemonade, which they gulped down gratefully.

"Oh, you girls are beautiful," Mrs. Turner drawled. She looked gorgeous herself in a long sky-blue gown, revealing a figure women half her age would envy. She made a beeline for Dawn. "Honey, this color is divine on you." Dawn peered down at her short strapless A-line dress and had to agree. She'd never thought orange was a flattering color on her, but the tangerine shade brought out her copper highlights and made the green in her eyes stand out. She'd logged some time by the pool with Jane and Todd over the past week, and her skin glowed golden against the satin fabric.

"I think those groomsmen are going to be falling all

over themselves to dance with you," Mrs. Turner added.

Dawn laughed, but her heart sank. She didn't want to flirt with Todd's friends. She didn't want any of them to touch her. She craved someone else's touch.

For the millionth time today, her mind played snapshots from Will and Sarah's wedding two years ago. The touching ceremony, Callan's speech, meeting his friends and mother, the dancing, the lovemaking. The memories assaulted her tenuous hold on her emotions.

She drew a shaky breath. *Stop crying over him. He's not worth it.*

She could add ruining Jane's wedding to the long list of grievances she had against Callan Marlowe.

Screw him. Her mantra had kept her strong over these past six months. Kept her strong when she'd started her new job and when she'd moved to a more modest apartment. Kept her going when she'd panicked because she didn't know what the hell she was doing and again when she'd led a successful volunteer drive. It had been with her when she'd gone way outside of her comfort zone to partner with a local news station to bring awareness to their organization and when she'd taken her first real case helping a little boy who needed a champion so badly. Her mantra had been with her every step of the way.

Screw him.

"You're going to create lines on your face with all that frowning," Jane said, elbowing Dawn.

"I'm not frowning."

"You are not allowed to be sad on the most important day of my life."

"I'm sorry. I really am so happy for you. I just can't help thinking about…"

"Him."

"Yeah. Him."

Jane hugged her as close as her makeup would allow. "Babe, you are going to have a blast at the reception. Have some shots and have fun. Maybe you'll go home with Prince Charming." She winked.

Dawn rolled her eyes. The men in Todd's good ol' boy crew weren't exactly her cup of tea. But, then again, maybe Jane was right. Have a few drinks and hook up for some revenge sex. That'd exorcise the demons right out of her. Mac seemed up for the job. He was Todd's business partner and the owner of the hardware store where Todd worked. He also happened to be Todd's oldest friend and someone Dawn and Jane had hung out with over the years. Objectively, he was a cute guy. Longish dark-brown hair, a powerful build from years of hauling lumber, and dancing brown eyes. If his behavior at the rehearsal dinner last night was any indication, he was totally into having a good time with her.

As they waited to enter the ceremony tent, Dawn gazed at her dearest friend. Jane could not look lovelier. This past week had been so much fun. It had been nice to be home and spend some quality time with her parents and friends. Dawn had kept her parents up to date on her life through regular phone calls, but this week she'd finally told them the details about her relationship with Callan, and they'd been so supportive. Being home made her realize how much she'd missed them.

During the ceremony, Dawn made eye contact with Mac. She smiled at him from across the way, and he smiled back. He'd flirted with her last night in a way he'd never done before. She hadn't thought much of it, but now she reconsidered.

She imagined herself kissing Mac. Threading her hands into his hair, sliding up against his chest. But when she raised her gaze, the man holding her didn't have dancing brown eyes. He had beautiful, complicated, searing hazel eyes.

Her breath caught, and she had to physically stop herself from shaking her head against the onslaught of Callan-laced memories. She needed to shove those memories back into the box. Hell, she needed to put him into a mental coffin and nail the damn thing shut.

Maybe Mac could be the hammer.

Dawn got a grip on herself and focused her attention back on the happy couple as they exchanged rings through tears of joy, though Jane still didn't have one smudge of mascara out of place. How did she do it? Dawn's grin was one hundred percent genuine when Todd grabbed Jane and laid a smacking wet kiss on her once they were declared man and wife. It was hard to be melancholy in the presence of such joy.

Mac offered his arm to Dawn, and they followed the bride and groom down the aisle and circled back to the grove of trees for more pictures. Under the fabric of his jacket, Mac's impressive bicep flexed, and he pulled her closer to him until his strong legs brushed hers with each step. They laughed and goofed around with the rest of the bridal party while the photographer snapped the camera around them. When picture duty was over, they joined the guests for drinks at the cocktail bar in the reception tent.

But as Mac sidled up beside Dawn and put his hand on her back, she instinctually shifted away from him. She couldn't help it. She didn't want him, plain and simple. He got the hint. He dropped his arm and engaged Jane's other single friends in conversation. Before long, his focus turned completely to Jane's sorority sister.

Dawn didn't care. She was delusional to think she could sexercise Callan out of her. And with Mac, of all people. Mac, whom she'd known since his wake and bake days. She lifted her hair from the sticky nape of her neck, wishing she had a scrunchie for her mass of curls. At least the sun was setting, the air shifting from blazing heat to simmering humidity.

Dawn mingled with the other guests, including her parents, former teachers, classmates, neighbors, and college friends. She smiled and laughed and joked until her face felt like it would crack. *Screw him.*

She tried her best not to be a pathetic heap of self-pity during the speeches, cake cutting, and first dances. *Screw him.*

She gamely joined in during a bridesmaid-led Electric Slide and danced with the little ring bearer when he bowed politely to her. *Screw him.*

She hooted with Jane's mom and old classmates when Todd pulled off Jane's garter with his teeth, and she made a show of diving for the bouquet even though they let Jane's perpetually single aunt catch the flowers. *Screw him.*

Dawn put on a good face, and the night crept along. Finally—blessedly—they were coming to the end of the night. The flower girls were slumped over, asleep, and the men had shed their jackets. The women had kicked off their high heels, and Jane's teenage cousins were done sneaking liquor from the bar. The bride and groom clung to each other as they made their rounds before saying goodbye. Dawn's own parents had left the reception an hour ago. Now Dawn sat alone at a round table, eyeing the wine stains dotting the white linen and picking absently at a piece of almond-flavored wedding cake.

She tried hard to not feel sorry for herself. To not to ache inside, thinking about what could have been. If only she hadn't told Mr. White about Callan's panic attacks, if only Callan had listened to her and understood she'd been trying to help, if only he hadn't blown up at her and used her as a scapegoat for his own issues, if only he'd seen a professional and gotten the help he needed. If only he'd called her. If only he'd said he was sorry. If only he'd cared enough to try to make *them* work. If only. If only. If only.

The beginning notes of a familiar seventies ballad blasted from the DJ's speakers. Dawn's throat tightened.

Oh, God. Not this song, not now.

She clenched her beer and took a long gulp to hide her trembling lower lip. Against her will, she was transported back to that night at the karaoke bar when Callan had sung this song to her, and she'd danced in his arms. She could still feel the rumble in his chest, feel the embrace of his strong arms.

She could still hear the beautiful tenor of his voice. *"You may be in love with me..."*

The beautiful tenor of his voice singing in her ear...

Singing in her ear...right now?

Dawn spun around and shot to her feet with a gasp.

Callan Marlowe stood right in front of her as if she'd conjured him from a wishing spell.

"What? How? Why are you here?" she sputtered.

He ran a hand through his hair. He looked good. Amazing, even. He wore a finely cut blue suit and white button-down shirt. The humidity hadn't wilted a thing on him. He was fresh as a daisy, like he'd just stepped out of the *GQ* center spread. But his eyes—they held so many emotions at once. Regret, guilt, fear. But also hope, excitement. And love. Her stomach flip-flopped.

"I spoke to Jane," he began slowly.

"She didn't tell me she'd spoken to you." Dawn shot Jane a look from across the reception floor, and her best friend grinned at her. Dawn frowned in return. Then Jane made a lewd gesture with her hands and mouth, and Dawn twisted back to Callan.

"I asked her, begged her not to tell you. We had a long talk, and she invited me to the wedding." He shoved his hands in his trouser pockets

"Have you been here the whole time?" Had he been watching her? Had he seen her trying so hard to fake her way through this wedding?

"I just arrived. I didn't want to create any distractions at the wedding." His lips quirked. "Even though Jane told me she loves drama."

"Sounds like Jane," Dawn grumbled.

"If it makes you feel any better, she did say that if I messed things up again, she'd track me down and cut off my balls. Slowly."

Dawn smiled reluctantly. "It's how she shows she cares."

Callan hesitated for a moment but then took his hands out of his pockets and grabbed her hands in his own. "Dawn, I am so sorry. I've missed you so much."

"You didn't call," she said stiffly.

Screw him. Was she going to let this guy worm his way back into her life? He had a track record of abandoning her and breaking her heart. But she ached to be with him. He wreaked havoc on her senses. She felt like she'd been starving for the past seven months, and now he'd appeared like a feast right before her eyes.

But she did have her pride, and she wasn't about to throw it away. She'd already done that too many times to count. She raised her chin.

Callan looked deep into her eyes, willing her to understand. "I acted inexcusably, horribly. I'm so ashamed of myself, of the words I said to you that day. I knew I'd been a total arsehole the second I left your flat."

"But you didn't call," Dawn said again. Confusion and anger took hold.

He shifted, pulling her closer. "I was so proud of myself, so convinced I was getting better. But I realize I'd placed the burden of my happiness onto you. I'd told myself you made me better, like a drug fighting a disease. I put that responsibility on *your* shoulders. But I know I am in control of my own happiness. You motivate me, you inspire me, but my actions and feelings are my own."

He took a breath. "When White Jr. confronted me and demanded medical reports, I blamed you, telling myself it was because you had betrayed me." He held up his hands to stop her from interjecting. "I know you didn't betray me. You were trying to help me keep my business. But I was so angry because I was faced with the truth. The truth that my relationships and my business hung in the balance because of my actions." He placed a palm to his chest.

"And I couldn't cope with it. After I'd processed what really happened, I couldn't go back to you and beg for your forgiveness. Not without—" He swallowed. "— Not without forgiving myself and taking responsibility for my own mental state."

She raised an eyebrow. "And you've come to realize all this because?"

"Because I've been seeing doctors. A team of them. You were absolutely right. I had to face my issues and stop running away."

"And what? Now you're magically better?" He was saying all the right things, but could she trust him?

He shook his head ruefully. "Hardly. I'm more self-aware now, and I realize I was unwell. I know six months isn't enough time to work through everything. It is a process, and it may take years. But I'm trying, and I'm committed, Dawn."

"Callan, I'm glad you are trying but..." She bit her lip. Hope rose inside her, but she tamped it down. She couldn't risk getting burned again. Could she?

"I'm more than trying, Dawn. I'm doing the work every day. And for the first time in almost five years, I can see a path out of the nightmare I've been living. I'm not there yet, but I will be. I won't give up on myself. Or on us," he added.

"Callan, how do I know what you're feeling is real? That you aren't just riding a high now that you are getting help?"

"Dawn, if these seven months of being without you have taught me anything, it is that I am in love with you. Desperately, madly in love with you."

Her mouth dropped open as his words sank in. He pressed his advantage. "I knew I was in love with you before Thanksgiving. I'd planned to tell you here, in Canton. But I was such a fool, and I ruined everything." He shook his head, and his eyes searched hers. "I know I have no right to ask, but would you give me one more chance? We can take things slow, at whatever pace you want. I will do anything to have you back in my life."

"You love me?" she asked faintly.

He nodded solemnly. "Yes, and I want everything. I want it all. No more bloody parameters around our relationship, no more fearing the past. I want to share *everything.* I want to share the future with you."

Here were the words she'd waited almost two years to hear. Could she believe them? She gazed into his eyes, and a seedling of hope bloomed. The words weren't empty platitudes. His face—his whole body—beamed the truth. He placed her hand on his heart, and it thumped wildly under her palm.

"I came here tonight because I couldn't stand being away from you any longer. I needed to make things right," he whispered.

"And you wanted to make a dramatic entrance," she said, nodding toward the DJ.

He grinned and shrugged. "The song was a bonus. It happened to be playing when I arrived and spotted you."

Do you believe in fate, Miss Dawn?

"Bill asked me once if I believed in fate," she said in a daze. His beautiful, changeable eyes glistened with apprehension and hope. She narrowed her eyes. "Did you realize you told him all about me when you sat beside him at a charity dinner?"

Callan blinked a couple times. Then he slapped his forehead and barked out a laugh. "Bloody hell, did I? I wondered how the old bugger knew about us."

She lifted an eyebrow. "He said you were 'deep in your cups' that night."

Callan winced. "I'm afraid I fell into a bit of a spiral after we parted in London. I had a few nights like that. Grieving for what was. Aching for what could have been."

"Callan Marlowe, you are frustrating and aggravating and have caused *me* a lot of heartache over these past two years." She punched his arm. And then threw him another punch. And another. Before she knew it, she was pummeling his chest, tears glistening in her eyes. He stood there and took it for a minute before he snagged her wrists and pulled her close.

He put his forehead to hers and closed his eyes. "I know. I am so, so sorry. Please give me a chance to make it right."

"It would be against my better judgment," she whispered back.

"I know," he said simply. He was done trying to convince her. She needed to make this decision herself.

Dawn sighed loudly. "But I'm screwed. Because I love you, too."

Shock washed over Callan's face. Then relief. Then joy. He laughed and picked her up in his arms. "I don't know which one of us is in more trouble."

"Me. Definitely me." She laughed.

And then he kissed her. Thoroughly and deeply. His hand snaked into her curls and cradled the back of her head as if she were a precious treasure. His warmth cocooned her, and she melted into him.

A round of applause rose, and they finally broke apart. Dawn's face heated when she saw the small crowd of guests watching them with smiles on their faces. Jane winked at her. Dawn laughed and rolled her eyes.

She turned back to Callan. "You certainly know how to put on a show." She grinned.

"Dawn, you are my sunshine. My love." Sincerity radiated through his entire being. "I will make a show every day of how much I love you."

"I don't need a show, Callan. I just need you."

He held her close and whispered, "Always."

Epilogue

Two Years Later

It's early morning. The first rays of the sun are peeking through the curtains but haven't reached the bed where Dawn and Aelia are sleeping. This time of day is my favorite. Aelia is slumbering in her bassinet beside our bed, and Dawn is curled up on the edge of the mattress, ready to soothe Aelia, even in sleep. They both look so peaceful, even though we were up all night nursing Aelia through her bouts of colic. I'm exhausted, and I know Dawn is too. But I don't mind. My heart bursts with love when I hear our one-month-old's cries because she is here and alive, something I'll never take for granted.

You taught me that.

When my doctor prescribed letter writing to me, I felt foolish writing to someone who would never read them. But now I can't imagine not writing to you; it has become an inexplicable gift. I can feel in my bones that you, somehow, hear me.

My world has changed so much these past two years. The business has grown, and I've hired some great people to take over the day-to-day operations so I can focus on strategy, which is my favorite part. I was inspired by your Aunt Gemma and Dawn to spend my days doing what I love.

I'm sad Gemma no longer works for me, but the feeling is minuscule compared to the pride I feel when I see the brilliant work she and Dawn are doing. They've helped so many children, and they are both fulfilled in their own way. Their happiness is mine as well.

If there is one thing I've learned over these past seven years, it's that doing what you love—and being with the people you love—is all that matters.

I wish with my whole heart you could be here for that lesson. I miss you so much.

When I look at Aelia, I see glimpses of you. But I want you to know Aelia is not a replacement of you. I will never forget you; you will live on in my heart forever. And Aelia will grow up knowing she has a big sister who is looking down on her from heaven.

Your presence is everywhere.

This Christmas, Dawn surprised me with photos of you. On the dresser, the bookshelf, the walls. Part of my therapy has been learning to not push you away. To learn I will never heal if I keep you hidden and buried. Dawn is helping me bring you into the light.

"She's a part of our family," she told me. But what really got me crying like a nutter was when she pointed to the photos of your mum. "And her too," Dawn said.

Because the truth is, I lost your mum twice, and I'm still coming to terms with it. I miss the woman I fell in love with at university. You would have loved her. You loved a version of her, but it wasn't the real Robyn. I'm so sorry you never got to know the happy, smart, and irreverent woman who was your mum.

But slowly, through talking about you and your mum often, through sharing photos and stories, through remembering the happy times and not just the sad ones,

I'm becoming more at peace. And I've never felt your presence as much as I do now.

Sometimes, when I close my eyes, I can feel your chubby legs in my lap, hear your little laugh as I make silly sounds. And I know now it's not a curse to remember you. It's not something dark and twisted I need to hide away. It's a gift.

You are my gift, Sophie Marlowe. And your daddy loves you more than you'll ever know.

A word about the author...

Katherine Grace began sneaking her sisters' romance novels at a young age and never stopped reading. Maybe that's why HEAs and true love are her obsession. An English major and former attorney, Katherine writes modern sexy romances set in the real world with characters who face real issues with resilience, humor, and all the feels.

www.authorkatherinegrace.com

Thank you for purchasing
this publication of The Wild Rose Press, Inc.

For questions or more information
contact us at
info@thewildrosepress.com.

The Wild Rose Press, Inc.
www.thewildrosepress.com